BLOODLACED

COURTNEY MAGUIRE

CITY OWL
PRESS

BLOODLACED
Youkai Bloodlines, Book 1

CITY OWL PRESS
www.cityowlpress.com

Cover Design by Mibl Art. All stock photos licensed appropriately.

Edited by Heather McCorkle.

For information on subsidiary rights, please contact the publisher at info@cityowlpress.com.

Print Edition ISBN: 978-1-64898-016-9

Digital Edition ISBN: 978-1-64898-015-2

Printed in the United States of America

To my soulmate without whom this world wouldn't exist

ONE

A Boy or a Girl?

I COULD HEAR THEM OUT THERE, BANTERING AND BARTERING, TRYING to agree on how much my life was worth. Would I fetch more than a horse? Would my new master's teacups be worth more than I was? I could almost laugh if it weren't so absurd.

Sitting on my knees, the tatami biting into my legs through my threadbare kimono, I ducked my head against it, my long black hair like a veil between me and the world. Behind it, I could be anywhere, like back in the arms of my mother, in a world I barely remembered but knew had to be better than this, smelling the powder on her skin, humming a tune I imagined was hers.

"Are you a boy or a girl?"

I tipped my head up as a small voice pierced my fantasy. A little boy, maybe eight or nine years old, squatted in the corner, his too-long legs tangled up underneath him. He wrinkled his nose as he studied me, his thin mouth puckered in confusion. His eyes were big as walnuts, but shadows lay under them.

"What do you think?" I returned, dropping back behind the shadow of my hair. The tatami creaked as he shuffled on his hands and knees toward me and tugged at my sleeves.

"Your kimono is like a girl," he said, "but you're big like a boy."

"Maybe I'm a giant."

He giggled, his big eyes sparkling. "You sound like a boy too. But your hair is long like a girl."

"Boys have long hair," I said, ruffling his shoulder-length locks.

"Not this long," he retorted, tugging on the ends. His face scrunched up, his tongue sticking out a little with the effort. "What's your name? If you tell me your name, I'll definitely know."

"Asagi." I couldn't help but laugh at the dejection on his little face.

"No fair!" he cried, balling his hands into pudgy fists. "Your name can be both!"

"Maybe I *am* both."

His jaw dropped, and he fell backward onto his bum on the dirty floor. "No way!" he gasped in childish disbelief. "You can't be both. How can you be both?"

"I'm magic," I said with a devilish wink, making him smile wide.

Our brief moment of levity dropped at the sound of raised voices, and our focus shifted to the shadows moving on the other side of the paper walls. My chest tightened, and my skin went cold. I wasn't particularly attached to this house, but starting over always held a certain terror. A new house, new rules, new dangers to avoid. I slid my fingers up my sleeve, found the short, thin cut just inside my elbow, and scratched my fingernails over it. A twinge of pain and the tension eased, allowing me to breathe a little easier.

"My mom died. Now, they don't know what to do with me," the boy said, his tone flat but his eyes glistening.

I knew, of course, of the kitchen maid struck down by a sudden fever and the son she left behind. The house wasn't so big that a death among us didn't shake us all.

"Why are they getting rid of you?"

I released a long, heavy breath. "They don't know what to do with me either."

The door snapped open, and our master stepped inside, followed closely by a middle-aged man with a shaved head and an expensive-looking burgundy kimono pulled tight across his round belly. He scratched at it and sucked at his teeth as he ran his cold eyes over us. I dropped my forehead to the tatami, and he stopped so close, I could see his toes.

"Up. Both of you."

Keeping my eyes lowered, I lifted to my feet in one smooth, practiced motion. The boy scrambled up and pressed himself to my side. I cringed as the old man raised a meaty hand to touch the ends of my hair, toying with it before pushing it back from my face.

"Well, well, what have we here?" His stinking breath rolled over me as he grabbed me by the chin, forcing my head up. I shivered involuntarily as his gaze dragged over my face and down, lingering around the loose-fitting collar of my kimono. He sucked his teeth again, squinting, judging, before shoving his hand squarely between my legs.

"Well, well," he repeated with a wide, sickening grin, "what *have* we here?"

He released me, and I crumpled a bit, gasping, heart pounding against my sternum. My gut clenched as his gaze dropped to the boy pressed against my hip. A familiar darkness swirled in his eyes that made my palms sweat, and I pushed the boy farther behind me.

"What are you to this boy?" He released a snorting laugh. "Are you his mother?"

"N-No, Goshujin-sama. No relation, Goshujin-sama."

He rocked back on his heels, mouth twisted into a cruel smile. "Fine. I'll take them both." He tossed a small bag of coins over his shoulder to our master, the paltry price for two lives. "I'd hate to break up a pair."

A wail burst from the boy, sending a rush of adrenaline burning through my veins. "No! I don't want to go!"

The old man—our new master—rolled his eyes and cursed. "Yutaka!"

A third man appeared, broad chested with a hard face and a sword on his hip, his expression blank and cold as a block of ice. Our master took a step back, gesturing to the boy with an irritated wave of his hand, and Yutaka lunged forward. The boy squealed, and I instinctively stepped between them. Without hesitation, Yutaka slapped a heavy hand on my shoulder and shoved me aside. He scooped the boy up and threw him kicking and screaming over his shoulder like a bag of rice. The boy was a fighter, but it wouldn't matter.

All fighting ever gets you is broken bones and bloodied noses and scars so deep they bleed into your soul until you learn to stop fighting.

As the boy's screams receded, the master's dark eyes turned back to me. "Are you going to come quietly, or shall we wait for Yutaka to return?"

Hands clasped at my waist to keep them from shaking, I bowed deeply and walked past him on wobbly knees. He followed close behind as I drifted down the narrow hallway toward the front of the house. A few faces popped out from behind doors, drawn by the commotion. Familiar faces I would never see again.

The boy was already in the back of a waiting horse cart, Yutaka looming over him with his hand on his sword. The boy's legs were folded up under him, his body coiled to strike. I threw myself between them, wrapping the boy up tight in my arms before he got the chance to lunge. My muscles tensed with the urge to flee, to snatch up that little boy and spirit him away from this horror, but I knew what the result would be. A cane if we were lucky. A sword if we weren't.

"Don't fight," I said to him in a gentle voice. "You'll only get hurt."

A deep laugh rumbled from behind me, and I lifted my head to see the master watching with an amused glint in his eye. "Children are a chore, aren't they? Especially children without mothers." The boy released a hiccupping sob against my chest, and I held him tighter as the master's eyes hardened. "You are his mother now, understand? I have neither the time nor the patience to teach him manners. If he steps out of line again, it will be your responsibility."

"Understood, Goshujin-sama."

The master hoisted himself up into the front of the horse cart, joined shortly after by Yutaka, and with a snap of the reins, the cart lurched into motion. We settled into a corner, the boy's tears gradually tapering off into a stream of sniffles.

"What's going to happen to us?" he asked through his tears.

"Nothing," I lied, pulling him closer to me. "We'll work. We'll be good and obedient, and in return, he'll take good care of us." I forced a smile when he looked up to me. "So you mustn't run, okay? Be a good boy." My throat tightened as he dropped his head into my lap, muffling his whimpers. "What's your name?" I asked, running my fingers gently through his hair.

"Tsukito." He sniffled.

"Just be a good boy, Tsukito," I said, blinking back my own tears as I prayed to any god who would listen. I was young, so much younger than him, when I learned to stop fighting.

Please, I silently pleaded, *don't let him be like me. Let him remain a child a little longer.*

TWO

Starting Over

THE RELATIVELY SMOOTH STREETS OF THE CITY GAVE WAY TO ROUGH country roads, some little more than a pair of ruts worn into the long grass. Wheat fields and tiered rice paddies ran all the way to the jagged horizon, and I imagined disappearing into them, imagined the mountains chewing me up in their sharp teeth, never to be seen again.

Tsukito had fallen asleep with his head in my lap, and it bobbed loosely with the motion of the cart. *You are his mother now.* I couldn't be his mother. I couldn't even be his father. But I wanted to protect him, with all my broken heart.

The cart pulled to a stop in front of a modestly built manor consisting of a main house and a small outbuilding surrounded by lush gardens. The entrance was guarded by a tall maple tree that had just started to turn, the tops flaming red against the gray sky. I gazed up at it with a shiver of nostalgia. It reminded me of a house where I worked as a teenager and one of the kindest masters I'd ever known. I thought he'd cared for me. I might have even loved him in my own, inexperienced way, but I was already damaged by then, and when his wife summoned me to her bed, I didn't know how to refuse. When he found us, he broke a cane over my back and sold me to a much less pleasant neighbor. A harsh lesson on the conditionality of love.

I gave Tsukito's shoulders a shake, and he woke with a groan, scrubbing dust and sleep from his eyes with his small fists. We were met at the gate by a middle-aged woman with gray hair sprouting from her temples. She bowed low as the master and Yutaka passed, rising only after they had disappeared into the house. Her eyes were tired, and they drifted over Tsukito and me with a careful indifference.

"Come with me," she said.

I took Tsukito's hand and followed her down a stone path to the outbuilding that served at the servants' quarters. It was made up of one long room, flanked on each end by closets full of futons and lined with rows of small wooden chests for our few personal belongings. Each chest was topped with a basin, a pitcher, and a small brass mirror. It was easy to imagine the place at night with wall-to-wall futons, close enough to feel our neighbor's breath on our necks as we slept.

Our escort pointed me toward one chest and Tsukito to another at the other end. Tsukito yanked the drawers of his chest open with the enthusiasm of a child, inspecting the few garments within and throwing me a wide grin. Only someone so innocent could go from fear to excitement so quickly, his horrible ordeal turning into just another new adventure in the space of a breath.

The woman observed us both with narrowed eyes. "Are you his—is he your son?"

I swallowed around the lump in my throat. "His mother is dead."

"Oh." Her eyes softened a bit.

"I'll take care of him."

She nodded sharply. "Fine." Her posture went rigid again as she turned and padded back toward the door. "You will be working in the kitchen. The boy in the stables." She rolled her eyes as we stared at her dumbly. "Well, come on."

Tsukito started sniffling again as he was handed off to an old man who could have been her father for the resemblance. The same narrow face, the same burst of gray, though more pronounced, reached well behind his ears. She then led me to the kitchen where she introduced me to a portly old woman who scrunched up her face and raked rheumy eyes over me.

"Are you a man or a woman?" she asked, her nose millimeters from mine. The same question I'd been asked a million times before. I only ever had one answer.

"I am Asagi."

THE WORK WAS HARD, BUT NOT UNREASONABLY SO. I SPENT MOST OF the day moving heavy bags of rice and washing dishes. Tsukito and I found each other again as the sun was going down, tired but in one piece. He'd worn blisters into his palms from mucking stalls, and I dragged him toward the well where I washed them out and wrapped them in strips of cotton cloth. He seemed completely unbothered, chattering on about a horse named Kousuke who was now his best friend, and I marveled once again at his resilience.

A kernel of dread formed in my stomach as a group of men gathered around the well. One or two gave me a sidelong glance before stripping down to their fundoshi and dumping buckets of water over their heads. I took Tsukito's hand and pulled him back toward the servants' quarters, which was, for the moment, still empty, but soon would be full of women doing essentially the same. I didn't have much time.

I rushed us both inside and slid the door shut. "Can you do something for me?" I asked him. He nodded quickly, eyes wide and a conspiratorial glint in his eye. "Stay right here and watch this door. Tell me if you see anyone coming."

"Okay," he said with a sly grin before plopping down in front of the door and peering through a tear in the shoji. For him, it was a game, a small act of rebellion in his otherwise structured life. But in reality, he was protecting me at my most exposed.

Heart racing, I rushed across the room to my tonsu. I stripped down to my nagajuban and filled a basin with water from the pitcher. With a deep, steadying breath, I bared myself down to my waist. Flat, broad chest, narrow hips, wide shoulders. A man's body. I was certain that most, if not all, of my fellow servants knew what I was, but knowing and *seeing* were two different things. If they saw me, they would forever see only this, something strange and unnatural, a man with a girl's face.

Pushing the thought away, I washed as quickly as I could in the basin. I had just traded my soiled nagajuban for a fresh yukata when Tsukito raised the alarm.

"They're coming!" he whisper-yelled as he scurried away from the door, and I only just managed to cover myself before the room flooded with feminine voices.

Our quarters exploded with activity. I clutched my collar and averted my eyes, but the women paid me little mind as they dressed, and the tension in my belly gradually unwound. Tsukito pranced around me as I pulled his futon out of the closet and laid it out for him, and even as I wrestled him into it, his boundless energy showed no sign of running out.

"Be still, boy," I grumbled as I combed his hair and scrubbed the dirt from his cheeks.

"Do you think they'll let me ride the horses?" he asked, rocking back and forth on his hips.

"No."

He pushed his bottom lip out in a dramatic pout. "Maybe when I'm older—"

"I don't think so, Tsukito. Lie down."

"Why not?" He wiggled under his blanket and released a great yawn. His eyelids grew heavy as if the futon had cast some spell on him to sap his energy.

"Because they're for working, not for riding. Now, sleep."

A pout still on his lips, he snuggled down into his futon and let his eyes fall closed. I tucked his blanket around him and had started to stand when he whipped a hand out and grasped my sleeve.

"Don't go, Asagi."

"That's enough, Tsukito," I said, shaking him off. "Go to sleep."

"But I'm scared. What if there are monsters?"

"There's no such thing as monsters."

"My mom always used to—"

"I'm not your mother."

He gasped and yanked his hand back as if I'd slapped it, his little brows pulling together and his eyes welling. I hesitated, cursing under my breath, before giving in with a groan.

"Fine. Just this once and only until you fall asleep."

He grinned and wiggled over enough for me to squeeze into the futon next to him. He curled into my chest, his head against my heart and his fists balled in my collar. My own exhaustion barreled down on me as I wound my arms around his shoulders. He was so small, so warm, and it felt like home.

THREE

Weaker Men

A SHARP KICK TO THE BOTTOM OF MY FOOT STARTLED ME AWAKE.
Tsukito still slept beside me, arms and legs splayed and mouth hanging
open. The air vibrated with the sounds of heavy breathing and soft
snores. I blinked in the dark, my mind resisting waking, until a rough
hand came down on my shoulder.

"Wake up, Asagi." Yutaka stood over me, his hard face pulled into a
scowl. The only light came from a paper lantern he'd left at the door,
and it cut sharp shadows over his heavy brow. "Goshujin-sama wants
you."

Head still thick with sleep, I carefully rearranged Tsukito's limbs and
slipped out of the futon. Yutaka stopped me with a rough grunt as I
headed toward the chest that held my clothes.

"I should get dressed—"

"Now," he barked, jabbing a finger toward the door.

A burst of adrenaline shocked my heart into a fast rhythm, burning
through the fog of exhaustion. I bowed in acknowledgement and pulled
my thin yukata tighter around myself. I'd plaited my hair into a braid
before bed, and I did my best to tame the frizz as I followed Yutaka into
the night.

"He needs water for his bath," Yutaka said. He thrust a bucket into my arms before picking up the lantern and marching toward the well.

We walked in a bubble of light that made the surrounding dark look impenetrable. The air was warm and dense from humidity, and my yukata stuck to my back and chest. I held the bucket tight in front of me. I might as well have been naked.

When we reached the well, Yutaka set the lantern down on its edge and took a step back. The sword on his hip flashed like a threat in the low light. He watched in silence, arms tightly crossed, as I tied the bucket to a rope and dropped it down.

Once the bucket was full and retrieved, Yutaka led me to the ofuro, a small building off the back of the house, connected by a narrow engawa. A fire burned low underneath it, heating the tub above, and Yutaka tossed another log on as we walked by. It released a gasp of smoke and sparks before settling back into a steady glow.

Yutaka stepped up onto the engawa, and I followed, careful not to slosh the water from my bucket. The door of the ofuro slid open in a burst of steam. The master was already there, his bulk folded into the cast-iron tub set into the floor with water up to his navel. He looked like a boiled duck, his skin flushed and puckered. A saké bottle sat on a bamboo tray beside him, likely contributing to the red in his cheeks.

Chest tight and nerves tingling, I sat the bucket down and bowed low before setting to work. His gaze itched over my skin as I poured the water slowly into the tub to give it time to warm, careful not to splash his legs. The water level rose steadily, covering his round belly and ending up just under his armpits.

"You are a pretty one, aren't you?" His voice was gravelly and slurred with drink.

"Thank you, Goshujin-sama," I said with a bow, though my body screamed with alarm.

"It's no wonder Itachi-san's son was so enamored with you."

Cold slithered down my spine at the mention of my former master. His son was young and softhearted, unlike his father. He'd been kind to me, nothing more.

The master laughed, drained his glass, and then shook it in my direction. I lowered myself to my knees at his side and took up the saké bottle to refill it.

His cheeks flushed darker, his gaze drifting to the exposed skin at my collar. "I admit, I was nearly fooled myself." He raised a finger to trace the line of my braid where it fell over my shoulder. "Is that why you look like this? To gain favor? To draw your master's eyes?"

"Pardon me, Goshujin-sama," I said, a zing of resentment sharpening my tongue, "but I have no control over a man's eyes."

He laughed so hard his belly shook, sending water splashing from the tub. Relief washed over me until he snatched me by the braid and yanked nearly sending me face first into the water. The saké bottle rolled across the floor as I scrambled to brace myself on the edge of the tub, scalp burning, the master's rank breath on my cheek.

"You think you're smart," he hissed, spit landing on my mouth and nose, "but everything about you is a lie. The way you dress. The way you speak. I will not be fooled, understand me?"

"Y-Yes, Goshujin-sama."

"Get out." He released me, and I fell over backward.

Heart pounding, I scrambled to my feet only to be knocked down again when he hurled his bamboo tray at me. The edge struck me square in the bridge of my nose. My vision exploded in a flash of light. A burst of blood filled my sinuses and spilled down my face. I tried to push myself up. The ground tilted, and my hand slipped on the varnished wood. Strong hands grabbed me under my arms, and I thrashed blindly against them as they pulled me away.

Finally, they released me, and I dropped onto the cool grass. I shivered despite the heat, choking on blood and tears. Anger boiled in my gut, and despair cooled in my veins. It was always like this. Always.

"Can you stand?"

I blinked back the fog to find Yutaka standing over me, glaring down in his usual disinterested fashion. My knees wobbled as I pulled myself upright, and he reached out a hand to steady me.

"Don't touch me," I snapped as I slapped it away. Somehow managing to stay on my feet despite the intense urge to vomit, I took a few unsteady steps toward the servants' quarters.

"Where are you going?"

"Back to bed."

"You should clean yourself up first."

I ignored him, spitting a mouthful of blood.

"You want your boy to see you like that?"

I stopped. A needle lanced through my heart at the thought of Tsukito's wide, fearful eyes when he saw my bloodstained face. I half pivoted back toward Yutaka, who watched me closely, his brows low over his eyes. After a moment, he turned without a word in the direction of the well.

He'd already pulled up a pail of water by the time I reached it. I sank down to the grass, my back against the wood frame, and he set the pail down beside me.

"It might be broken," he said as he whipped a rag off a nearby clothesline and handed it to me.

"It's not broken." I dunked the rag in the cool water and pressed it against my nose.

"You sure?"

"I know what a broken nose feels like."

"This happen to you a lot?"

I laughed bitterly. "Once or twice."

"Why?"

I sighed. "I'm a man who looks like a woman. Who *wants* to look like a woman. I don't...make sense to people." I lowered the rag and sniffed. "People are afraid of what they don't understand."

Yutaka's brows pulled down even lower, his eyes practically disappearing beneath them. "And weaker men want to destroy the things they fear."

I lowered my eyes to the rag in my hands, now spotted with blood, and ran it through my fingers. "What kind of man are you, Yutaka-san?" I asked, my gaze falling once again on the sword at his hip. "Would you try to destroy me?"

Silence stretched long and brittle. Yutaka didn't move, but his figure softened. His fingers loosened around his sword, his shoulders relaxed, and when he spoke, his voice was gentle and warm.

"I'm not afraid of you," he said before leaving me alone in the dark.

FOUR

Hurt

I slept what was left of the night in fitful snatches. When I woke, the sky was gray with the coming dawn, and our quarters were already bustling. A headache throbbed behind my eyes, a steady reminder of the night before. I touched the bridge of my nose and told myself it could have been worse, much worse, that I did nothing wrong, yet the shame was still there cooling beneath my skin.

I groaned and pushed upright. My gaze swung down the line of bodies to Tsukito's futon, and my heart lurched when I found it empty.

"Where's the boy?" I asked to no one in particular.

"He went to the well with the men," answered Kimiko, the girl in the spot next to me, her hair bundled up in her hands and a leather strap pinched between her teeth. All the ladies wore kimono in deep blue, and it made her fair skin glow. Her eyes were striking. A perfect almond shape lined with a ring of black and a delicate shade of brown.

"I should go…" I started to stand, but a wave of dizziness sent me back down.

"Take it easy. He'll be okay," she said, laying a hand on my arm. "They like him. He's a sweet boy."

I released a long breath in an effort to let go of the tension, but it sat like a knot in my belly. He was fine, safe under the watchful eye of the others, but I knew I wouldn't feel satisfied until I saw him with my own eyes.

I pivoted on my knees to face the tonsu against the wall. It was a scuffed cherrywood chest with tarnished brass fittings. I tugged the top drawer open to find a scant collection of undergarments and accessories. The bottom drawer was deeper and held three kimono. Dark gray, like the men.

I slammed the drawer shut with a curse. My eyes burned, and pressure built in my chest until I couldn't breathe.

"I'm sorry," Kimiko said, laying a hand on my back. "When he told us someone new was coming…he wouldn't let us change them."

I pressed my fingers against the space between my eyes, the seat of my headache, until I saw stars, and the pressure in my chest eased as my body focused on this different kind of pain.

"You can wear one of mine."

I shook my head. "You'll only get into trouble."

Her eyes pinched, and her lips trembled. "It'll get easier, you know," she said gently. "It's only because you're new. Eventually he'll get bored and find someone else to pick on."

I nodded, though I didn't believe it. I was different. I would always be different, which made me an easy target. A flutter of warmth permeated through the cold when I thought of Yutaka's words the night before.

Weaker men.

Hardened with new determination, I pulled a kimono out of the drawer and cradled it in my lap. As if in response to my nervousness, Kimiko stood and slid open the door of the futon closet. I stepped inside with a grateful smile and used the relative privacy to slip out of my bloodstained yukata and into the kimono. I wore it long rather than bunched up around my knees like the men. The sleeves were short, but there was nothing I could do about that. In an effort to simulate curves I didn't have, I wrapped it tightly around my hips and loose around my chest.

When I emerged, Kimiko had left, but her charcoal pencil lay on top of her tonsu. I plucked it up and, with the solemnity of a religious ritual, lined my eyes and brushed out my hair so it fell long and loose over my shoulders. As I hid my true face, the more fragile part of me slid back and something stronger moved forward to take its place.

He'd tried to weaken me, but instead he'd created something androgynous and otherworldly. Something he couldn't touch.

The sun had burned the sky orange by the time I made it outside to fetch Tsukito. I found him as promised at the well, running circles around a group of bathing men. He had his yukata pulled down and tied around his waist. One of them dumped a pail of water over his head, and his boyish laugh rang through the garden, sending my heart soaring. His joy was infectious, and I saw it on the faces of everyone around him.

"Asagi!" He threw up his arms, sending a spray of water in every direction before launching himself at me. I staggered backward as he latched onto my waist.

"Easy, boy. You're soaking wet."

"You look so pretty!" he said.

I melted a little. "And you look a mess." I went down on my knees and swept my hand through his wet hair. "What have you been up to?"

"Bathing. Like a man." He planted his fists on his hips and puffed out his chest. "Hey, what happened to your nose?"

I flinched and brought my hand up to my face. "Oh. Nothing. Just what happens when you wander around in the dark in a strange place."

His face pinched, and before I could stop him, he grasped my face in his hands and planted a kiss on the bridge of my nose.

"What was that for?" I asked, blinking.

"My mom used to do that," he said, his eyes going far away. "She said love makes everything hurt less."

My throat constricted, and my heart did a little flip. "Smart lady, your mom."

"Yeah. I miss her." He sniffed and wiped his nose with the back of his hand. "But you're pretty good too."

Warmth exploded through my chest. My eyes burned. He was right. It did hurt less. But it hurt more too. The injustice, the unfairness of it all. He'd lost his mother and his home, been tossed into unsafe waters with an unfit replacement, yet he still found a way to smile. A heart like his was rare, and the world seemed determined to stomp it out.

The back doors of the house slid open, and my soft mood soured as the master stepped onto the engawa. Yutaka followed close behind, expression stoic as usual. His gaze stopped on me for the smallest of moments before jerking away, and something about it made my stomach ache. The master's gaze stopped too, only his lingered. First on me, then on Tsukito, and heated in a way that sent a painful fire through my veins.

Hands shaking, I tugged Tsukito's yukata back up over his shoulders. "Let's get you dressed—"

"Asagi."

My stomach sank as the master called my name. I stood and turned to face him, tucking Tsukito behind my back before bowing low. Even with my eyes on the ground, I felt his stare burning into me.

"I trust you slept well."

"Yes, Goshujin-sama."

"And your boy?" He rocked back and forth on his heels and thrust his big belly out like a walrus. "How is he adjusting?"

"Fine, Goshujin-sama."

A long, dense silence fell between us, punctuated by that awful sucking of his teeth. He leaned forward, stretching as close to us as he could without stepping off the engawa.

"It seems someone has bled all over the floor of the ofuro. Clean it up."

"Yes, Goshujin-sama."

I didn't lift my head until the door snapped closed behind him. Panting as if I'd just run a lap around the manor, I took Tsukito by the shoulders and pushed him back toward the servants' quarters. He obeyed with surprisingly few complaints, and as I helped him into his kimono, I noticed a hardness to his posture that wasn't there before.

"He hurts people sometimes," he said in a small voice.

I struggled to keep my tone light, though my heart was in my throat. "Where did you hear that?"

"The others." He dug his toes into the tatami and tugged on the edge of his obi.

"Don't be afraid. He won't hurt you. As long as you work hard and do as you're told—"

"Did he hurt you?"

Tears leaped to my eyes. I turned my face away to hide them. I didn't want to lie, but I also wanted to protect him from that ugliness, to let him stay that happy little boy for as long as possible.

"I'll protect you." His hands balled into little fists, and his face twisted into a determined scowl. "If he hurts you, I'll hurt him back."

My mouth went dry. I grasped him firmly by the shoulders. "No, Tsukito."

"Why?"

"Because I said no."

"But I'm strong." He raised his fists, and I wrapped my hands around them.

"I know you are. You're the strongest little boy I've ever met, but it's my job to protect you, understand?"

He lowered his hands, his scowl devolving into a pout. He vibrated with anger and frustration. It scared me. I knew the helplessness he felt, knew it so deeply it had fused with my bones.

"Don't worry. He can't hurt me," I said, pinching his nose. "I'm magic, remember?"

THE BLOOD TOLD A STORY I DIDN'T WANT TO SEE. A TRAIL OF DROPS where I staggered. A pool where I fell. A streak where Yutaka dragged me down from the engawa and onto the grass. The blow to the head had made everything foggy, but it was here in savage, undeniable clarity.

My forehead throbbed, and I pressed my fingers against it. Bile burned in my throat, and I swallowed it back. The pail in my hand felt full of stones. I let it fall heavily by my feet.

"Just clean it up." I dropped to my knees by the bucket. "Clean it up, and it'll be like it never happened."

I pulled the horsehair brush out of the soapy water and scrubbed at spots on the wood. I wanted them to disappear, but they just got bigger. The suds turned pink and then red until it was all I could see.

"Why do you antagonize him?"

I jumped at the hard voice behind me. A chill ran up my back, though a surprisingly not unpleasant one.

"What makes you think that?"

"The paint on your face, for one." I tensed as Yutaka's heavy footfalls drew closer.

I laughed a wet laugh. "You think a different kimono and a clean face will change anything?"

"It might make you less of a target."

I threw the brush in the bucket, spraying water all over the floor, and stood so fast I nearly took out his nose. "This is what I am." My voice cracked, and I cringed as its baritone reverberated off the walls. "Do you think he's the first master to punish me just for existing? He's not even the worst of them. I have bled far more than this for the *weakness* of men."

A shard of panic cut through me. *Baka! He's the master's right hand. What have you done?* We were close, so close he'd hardly have to raise his hand to strike me, but he didn't move.

I took two jerky steps back, out of arm's reach, and bowed low. "I'm sorry, Yutaka-san. I spoke out of place."

Sweat beaded on my brow as he took one long step forward. He cupped my chin in his hand, rough and calloused from sword training and hard work, and urged me upright with a gentle pressure. He held me there, back straight and head up, and I had no choice but to look him in the eye. The coldness I'd grown used to was still there, but at this distance, it looked different. It wasn't malice or disgust or even pity, but a shield. A shield that bulged and strained with the weight of what was behind it. His grip shifted, and he brushed the pad of his thumb gently down my swollen nose before taking a sharp step back and disappearing into the house.

FIVE

The Master's Eye

IT TOOK HALF THE DAY BEFORE I STOPPED SEEING BLOOD. THE SUN burned through the clouds, and even with all the shutters open, the ofuro turned into a sweatbox. I didn't mind it, though. I found it cleansing, and with every drop, the lines of my memory blurred a little more until the night before felt like a bad dream.

My job nearly done, I hunched over the well, my hair tied into a bun and a cool rag against the back of my neck. A bead of sweat rolled off the end of my nose. I traced its trail with my fingertip.

Love makes everything hurt less.

"BOO!"

I nearly went headfirst into the well as Tsukito's body slammed into my back. The air rang with a stream of giggles as he bounced a circle around me. My irritation dissolved into relief.

"What are you doing, boy? Don't you have work to do?"

"I'm done," he said, throwing up his arms in triumph.

"Good. You can help me with this, then." I pulled up a bucket of water and dropped it at his feet. "Fresh water for the bath."

He made a sour face at me before grasping the handle and waddling with it across the garden. A laugh bubbling in my chest, I pulled up a second bucket and followed. We arrived together, and with much more ceremony than the task required, he heaved the bucket over his head and dumped. More water ended up on the floor than in the tub. My heart floated. I'd spent all day in here, but only with his sweet voice in my ears did it feel clean.

After a triumphant lap of the tub, Tsukito scooped up both our buckets and pranced down the engawa as I closed the shutters. I turned in time to see the back doors of the house slide open. My blood froze. I sprinted after him and snatched him by the collar. He yelped as I pulled him to the side and forced his head down into a bow just as the master emerged. I stood beside him, head lowered and gaze on my toes, praying he would walk past.

He stopped.

My mouth went dry as he rocked back on his heels, the boards creaking under his weight. Yutaka was there too, his presence like a cool breeze across my skin. I wanted to look up. I wanted to know if he was looking at me, but I didn't dare.

The master was looking. I felt it like a brand down the nape of my bent neck. He blew a heavy breath out his nose like a bull, tracing the edge of his obi with his fingers. My stomach wrenched, and my sweat turned cold. The boards creaked again as he shifted his weight toward Tsukito. I cut my eyes to the side and caught him tucking his finger under his chin, tipping his head up.

"You're as pretty as your mother, aren't you?"

Cold rushed through me like falling through thin ice. My head reeled, and I couldn't breathe. My heart pounded. My ears rang. I clenched my fists so tight my fingernails dug into my palms. I wanted to slap his hand away, to bend his finger back until it broke.

His weight shifted again, and he was gone, taking Yutaka with him. The tourniquet around my lungs loosened, and my breath released in a choking gasp. My muscles trembled as they freed some of their tension, and I would have fallen had Tsukito not been there to prop me up.

"Are you okay?"

"Yes, I'm…" I took a step, swayed, and braced against a pillar. "It's the heat. I think I need to sit down."

Tsukito held my hand as I lowered myself down onto the edge of the engawa. He ran off to the well, returning with a ladle full of water. I took it gratefully, and my roiling stomach calmed.

"Did I do something wrong?" he asked, his small brows bunching over his nose.

"No. You did just fine." I offered him a smile that felt unconvincing even to me.

"How did he know?"

"Know what?" I asked, still struggling to control my breathing.

"That my mother was pretty?"

My throat constricted, and tears burned my eyes. I knew, of course. I knew by the hoarseness of his voice, his heavy breathing, his fingers twitching with the restrained urge to touch. He'd said it before he brought us here. *You are his mother now.* He was comparing him to me, which meant only one thing. The thing I feared more than a hundred broken noses.

Tsukito had drawn our master's eye.

THE NEXT DAY, I STOLE A KIMONO. THE SERVANTS' LAUNDRY HAD been done the day before, and come morning, the lines were adorned with deep-blue garments drying in the sun. I sneaked out in the early morning and pulled one down. Kimiko gave me a sly look when I emerged from the closet wearing it, the corners of her mouth turning up in approval at my rebellion.

But it wasn't rebellion. I'd made a decision that night with Tsukito tucked up against my chest. I wouldn't let him be broken. I wouldn't let that darkness in our master's eyes swallow him up as another's had me so many years before.

I'd picked an auspicious day. Whatever stir might have been caused by my change in appearance was overruled by panic. We were hosting a traveling merchant and his company, and the kitchen buzzed with energy as the women rushed to prepare tea and wagashi shaped like delicate pink flowers for our guests. Steam from boiling water made the air heavy, and rice flour clung to every surface. The old woman barked orders over our heads as we kneaded dough until our hands ached.

"BOO!"

I yelped as a weight slammed into my back, nearly knocking me face first into the dough I was kneading. I was the first station in an assembly line of ladies preparing steamed buns for that night's dinner. Tsukito threw his arms around my neck from behind, a mischievous finger reaching out to poke at the dough.

"What's gotten into you, boy?" He poured a stream of giggles into my ear. I swatted his hand away, leaving a patch of rice flour on his sleeve.

"It smells so good," he chimed. "Can't I have one, Asagi? Please?"

"You cannot. They're for the master and his guests."

His bottom lip protruded in a pout, and he slid off my back into a dejected pile at my hip. Sana, a sweet-faced girl with a generous smile, lifted the lid off the pot on the fire, filling the room with a burst of steam.

"Oh, lighten up, Asagi," she chided. "There's plenty enough to go around."

Tsukito's face brightened as she lifted a bun out of the pot with bamboo tongs and wiggled it in his direction, only to darken again when I shooed it away.

"And if he's caught with it, he'll get the cane for stealing."

Sana flinched, her smile wavering. She dropped her gaze and let the bun fall back into the pot. Tsukito laid his head on my thigh with a sigh, his eyes longingly following the path of my hands through the dough. A burst of warmth filled my chest as his little fingers traced patterns in the flour on the floor around my knees. He was still only a boy, but already I could see the man emerging in the height of his cheekbones and the sharp angles of his jaw. I gave his ear a pinch, and his smile returned as he squirmed and swatted me away.

"Asagi."

My head jerked up at the sound of my name. Yutaka stood in the doorway, his grim figure casting a shadow over the room. His gaze swept over the knot of ladies gathered around the fire before stopping on me.

I brushed the flour from my hands and stood. Heat bit at my cheeks as his gaze bounced over me, the muscles in his jaw tightening. For a long moment, far longer than what was proper, his eyes locked with mine.

"Clean yourself up," he said, voice gruff and guttural. "He wants you to serve."

I bowed low in acknowledgement, not lifting my head again until the floorboards creaked with his departure. My heart struggled against the panic clogging my veins. Tsukito watched the whole exchange with wide, worried eyes, the weight of the air telling him something was wrong even if he didn't understand what.

"Go back to the stables, Tsu-chan, before somebody misses you."

"But, Asagi—"

"Do as I say, boy," I snapped.

He flinched. Face pinched and eyes watery, he jumped to his feet and ran from the room.

Shaking off a cold splash of guilt, I peeled off my apron and rinsed my hands in a shallow pail of water. Sana appeared behind me to help smooth out a few strands of hair that had pulled loose from the round bun at my crown. I released the tasuki binding up my sleeves and shook them out.

Sana loaded up a tray with a teapot and a plate of wagashi. It rattled when she placed it in my hands. "Relax. You're invisible to them." She laid her hands over mine until they stopped shaking. "Just keep your eyes down, don't speak unless spoken to, and don't spill anything."

I nodded and took a deep breath to steady my nerves. This was my chance. My chance to show our master that I wouldn't break, a subtle challenge I was sure he would accept.

My heart beat loud in my ears as I ducked out of the kitchen and started toward the sitting room where we received our guests. The hallway was impossibly long, its walls pressing in on me until I could hardly breathe. I stopped outside the door, closed my eyes, and saw Tsukito's face.

It had to be me.

I dropped to my knees and carefully slid the door open. My master sat in the center of the room on his knees, back as straight as his round belly would allow. My stomach lurched as I spotted Yutaka seated against the wall behind him, posture rigid and eyes wary. Across from him in a similar position was a much smaller man in a purple kimono, his delicate features set in a friendly yet guarded expression, with an older man I assumed was his attendant stationed within arm's reach behind him.

None of them looked up as I touched my forehead to the floor. *You are invisible to them.* I picked up my tray and eased into the room, moving toward them with careful, almost silent steps. I set the tray down between them. The gentle breeze allowed in by the open shutters carried the sharp scent of the tea, whipping it around the room as I poured first my master's glass and then his guests'. Something itched along my spine. I lifted my gaze just enough to catch Yutaka's hard stare.

I jerked, causing the teapot to rattle against the edge of our guest's cup. He reached out to steady it, and his warm brown eyes met mine.

"I'm so sorry, Mahiro-san." My master's voice sent a tremor of panic through my muscles. "Asagi is new to my house and still in need of some polish, it seems."

I bowed low in apology, mouth dry and palms sweating. Avoiding my master's glare, I withdrew to the back of the room and positioned myself next to Yutaka.

"Stop it." I squeezed the words between my teeth just loud enough for him to hear, my gaze pinned to my knees.

"Stop what?"

"Looking at me."

"You draw attention." The words came out slowly, each one barbed.

I scowled and balled my hands into fists on my thighs. My attention swung back to the men at the center of the room. "Who is he?"

"Arakawa Mahiro. He controls half the rice in Musashi Province."

A hollow sound made me sit up straighter. My master tapped his empty teacup against the tray. I hurried to his side and took up the teapot again. When I offered to refill our guest's glass, he quickly drained what was left and replaced the cup upside down.

"I appreciate your hospitality," he started, "but the road has been long, so if you don't mind…"

"Of course." My master gestured to Yutaka. "Yutaka-san will show you to your room."

He stopped him with a raised hand. "No need. I'll find my way." He gave a slight bow before rising to his feet, followed closely by his attendant. I lowered my forehead to the floor, listening to the soft sounds of his footfalls and the snap of the sliding door.

"What are you up to, *girl?*" Pain burst through my scalp as my master grabbed my bun and gave it a fierce yank. He hunched over me and growled the words against my ear, his spit painting my cheek. "You think you can flounce around in here like a whore——"

"N-No, Goshujin-sama." I scrambled for balance, the skin of my brow burning as it ground into the tatami.

"——bat your eyes at Mahiro and he'd save you?" He released me long enough to flip me onto my back and take hold of my throat. "You think you can infect us all with your perversion, don't you?"

I opened my mouth to protest, but the words were pinched off in his grip. My lungs burned. My vision darkened. A shrill voice pierced the fog engulfing my consciousness.

"Stop!" A small body hurled itself into the room, knocking over the tea tray and slamming into our master's hulking form. The grip on my throat released, and I sucked in a lungful of air.

"Tsu-chan!"

I coughed and croaked out a sound of protest as Yutaka entered the fray. He grabbed the boy under his arms and peeled him off our master. Tsukito's long, spindly legs thrashed in the air as Yutaka hoisted him up and tossed him to the other side of the room.

My heart lurched when Yutaka reached for his sword. "Yutaka-san, please——"

Shoulders tense, head lowered, his back filled my vision like a wall of granite. His blade flashed as he pulled it from its sheath. A scream balled itself in my throat. He extracted the sheath from his obi with his opposite hands and raised it high.

I threw myself around his legs and covered Tsukito's body with mine. The sheath's downward arc halted just short of my shoulders.

"Please. He's just a boy." Tears poured hot down my face.

Yutaka rocked back on his heels, a muscle twitching in his jaw. He cast a glance over his shoulder at our master, who sat on his haunches, red-faced and spitting.

"Teach him some manners. One strike for every broken dish." Our master lumbered to his feet and thrust a fat finger in our direction. "If his *mother* refuses to move, let him take the pain instead."

Tsukito released a piercing wail. I curled my body around him. I could take it. It was my fault after all. For being strange. For being an improper mother to a boy who needed one. I laid a hand tight over his eyes and pressed my lips against his ear.

"We're not here." My voice caught, and my whole body shook. "This isn't happening."

I squeezed my own eyes shut as Yutaka squared himself up again and raised his sheath. He sucked in a deep breath, choppy and ragged.

The first strike came down like an explosion across my back. I bit down on a cry of pain. Tsukito released it for me, his whole body lurching with sobs. Another strike and my mind went dark. My mother's song drifted to the surface. It coated my skin and leaked from my lips until it was all I knew.

Four broken dishes. Four strikes. I kept singing. The beating stopped, but the pain continued, rolling through muscle and bone like peals of thunder. Multiple pairs of hands and a strong back carried me to the servants' quarters and dropped me into a futon made of needles.

My first real awareness was Tsukito crouched over me, his forehead pressed to mine and tears stinging my rug-burned face. My stomach twisted. He shouldn't see this. I didn't want him to see this.

"Take him away," I said, even as I reached for him. "Get him out of here."

"Asagi, I'm sorry. Please let me stay."

My heart broke at the sound of his pleas. Sana folded him into her chest and carried him outside. The moment his cries faded, I dissolved into shivering groans. Kimiko whispered soothing words in my ear as my muscles twitched against the hot pokers prodding them. She tried to peel my kimono back, but I clutched my collar.

"Asagi, please," she said gently. "I need to see how bad—"

"No." Shame ripped through me. Being bare in front of her was more than I could take. "Just go before he comes for you too."

She let out a long breath and placed a kiss on my temple before standing. Her footsteps receded and the door slid closed, dropping me into thick silence. I pressed my nose into the futon and focused on the pain. It was familiar, almost comforting. I sank into it, letting it drown out the anger and fear. Pain could be dealt with, could be treated, and would eventually fade. If only everything were so easy.

SIX

Love

I KNEW IT WAS HIM THE MOMENT THE DOOR OPENED. THE AIR solidified, and my body throbbed in response. I didn't move. His heavy footsteps drew closer and circled around me, followed by the weight of him dropping to his knees.

"Why are you here?"

"I…brought you this." I opened my eyes enough to see Yutaka's hands curled around a small glass tub filled with something viscous. "It's good for bruises."

I pushed upright, sending splinters of pain cascading from my shoulders to my waist. Yutaka reached out to help me. I flinched, and he pulled back. He wore the same stoic expression as always, only now there was darkness under his eyes and deep lines around his mouth I was sure weren't there before.

"Why do you do this to yourself?"

I released a choking laugh. "To *myself?*"

"You intentionally anger him."

"My existence angers him. You think anything I do or don't do will change anything?"

"You could stay out of his sight. Be less…"

I narrowed my eyes. "Less what?"

"Conspicuous."

"Like a girl, you mean." The lines around his mouth deepened. I laughed again and, despite the pain, leaned forward into his personal space. He swallowed hard but didn't move. "You don't understand anything, do you?"

"Maybe I understand more than you think."

I blinked and sat back. Something hung in the air between us, thick like smoke but impossible to grasp. His gaze dropped to the container in his hand, the skin on his neck darkening as if he'd just given up some secret.

"Turn around."

I balked. "No."

"You can't do this yourself." The muscles in his jaw twitched as he pulled the lid off the tub. "Turn around."

"Or what, you'll hit me?"

I regretted the words the moment they left my lips. Yutaka's shoulders dropped, and the shield behind his eyes cracked a little. When he spoke, the words were tattered and broken.

"I don't want to hurt you."

Tears flooded my eyes until I had to turn around so he wouldn't see. He loosened my obi and tugged my kimono down just enough to expose my shoulders and upper back. From his sharp intake of breath, I knew it must have been bad. He spat a curse followed by the rasp of calloused skin as he rubbed a dollop of ointment between his palms.

I gasped at the first touch. I thought his hands would be rough, that they would hurt, but they drifted over my bruises with such tenderness and care it made my chest ache. The ointment warmed as he spread it over my skin. My sore muscles unwound, and something deep inside me unwound too. Something long dormant and almost forgotten. His touch communicated all the things hidden in his long looks and his silences. I leaned into him as he pushed his way lower beneath my kimono, and it did hurt, but even the pain was sweet.

Love makes everything hurt less.

I stiffened and pulled away from him with a gasp, sending a shard of pain up my spine. His brows knotted as I tugged my kimono up tight over my chest, ducking my head against the heat in my cheeks.

"Please, leave." My voice sounded hoarse and strange to my ears.

"Asagi—"

"Please."

His eyes darkened. I thought he would argue, part of me wanted him to, but he just nodded once sharply before lifting to his feet. A cold swell of loneliness surged through me as the scrape of the tatami receded and the door slid open and closed. I didn't watch him leave. I couldn't. I was weak and too afraid of what would happen if I called him back.

THE NEXT DAY, I COULD HARDLY LIFT MY ARMS. TSUKITO HELPED ME brush and plait my hair. Something had changed between us, or in him, as if he'd grown up overnight. His laugh was more careful, his playfulness tempered, and my throat grew tight as he walked out with the men to start his day. Not ran out full of wild, youthful exuberance —walked.

The sun had just begun fighting off the chill of the impending fall as I struggled to pull a pail of water up from the well. My back and shoulders screamed with every pull, and the rope burned through my hands as my grip faltered and eventually gave out.

A big hand whipped out to grab the rope, halting the bucket's fall. Yutaka stood tall and imposing beside me, glare fixed on the rope as he pulled it up hand over hand. I shrank away. Something had changed between us too, and it made me feel strange. I flushed, like a fire burned inside me. His nearness only made it burn higher, and I wasn't sure I liked it.

"You shouldn't be doing this with your injuries," he said.

"I could have managed."

"Really?" He arched an eyebrow at me before feigning dropping the bucket back into the well.

I lurched forward to rescue it, and the corner of his mouth lifted. It was the first time I'd seen him even come close to smiling. It made my cheeks hot.

"Yes. Really." I pulled the bucket off the edge of the well and let it fall heavily to the ground, splashing a fair amount of its contents over our feet. Heat ran all the way down my neck as I struggled to lift and drag it toward the kitchen, stopping every three steps along the way.

Yutaka huffed and nudged me aside. He lifted the bucket easily with one hand and traipsed toward the house.

I ran around in front of him and wrapped my hands around the handle behind his. "Don't you have something better to do than annoy me?" He shrugged me off and kept walking. "Stop. What are you trying to do?"

"I'm trying to help you," he growled.

"You can't help me." Frustrated tears leaped to my eyes, and I blinked them back. "You can't intervene in his rages. You can't hesitate when he tells you to hit me. And you can't touch me after." A wet ball of emotion lodged in my throat. I nearly choked on it. "You can't...touch me."

He flinched. "Asagi—"

"How do you think this ends, Yutaka-san?" I couldn't stop the tremble in my voice. "If you don't want to hurt me, stay away from me."

He blinked once before his expression shuttered completely. He rocked back on his heels, pivoted, and trudged toward the house, the shape of his back an ink blot on the rising sun. The bucket lay on the ground at my feet, its entire contents spilled onto the grass.

OUR GUEST WOULD BE LEAVING THAT MORNING, AND DESPITE everything, I was still expected to serve his breakfast. Sana loaded down a set of trays with rice, miso, and grilled fish and sent me hobbling down the hall to the sitting room. Even that small weight made my shoulders burn, and I struggled against the tremors in my arms as I announced my entrance and laid out the trays. The party sat arranged just as before, only Yutaka was absent, and it made the room feel colder.

I took position behind my master as before, keeping my eyes down to prevent the misinterpretations that resulted in my last beating. They ate mostly in silence, broken only by polite comments on the food, before our guest announced his departure. My master escorted him out, leaving me alone to clean up.

"I see the way he looks at you."

I jumped at the master's voice from behind me. My gaze had drifted to Yutaka's spot in the corner as I cleaned. I jerked away. My heart slammed against my sternum. Did he mean Yutaka? He couldn't have seen. There was nothing to see. Yutaka looked at rocks with more warmth than me.

"Am I going to have to keep you in a cage to prevent you infecting my entire house with your perversion?" The words came out barely audible from between his clenched teeth. His shadow darkened the tatami around me as he drew closer. He flicked my braid with one finger, sending it over my shoulder and exposing the back of my neck. He dragged his fingertip along the edge of my collar and touched the exposed bruising there. "Maybe I should keep you close. Keep an eye on you."

I broke into an all-over sweat. My muscles coiled with the need to lash out. Sharp-edged words piled up on my tongue. I wanted to sling them, to cut him mercilessly no matter the consequences, anything to get his hands off me. But then the wind shifted, carrying with it Tsukito's high, joyous laugh. A shudder ran through me, equal parts resignation and relief. I had drawn the master's eye.

"As it pleases you, Goshujin-sama."

SEVEN

Monsters

I CARRIED THE WEIGHT OF THAT TOUCH ALL DAY, PRESSING DOWN ON the back of my neck like an anvil. No one objected when I slipped away from my duties early and returned to the servants' quarters. I knelt in front of my tonsu, gaze resting on the jar of ointment sitting on top. My back ached, but it was overshadowed by a sharper pain, less tangible but strong enough to take my breath away.

Maybe I should keep you close.

Adrenaline burned through my veins so hot I doubled over. I wanted to scream. I wanted to claw the skin off my neck. I wanted to run.

Approaching voices shook me from my thoughts. I took a deep, ragged breath and straightened. The door opened, and the familiar sound of feminine voices trickled over me. I wanted to absorb them, to wear them like armor against what was coming.

I pulled open the top drawer and extracted the few things that could be considered mine: a couple of yukata, those hateful gray kimono, a charcoal pencil Kimiko had given me. I arranged them in a bundle beside me. While everyone else carried on with their nightly routine, I waited.

My head popped up as Tsukito's wild energy entered the room and bounded toward me. He stopped short of his usual tackle, dropping into a bundle of legs beside me instead.

"Look what Kota taught me! Look!" He shook the short length of rope he carried in front of my nose. His lips pursed, and his brows lowered as he wound it in his hand to produce a simple slip knot. He held it up proudly, eyes bright. "Look!"

A laugh bubbled up in my chest even as my vision blurred. His smile faltered a little, and he leaned forward, curling his hand around mine.

"Are you okay? Does your back hurt?" He jumped up again and circled around behind me to tug at my braid. "Do you need help with your hair? I can brush it for you if it hurts."

"I'm fine, Tsu-chan." I grabbed his arm and tugged him back down beside me. "Be still for a second and sit with me."

He grinned and settled against my hip, his head resting against my arm. I lowered my nose into his hair and breathed him in deep. I wanted to remember that smell forever. The smell of sunshine and stables and insatiable youth.

Tsukito stiffened as his gaze fell on my little bundle. "What's that?" he asked, voice tight with panic. He looked up at me with wide, watery eyes. "What's going on?"

As if summoned by his question, the door slid open, and Yutaka appeared. Movement halted and voices hushed. He didn't say anything, just stood in the doorway, eyes on me and a hand on his sword.

Tsukito's focus jumped wildly between me and Yutaka. "You're leaving?" He gripped my sleeve and tears slid down his cheeks. "You can't leave."

"I'm not leaving. I'll be right there," I said, pointing through the wall to the main house. It might as well have been on the moon.

"But...who will keep the monsters away?"

Something broke inside me just then. I threw my arms around him and pulled him to my chest. "I'll keep them away," I said, swallowing my tears. "Even if you can't see me, I'll always be fighting them. I promise. So don't be afraid."

I pressed about a hundred kisses into his hair as he wept into my collar. Yutaka cleared his throat. With a feeling like ripping off my own skin, I tore away from Tsukito, gathered my meager belongings in my arms, and left without looking back.

Yutaka led me in silence through the garden and to a room in the back of the house. It was not so much a room as a closet with a worn-looking futon shoved in the corner. Situated directly between the kitchen and the toilet, fumes leaked in from both, making the whole place stink of something rancid. Wind whistled through damaged shoji, a promise of cold nights to come.

I took one small step forward. My cage. A place to keep me away from other men. And close to him. My stomach turned, and I braced against the wall to keep from falling. This was the plan all along though, wasn't it? To keep his attention on me and away from the boy. I should have been proud. Instead, I felt sick.

"You'll act as his attendant." I startled at Yutaka's gruff voice from behind me. "You'll serve his meals, help him dress. Stay close, but don't get in the way. He'll call for you if—"

"Be careful, Yutaka-san." I half turned to find him staring at me, lips tight and brows pulled low. "'I see the way he looks at you.' That's what he said to me."

Yutaka flinched and looked away. Silence fell thick around us, the room suddenly stifling. Yutaka shifted his feet, opened his mouth as if to speak, but just huffed and snapped the door shut.

"ASAGI!"

I jerked awake at the slurred and guttural sound of my name shouted from somewhere outside. For a disoriented moment, I forgot where I was. The space between shouts was too still, too quiet, the dark lying heavy and too close around me.

Another shout knocked loose the remains of my sleep. I leaped out of bed and hit my head on a low shelf. Cursing and rubbing at my sore scalp, I gathered myself the best I could before stumbling into the hallway. The house was dark except for a flickering lamp somewhere in the direction of the master's room. I rushed toward it, narrowly dodging a thrown saké glass as I rounded the corner.

"ASA—oh, there you are." He grunted from among a pile of cushions. His yukata hung loose and exposed the entirety of his belly, and his obi clung for dear life to his hips. The room looked as if he'd thrown some sort of fit. Flower vases were toppled, art had been knocked from the walls, and drawers tossed.

"I'm sorry to keep you waiting, Goshujin-sama." I bowed low but kept my eyes up in case he thought to throw something else.

"I've run out of saké."

"I'll look in the kitchen, Goshujin-sama."

"No. There's another bottle here, somewhere. I just can't find it." He rolled around in his cushions like a toddler who'd just learned to sit up. "Find it for me."

I swallowed a groan and bowed again before stepping into the room. The whole place stank of liquor and sweat. I made a circuit of the room, poking around piles of clothes and bedding with one finger, his eyes burning across my skin. I found the offending bottle tucked under his futon. His bloodshot eyes lit up. I ducked back out into the hall for his thrown cup, excavated a chabudai from the wreckage, and laid it at his side.

"Is that all, Goshujin-sama?" I asked after pouring his glass.

He scooped up his glass, knocked it back, and held it out for another fill. I complied and bowed to take my leave, but before I could straighten, his hand was on my neck. Every muscle locked as he tugged back the collar of my yukata and traced my bruises. It was like what Yutaka had done, yet completely different.

"It must have hurt when he beat you." His voice took on a husky quality, and bile rose in my throat.

"Yes, Goshujin-sama."

"Did you learn your lesson?"

"Yes, Goshujin-sama."

"I don't think you did."

I yelped as he yanked at my yukata and pulled it down off my shoulder. I clutched at my collar in a desperate bid to keep it closed.

"Or you wouldn't have come into my room so inappropriately dressed."

I could have made excuses, told him he woke me from my sleep. I could have apologized, groveled, begged for forgiveness, but it wouldn't have mattered. A black fog crept into the edge of my vision as his hand slithered down my back.

"What do you have under there?" His lips were close to my ear, hot breath painting my cheek. "A shriveled little cock?"

I'm not here. I'm not here. I'm somewhere else. I'm not here.

"Show it to me."

I closed my eyes. I didn't want to see his flushed cheeks, his dilated pupils, the bulge forming between his legs. My mother's song whispered to me from somewhere inside. It grew louder as I rose to my feet, and by the time my yukata hit the floor, it was all I could hear.

EIGHT

The Toad and the Moon

THE FIRST THING I WAS AWARE OF WAS THE ACHE. THAT TERRIBLE, nauseating ache that told me I'd been violated in some unthinkable way. Then the stickiness of my thighs, the scrape of my rumpled yukata. My scalp burned, and my braid lay tattered over my shoulder. I stood in the hallway in pitch dark, the master's closed door behind me, his stink all around me.

I tried to take a step, just one single step, but my bones had turned to noodles, and I fell headlong into the wall in front of me. I shook so hard my teeth chattered, and my skin broke out into a cold sweat.

"Asagi?"

A gruff but familiar voice materialized from the fog. A small light appeared in the hall, accompanied by a broad shadow. My heart jerked into a strange rhythm, and I leaned toward it.

"Yu…"

My stomach lurched. I fell to my knees as its contents splattered to the floor. The light rushed toward me, filled my vision, and then the world went dark again.

THERE WAS A MAN IN MY ROOM.

I awoke with a scream in my throat. I kicked away from the presence, slamming my back into the wall. A dark shadow sat against the door, a flickering oil lamp on the floor beside him. I squinted against the glare framing broad shoulders, strong hands, hard features.

Yutaka.

He didn't move, and for a moment, I thought I hallucinated him. He sat with one knee up, one arm resting on it, only his eyes visible over the top of it. They were rimmed with red. Only after my heart slowed did I realize he had cleaned me and changed my clothes, and a profound shame tore through me.

"You can't be in here," I croaked.

"I know."

He didn't leave, and I was at once angry and relieved.

"What did he do to you?"

"I think you know what he did."

He flinched, and his gaze dropped to the floor. Maybe he was hoping for a different answer.

"You knew this would happen."

I released a shaky breath and let my head fall back against the wall. "I've known what he wanted since the first day. I could see it in his eyes. How angry it made him."

"Then why—"

"Because I saw the same thing when he looked at Tsukito." Bitterness crawled up my throat, and I thought I would be sick again. "He's just a boy. It has to be me."

He balled his hand into a fist and squeezed his eyes closed.

A dark laugh rose in my throat. "What, are you going to avenge me?"

"Must you always belittle my feelings?" he hissed.

"Your feelings are misplaced." I wanted the words to be barbed, but they were flat, like words said over a grave. "I am below your station. You may as well fall in love with a toad. And I with the moon."

His shoulders slumped, the anger in his eyes replaced by an exquisite pain. That great black ball of loneliness welled up inside me again. I wanted to reach out, to take comfort in his presence, but the space between us was uncrossable.

"You can't be in here," I repeated, the words broken up by tears.

"I know."

NINE

A Safe Place

WEEKS SLID BY ALMOST WITHOUT NOTICE, MARKED ONLY BY THE
biting wind that leaked through my walls, signaling the change of
season. I traversed my days like a clockwork toy, wound up and released
without awareness or guidance. Life went on around me, but I was blind
to it. I bumped into walls, tripped over my own feet, waiting only for the
slow and inevitable wind down.

By moving me out of the servants' quarters, the master succeeded in
isolating me from the rest of the house. Attending to his needs occupied
every second of my time, my sole contact with the others was my brief
appearances in the kitchen to fetch his meals. Sana did her best to keep
me apprised of what was happening, especially as it came to Tsukito.
He'd grown out of his shoes. He'd had a birthday. He was strong and
smart but woke almost every night from nightmares and asked about me
daily.

I missed him. I missed his lilting voice and him crawling into my bed
every night. My heart tore itself to pieces with every beat, but I didn't
dare see him. He'd take one look at my sunken eyes and sallow
complexion and *know*. I couldn't risk him doing something foolish to
protect me, so I told Sana to tell him I was fine, that I was happy in my
new position and thought of him every day.

The truth was, I thought of him every second until I worked myself
into such a worry I fell sick. Yutaka found me collapsed in the hallway,
the master's breakfast scattered around me. Next I knew, I was back in
my frigid and stinking room with a doctor hovering over me, shivering
and sweating and racked with searing pain.

I felt the cold hand of death, felt it dragging me down as I struggled
to stay afloat, felt the temptation to stop fighting and let myself sink. But
as the darkness closed in, a tiny light fluttered in the distance, small and
warm and so bright. I reached for it, cupped it in my hands, pulled it to
my chest, and found myself surrounded by the smell of the stables and
sunshine.

I cracked my eyes open to find something warm and trembling
pressed against my chest. Tsukito lay curled up against me, head buried
in my chest and hands bunched in my collar. He slept fitfully, cheeks
flushed and eyes moving rapidly behind his eyelids. His lips parted, and
he mumbled something in his sleep.

"Okaasan…"

I opened my mouth to speak, but it came out a groan. Tsukito's eyes
popped open.

"Asagi!" His sweet voice stitched the pieces of my broken heart back
together.

"What are you doing, boy? Go back to your own bed," I croaked
even as my body instinctively curled around him.

"They said you were sick."

"If he finds you here…"

"He won't. Nika-chan sneaked me in."

My eyes rolled toward the door where one of the servant girls
peeked inside. She gave me a small smile before sliding the door shut. I
released a long sigh as I buried my nose in his hair, and something
uncoiled inside me.

"I've missed you," I said, tears streaming down my nose. I knew I
should have pushed him away, should have told him lies and sent him
back to the relative safety of the servants' quarters, but I didn't have the
strength.

"Is he hurting you?" he asked after a long silence. I didn't want to lie to him, so I stayed silent. His body tensed, his expression hardening into something so unnatural on him it scared me.

"Promise me," I said, drawing on my last reserves to hold myself together. "Promise me you won't misbehave. No matter what happens—"

"Asagi—"

"Promise me, Tsukito." I clung to him as the room tipped. My vision clouded with images of him enacting some childish revenge and the bloody aftermath. "Please, just promise me you'll be a good boy. Promise me…"

I repeated my plea over and over, the words barely a breath until they gave out entirely. I clung to Tsukito in the encroaching darkness, and even with pain lancing through every one of my muscles, I was no longer tempted to sink.

My health improved dramatically after that night. They said it was nothing short of a miracle. By the following afternoon, I was able to sit up and even eat a little of the bland porridge the girls brought to me. Every day I got stronger, and every night Tsukito would sneak into my room and curl up against my chest while I selfishly prayed for the sun to stay hidden forever.

It was on just such a night, with Tsukito tucked up against me and jabbering away about the antics of the stable boys, that the door flung open and the master stood ominously behind it. I jumped out of the bed and to my feet, pulling Tsukito behind me. The master's face jerked as his gaze fell on the boy before settling into something even more menacing. His eyes gleamed darkly, his lips twitching into an almost smile as he watched my face go pale.

"I see you're feeling better," he growled.

"Y-Yes, Goshujin-sama," I answered.

"I've spoken to the doctor," he said. "You're ready to go back to work."

I gave a bow of acknowledgement. We stood in heavy silence, the only thing breaking it that dreadful sound of the master sucking on his teeth. My grip tightened on Tsukito's arm where I held him behind me. The master studied us as he had that first day, measuring us up like livestock. My palms started to sweat.

"I need you in my room." His gaze cut to Tsukito with a sickening heat. "Bring the boy with you." With that, he turned and sauntered off.

Blood rushed in my ears, and my chest felt tight. Every muscle tensed. My entire body screamed, *Run! Get him away from this place!* But where could we go? Who would help us? The invisible and the unwanted. Where could we possibly hide that our master's hand couldn't reach?

"I want you to do something for me." I dropped down on my knees in front of Tsukito and took both his hands in mine. "I want you to close your eyes and think about a place where you feel safe. Can you do that?"

"Yes," he said, squeezing his eyes shut.

"Can you see it?" I asked. He nodded, his face scrunching up and his tongue poking out a little. "Good. Now I want you to bury it deep inside your heart. Somewhere no one else can get to it. And when something bad happens, I want you to go there."

"But why—"

"Because our hearts are the only thing that's ours to control. It's the only thing he can't touch."

His eyes opened, shining with the first shimmer of fear. I brought his hands to my lips, kissed each one, and with my heart tearing itself to pieces all over again, led him out into the hall.

TEN

Powerless

Heart pounding, throat dry, my body tense with panic, I clutched Tsukito's hand in mine as we made the short walk down the hall to the master's room. We passed Nika on the way, who bore a fresh bruise on her cheek. Her eyes welled at the sight of us. I turned my face away. It wasn't her fault, but still I couldn't look at her.

When we reached his door, I dropped to my knees, instructing Tsukito to do the same. Once again, I thought about running, but fear of the cane nailed me to the spot. Phantom pain splintered across my back, and I looked over at Tsukito's small form. I could survive it, but could he?

The master cleared his throat loudly from the other side of the door. Without rising, I slid the door open. Tsukito and I both touched our foreheads to the tatami before slipping inside and closing the door behind us. The master stood against the back wall, a saké cup in his hand and an evil twist to his lips.

We stood before him with our heads lowered. Tsukito stood very close to me and sneaked his hand into the folds of my clothes as the master took one long step forward. My mouth went dry as he slipped his finger under Tsukito's chin and tipped his head up.

"You really do take after each other, Asagi. One could believe he was actually your son."

Without thinking, I thrust myself between them, forcing the master to take a staggering step back. Anger flared in his eyes, and adrenaline zapped through my veins.

"Please, Goshujin-sama," I said, voice tight and tremulous. "I'm sorry he sneaked in when he wasn't supposed to. It's my fault for not teaching him properly. Punish me."

"Get out," he barked.

I didn't move. "Please, Goshujin-sama."

"I thought your *mother* would make a good attendant," he snarled around me, "but he is disobedient. Perhaps you'd like to work for me instead."

"No, Goshujin-sama, please. He's just a—"

My pleas broke off as the master swung his meaty fist into my ribs, sending me gasping to my knees. Tsukito screamed and hurled himself at the master, who caught him easily by the wrists.

"Yutaka!"

The door burst open and Yutaka appeared, wide-eyed and hand on his sword. He hesitated an instant before lurching forward and hauling me kicking and screaming to my feet by my armpits.

I clawed at the air for something, anything to stop my inevitable backward momentum. Tsukito cried my name over and over, his arms outstretched just beyond my reach as he struggled in the master's grasp. My lungs burned. My heels scraped across the tatami. Paper walls tore under my flailing hands as Yutaka dragged me out and down the hall.

"Let me go!"

Yutaka growled as he threw me into my room. I fell against the back wall, floundered, found my feet, and sprang forward again. I couldn't see, couldn't think. I only knew I had to get Tsukito out of that room.

"Stop, Asagi." He easily thwarted my tackle with a shoulder in my solar plexus.

"Get out of my way, Yutaka. I have to stop him. He's just a boy." He didn't move. I beat my fists into his chest, and he grabbed me by the forearms to hold me at bay. "How could you? You know what he'll do to him. Why won't you let me go?"

"He'll want your head if you go back in there."

"I don't care."

"Who do you think he'll send after it?"

I froze. For the first time, I saw the bare, raw pain in his eyes. I felt how his hands trembled where they held me, heard his voice shake.

"Please, don't do that to me."

All the strength drained out of me like a punctured balloon. It was useless. Me, Tsukito, even Yutaka, we were all nothing to him. We were just pieces on a game board he could move around to do his bidding. No matter how I raged, the master was the master. We were his property, to do with as he wished. I had no more power against him than a rabbit did against a fox.

My legs gave out, and I sank to the floor. Yutaka came down with me, his arms around me the only thing keeping me from dissolving altogether. I wailed into his chest, alternating beating against it and clinging to it. I knew he was right. There was only one way this could end. And I was so angry.

He held me long after I'd exhausted myself. He pulled away only after the master called his name from down the hall. Before he left, he pressed his forehead against mine, and in that silence, I knew him—his pain, his regret, his powerlessness. I might have forgiven him then. I needed to forgive him, and he needed to be forgiven. We had nothing else.

I stayed up all night, but Tsukito never returned to my room. Yutaka reappeared sometime after sunrise, his eyes red, the skin beneath them bruised and raw. Another man stood behind him, which could mean only one thing.

The master was done with me.

An iron door came slamming down inside me, leaving me so cold I couldn't stop shaking. I moved like a sleepwalker as Yutaka eased me to my feet and escorted me out of the house to an awaiting horse cart. I hesitated before stepping into it, casting a long look over my shoulder at the house.

"It'll be better for you." Yutaka stepped up close to me, his strained words barely reaching my ear. My eyes burned, and my throat constricted.

"How can it be better when I'm leaving my heart behind?"

ELEVEN

Girl

———

THE CART TOOK ME TO ANOTHER HOUSE A HALF DAY'S RIDE AWAY IN Musashi Province, just outside Edo. Rolling hills dropped into marshy flatlands as we crossed the river basin. A patchwork of farms spread like a blanket over the lowlands, most bare, a few sporting hearty winter crops fighting against the early snows. I felt every mile of that road as if it were marked in bruises, my heart pulled thinner the farther we rode.

I dropped into a fitful sleep only to be jerked out of it at the remembered sound of Tsukito's screams and the master's vile grin. Part of me wondered when exactly he had sold me. Bitterness welled up in me when I realized it could have only been when I started to recover from my illness. When he had decided I was broken and no longer worth keeping, like a piece of cracked china.

The cold leeched all the way into my bones, and I shivered uncontrollably as the driver pulled the cart to a stop. He yanked me roughly to my feet. With a hand under my arm, he dragged me stiff legged and stumbling to the gate of a house not unlike the one I had just left. Sloping brown roofs and blue-green treetops poked their heads over a stone wall. An elderly gentleman in a modest gray kimono and heavy haori stood just outside. He jumped to attention as we approached.

"I've come with——"

"Yes, yes, that's quite enough," the old man interjected, waving his hands and swinging a little purse full of coins. The brute beside me blinked, clapping his mouth shut as the old man pressed the pouch into his palm and pried his hand from my arm. "I'll take it from here, thank you."

Confused and more than a little crestfallen at the shift in power, the driver clutched his meaty hand around the coins and pulled himself back up onto the cart.

"Shoo! Shoo!" the old man shouted as the cart pulled away, kicking at the dust and making obscene gestures in his wake. "Savages." He spat on the ground before stomping to the gate and pushing open a small wooden door. He disappeared through it, his head popping back into view a second later. "Well, come on, girl!"

Girl. He vanished again before I could correct him. Arms wrapped tightly around myself, I ducked through the small opening and into a lush garden abloom with winter flowers. The old man shuffled down the stone path to a wide house encased in bright-white screens, closed up tight against the chill. He kicked out of his sandals and gestured for me to follow before sliding the screen open just wide enough for the two of us to squeeze through.

The difference between the inside and the outside was astounding. A fire crackled in a sunken brazier in the center of the room, warming the air until it glowed. Light danced over elaborately painted screens, making the animals depicted on them seem to move, turning the wide expanse of tatami into a forest teeming with life. Next to the brazier sat a small man, his entire lower half hidden under a chabudai and a thick robe draped over his back. He didn't look up when we entered, focused on the brush in his hand and the stack of papers before him.

Straightening his haori, the old man at my side gestured me forward and cleared his throat softly. "Pardon me, Mahiro-sama," he said, bowing low. "The new girl has arrived."

The small man lifted his head, blinking as he struggled to adjust his focus. "Ah! Thank you, Ryuichi," he exclaimed, dropping his brush and hopping gleefully to his feet. "You must be Asagi. My name is Arakawa Mahiro. Hajimemashite."

Still unable to unlock my jaw, I bowed in acknowledgement. Arakawa Mahiro. Was he the master of this house? Compared to my previous master, he couldn't be more opposite. The oversized robe over his shoulders dwarfed his slim, small frame, giving him a childlike appearance. His already narrow eyes practically disappeared as his dainty mouth pulled into a warm smile. His gaze didn't burn with lechery as he looked me over, but rather a gentle concern. A memory whispered at the back of my mind, but my grief drowned it out.

"My, did you travel all this way without a coat?" he asked, eyes widening. "You must be freezing. I absolutely detest being cold. It takes a special sort of cruelty—"

He whipped the robe off his back, revealing a bright-purple kimono. He moved to drape it over me, stopping short when I flinched away from his raised hands. He sucked in a breath, his cheerful expression dropping with understanding, and pulled his arms back.

"I am…aware of the sort of house you came from," he said in a low voice, laying the robe over my hands instead. "I promise you, you'll have none of that to fear from me."

Swallowing hard, I bowed my thanks and wrapped the robe around me. It felt delicious, warm from his body heat and the nearby fire. Muscles unwound as the cold melted away. He'd given me the coat off his back. No master I'd ever had would dream of doing such a thing. A flicker of hope lit inside me as he graced me once again with a kind smile, but I held it at a suspicious distance.

"Kira!" At Mahiro's call, a petite young girl appeared and scurried to his side with a quick bow. "Asagi will be joining you in the kitchen starting tomorrow. In the meantime, would you please find her a fresh kimono and show her to the servants' quarters so she can settle in?"

Her.

"Yes, Mahiro-sama," she said in a girlish voice, bowing again.

"Feel free to take the rest of the day to get acquainted with the property. You must be exhausted," Mahiro said, turning his attention back to me. "Kira here is one of my best girls. If you have any questions, she will happily answer them for you."

"This way, Asagi-san." She touched my elbow and gestured for me to follow.

I bowed to Mahiro, who nodded and winked, sending a rush of warmth to my cheeks.

I followed Kira down a dim hallway toward the back of the house. She moved quickly despite a slight limp that gave her a shuffling gait. Her tightly bound hair came loose in little tufts at her hairline that bounced as she walked. She pointed to doors as we passed, rattling off their uses: parlor, guest room, dining room. I curled my fingers in the robe clinging to my shoulders as I struggled to keep up, committing each of them to memory, until she stopped so abruptly I nearly ran her over.

"Closet," she said, sliding open the door to a large storage area with a flamboyant sweep of her arm. The back wall was lined with shelves up to the ceiling, each carrying a load of kimono boxes. She turned to study me, squinting dark eyes and pursing berry-colored lips. "You're so tall…"

My shoulders slumped, and I lowered my head as she poked through boxes of drab gray and brown garments. She fetched a stool and climbed on it, fishing around over her head on the topmost shelf until she pulled out a dusty box with a triumphant squeak.

"This should do for now," she said, shoving the box into my hands, "until we can get you something of your own."

My own? What was this place?

Kira closed the closet door with a snap and took off down the hallway again. I had to run to catch up. I nearly lost her around a corner before she stopped again at a dead end bordered all around by doors.

"This wing is for the women," she said. "Four to a room. You'll be in here with me." Another sweep of her arm revealed a modest six-mat room with a row of small tonsu along the back wall and a pile of futon in the corner. "The one on the end is empty," she said, gesturing toward the tonsu. "There's water in the pitcher if you want to wash up."

Clutching the kimono box to my chest, I took one slow step into the room. It didn't seem real. It didn't seem *fair*. Hell I was used to, maybe even deserved after all that had happened. This was…

"You don't have to be afraid," Kira said, sensing my hesitation. I looked over my shoulder to find her leaning on the doorframe, a dreamy look in her eyes. "Mahiro-sama rescued me from someplace awful too. I remember how hard it was to accept that things could be better. But he's a good man. A *really* good man." She smiled softly, cheeks pink with adoration. "You can trust it, I promise."

I took a deep breath to still my nerves and bowed. Kira popped off the wall and vanished down the hall with promises to check on me later, leaving me alone. The effects of my long journey hit me all at once, and I fell to my knees in front of my tonsu. Tears pushed hard on the backs of my eyes. Tsukito would love it here, would flourish here. He could be the happy little boy he deserved to be. I slammed the kimono box down on top of the tonsu, cursing the fates for being so cruel.

"Get ahold of yourself, Asagi," I growled, scrubbing at my face. Like everything else, it was out of my hands. I had a new master now.

Sniffling, I reached for the pitcher and basin in the far corner of the room and pulled it toward me. I slipped out of the robe Mahiro had given me and, heat rising in my face again, held it for an indulgent moment to my nose. It smelled like sweet smoke and flowers. I folded it carefully, setting it on the floor to my left before tugging my hair loose of its braid and letting it fall down my back. I groaned as I ran my fingers through my tangled locks, gritty with dirt and oil. I desperately needed a wash.

Taking a quick glance behind me to make sure the door was closed and I was alone, I stripped down to my nagajuban and loosened the collar until it draped off my shoulders. I pulled the length of my hair forward until it hung over the basin and poured a thin stream of water over it. With a wooden comb I found in the top drawer of the tonsu, I brushed it through, loosening the knots and stripping the buildup until it shone. Satisfied, I tossed it back over my shoulder, shaking out the remaining water clinging to it.

I closed my eyes for a moment before I slipped my arms out of my nagajuban and let it pool around my waist. Ignoring the deep-yellow bruise flowering over my rib cage, I let my mind drift into fantasy as I filled the basin with water and plunged a clean cloth into it. I imagined I was a proper lady bathing herself under the soft glow of moonlight, surrounded by beautiful things. Something sacred and untouched.

A shrill scream from behind me made me jump to my feet. *Kira!* I yanked my nagajuban back into place, but it was too late.

Hands clapped over her mouth, eyes wide, Kira stared at me from the doorway as if she'd walked in on a monster shedding its skin. In a way, I suppose she had.

"Kira-san…"

Her eyes widened even further, and she drew back at the sound of my deep voice.

"Kira-san, please don't—"

Like a bolt, she took off down the hallway. Fear sliced through me as she called Mahiro's name, and I flew after her. She meant to tell Mahiro! To tell him that I wasn't what he thought I was, that the girl he'd bought wasn't a girl at all. That she was some kind of deviant, a pervert, a freak.

I grabbed at the back of her kimono, but she slipped out of my hands just as we rounded the corner to the main room. Mahiro was already on his feet, surely roused by her cries, and she threw herself onto her knees in his path.

"Mahiro-sama!" she whimpered, shaking and pointing an evil finger at me. "She's a—he's a—she's a he!"

I froze and my stomach dropped to my feet as Mahiro's gaze swung in my direction. Panic blurred my vision, and I fell to my knees before him, pressing my forehead to the floor.

"I'm sorry, Goshujin-sama," I said, the words tumbling out of me. "I didn't mean to—I wasn't trying to deceive you, Goshujin-sama." I cringed, the sound of my voice offensive to my own ears. "Please…don't put me out."

"Put you out?" Mahiro said with a soft laugh. "Why on earth would I do that?"

I gasped, but didn't dare raise my head. "Because I'm not…what you wanted."

"Oh, Asagi…" A slight rustling and then a swath of purple appeared at the edge of my vision. A gentle hand touched my shoulder, then under my chin, lifting my head until I had no choice but to look into his face. "You are exactly what I wanted."

TWELVE

Mourning

I DIDN'T KNOW IF IT WAS HIS WORDS, HIS GENTLE TOUCH, OR JUST HIS quiet presence, but my panic evaporated. It didn't disappear but hung in the air like a dense fog around us, blocking out everything else. There was no Kira, no deceit, no tarnished past, only a storm of pointless emotion with Mahiro at its epicenter, the peaceful eye shielding me from the tempest.

He brushed a tear from my cheek. Without thinking, I let my head fall into his chest. He released a small shocked laugh. Remembering myself, I jerked back. The connection broken, the mist condensed and rained down on me again, plunging me into a typhoon of fear.

"I'm sorry—"

Mahiro raised his hand to stop me. He pulled himself to his feet, smoothing his kimono as he turned back to Kira. "It seems I owe Kira an apology."

Kira blinked, her face still pale with shock and her hands clutched at her chest. "You knew?"

"Of course I knew," Mahiro answered with a laugh. "Do you think me blind, dear?"

Kira blushed and shook her head.

"Besides, we have met before."

I sucked in a breath as a wave of foggy, disparate memories washed over me. A purple kimono. A small man with kind eyes and half the rice in Musashi Prefecture.

Mahiro tipped his head in a small nod as the pieces came together. Our visitor. A trickle of shame ran down my back as I wondered if he'd seen the beating I received that day. Likely he at least heard it. Was that why I was here?

He addressed Kira once again. "I hope this doesn't affect your relationship."

"N-No, Mahiro-sama" she said, though her expression looked unsure.

"Good." Mahiro walked past her, dropping back down next to the brazier with his back to us. Kira danced a little circle on the tatami before disappearing in what I could only presume was the direction of the kitchen. I stood and took a single step toward the servants' quarters before stopping.

"Excuse me, Goshujin-sama. About my room…" Mahiro pivoted on his hip and gave me a questioning look. "Should I move? With the men?"

"Would you be more comfortable there?"

I hesitated a moment, dread welling in the pit of my stomach, and shook my head.

"Then I guess that is between you and your roommates, ne?"

"Yes, sir."

"Oh, and Asagi," he said, stopping me as I turned to leave. "When you are finished dressing, could you return my robe? I am catching a chill."

I blushed fiercely, suddenly aware of my inappropriate attire, and bowed in acknowledgement. Flustered and pulling at the collar of my nagajuban, I hurried back down the hall to my room. I fell through the door and snapped it shut behind me. Panting, heart ricocheting off my ribs, I slid to the floor. I fell into a fit of sobs, realizing despite all the guilt and shame how much I wanted this place, how much I desperately needed to feel safe, to trust my master as Kira did.

Mahiro was so kind, so patient and understanding, it just couldn't be real. He knew what I was from the start. Why didn't he correct the old man when he introduced me? Was it some kind of courtesy? But for who, me or the old man? And why *didn't* he warn Kira when she would surely house me with the women?

In his eyes, I wasn't a perversion. I wasn't an infection that would corrupt his house. I wasn't something to hate, or fear, or destroy.

I was just Asagi.

I shook my head as if I could throw off the questions and told myself it didn't matter. Gathering myself, I pushed away from the wall, snatched up the still-wet cloth from the basin and scrubbed my face. I quickly shook out the long-sleeved kimono Kira had provided me and threw it on. As predicted, it was too small, hugging my shoulders and showing a scandalous amount of leg, but infinitely better than the insult I'd been given before.

I pulled my socks up as high as they would go, gathered up Mahiro's robe and headed back down the hall. As I rounded the corner, I ran smack into Kira. She yelped and pulled away, looking at first as if she wanted to flee, but ultimately decided to stand her ground. Head high, arms crossed over her chest, she stared me down with a mix of curiosity and hostility that made me want to sink into the floor.

"I'm sorry for misleading you," I said.

Kira lowered her eyes and shuffled her feet, tugging at a tuft of hair at the nape of her neck. "So…" she started,. "you're certainly not a woman, but you're not really a man either, are you?"

The grand question. I bit down on the urge to say something spiteful. "Maybe I'm both. Maybe neither." Kira's brow furrowed, and her small lips puckered. "If I make you uncomfortable, I can move—"

"With the men? No way." Her gaze jerked back up to mine. "They will eat you alive." She tapped her foot, tugging on her hair again as she considered, the hostility in her eyes replaced by genuine concern. "You can stay," she said finally with a huff. She pointed a threatening finger toward my crotch. "If I catch you looking at my tits, I'll make you a full woman, understand?"

"Understood," I said with a quick bow. I found myself admiring her, her feistiness and confidence. She nodded, the matter settled, and stepped aside to let me pass.

I found Mahiro right where I left him, hunched over his papers in the glow of the firelight. A pot of tea steamed on a tray next to him, filling the air with its sharp aroma. He reached for it, shivering and rubbing his arms, but stopped short as he caught me in his peripheral vision.

"Oh, Asagi." His face lit up, and he beckoned to me with a wave of his hands.

"I'm sorry to keep you waiting, Goshujin-sama." I bowed before quickly closing the distance to drape the robe over his shoulders. He sighed in relief, pulling it practically up to his nose. I knelt at his side, took up the teapot and poured the green tea into a gold-embossed cup. Mahiro poked his fingers out of the robe, wiggling them in my direction, and I passed the cup into them.

"You are wonderful," he said, his face emerging from the robe to take a long sip.

I bowed, my cheeks hot. How was I wonderful? When I started to stand, he stopped me with a hand on my arm.

"Would you sit with me?"

"Goshujin-sama?"

"I am so bored with all this," he said, kicking at the little table in front of him. "The business of running a house is tedious. Your presence would be a welcome distraction."

I nodded and settled back down, topping off his teacup when he held it out to me. He hummed as he drank, closing his eyes and savoring the warmth. He was, in a word, mesmerizing. Despite the impropriety, my gaze drifted up to watch his eyelids flutter, dark lashes on cheeks slightly reddened from the cold. Once again my fears and worries melted away, replaced by an unfamiliar serenity. Part of me wanted to resist it, to hang on to the anxiety that had become so familiar. Comfortable was dangerous. It was like sitting on a pillow over a pit of vipers. Any instant, it could be snatched away, dropping me unaware and unprotected to my doom.

"How are you settling in?" he asked, his dainty lips hovering just over the edge of the teacup. Steam curled around his nose. "Are you comfortable? Aside from Kira's outburst, of course."

"Yes, Goshujin-sama. Thank you." Warmth rose in my cheeks, and I lowered my eyes, picking at the edge of my fingernail.

"I must apologize for her," he said. "She is a good girl, but excitable."

"It's no problem, Goshujin-sama. It's not an uncommon reaction."

"Even so, I would expect better from her." His nose wrinkled in distaste.

"You won't punish her, will you?" I said, a note of concern in my voice.

"No, of course not." He held out his teacup, and I refilled it again as we dropped into a thoughtful silence. My gaze ventured upward again, this time focusing on his slim fingers around the cup. "How long were you with your previous house?"

"Oh, um…" I swallowed hard, my heart skipping a bit. "A little less than a year, Goshujin-sama."

"Not long at all," he said, his eyebrows bouncing. "Though, with that beast, I am sure it felt like an eternity. You must be happy to be free of that place."

I opened my mouth to express gratitude, but the answer stuck in my throat as a cold knife of loneliness sliced through me. Tears sloshed around inside me again, and I clenched my fists in my kimono in an effort to hold them in. Mahiro's bright expression flickered as he noticed my silence.

"Or perhaps not," he said softly, his teacup dropping to rest on his knees. "Did you leave someone behind?"

I nodded, dabbing at the corners of my eyes with my fingertips.

"A lover?"

Yutaka's face flashed in my vision, and I pushed it away. "No, sir."

Mahiro arched an eyebrow, eyes narrowing. "No?"

"There was…a boy."

His face softened. "How old?"

"Nine…" I paused as I remembered his missed birthday. "No. Ten."

"Your son?"

"No, Goshujin-sama."

"But you love him as one."

"Yes, Goshujin-sama." My mangled heart burst, and I pressed my hand to my mouth. When was the last time I told him I loved him? Had I ever told him? Regret piled hard upon my guilt. Surely, he knew how much he meant to me, that I would suffer that man's abuses a hundred times over if we could just trade places. But that there was room for doubt made me hate myself more than ever.

Mahiro placed a hand over mine on my lap. His fingers were warm from his tea and soft as velvet.

"Why me?"

His eyebrows shot up. "I'm sorry?"

"Why me and not the boy?" My breath snagged on each word. The voice in my head screamed *Stop, Asagi!* but I pressed on. "Of all the people—"

He leaned forward, placing both hands on my knees, and I swatted them away. "Asagi—"

"He's just a boy. And you left him alone with that—with that monster."

"If I could save every soul in that house, I would." His words took on a hard edge, though his eyes were pained. "But it is not in my power. I saw an opportunity with you, and I took it."

I gulped deep breaths as I struggled to compose myself. I should have been grateful. I was grateful. But I couldn't help feeling like my life had been traded for his.

"I'm sorry, Goshujin-sama." I wiped my eyes and lowered my head to the floor.

"No, I am sorry." He touched my shoulder. "Here I am, asking you to entertain me when I have not even given you the time to properly mourn your losses." His eyes met mine, clear and sympathetic and earnest, and that comfortable feeling draped itself over me once again. He gave my knee a gentle pat. "Now, go on and get some rest. Tomorrow is a new day."

I wiped the tears from my face and bowed low before standing and returning to my room. Once there, I curled up on my futon, a pillow clutched in my arms, and cried until I was empty.

THIRTEEN

Utopia

I DIDN'T KNOW I HAD FALLEN ASLEEP UNTIL KIRA SHOOK ME AWAKE. Though still dark, I had the impression it was morning.

"Wake up, sleepyhead," Kira chimed. "Time for your first day of work."

I groaned and rolled onto my back, scrubbing my raw eyes. A single oil lamp flickered in the corner, giving everything a yellow glow. Kira grinned at me as she tugged her hair into place, stray tufts popping out almost immediately, and gestured to the two other girls who shared our room.

"This is Kaoru"—she pointed first to a portly but pleasant-looking woman tugging at her obi, then to a rail thin and severe-looking girl —"and that is Haruko." They both nodded in acknowledgment, regarding me with an intense curiosity that made me squirm. "I told them all about you, and they don't mind," Kira added from behind her hand.

"Why do you dress like a girl?" Kaoru asked, still struggling with her obi.

"Why do you?" I replied, the answer coming out more snide than I intended and making Kira laugh.

"Come on, girls," she said, smacking them about the shoulders and rushing them out of the room. "Don't you have work to do?" She followed close behind them, popping her head back in and winking at me. "Find me in the kitchen when you're ready. Don't take too long, okay?"

I grunted a response, and she disappeared with a wave. I lay staring at the ceiling for a moment, taking deep breaths and mentally preparing for what was to come. The first day at a new house was always challenging, both mentally and physically. A new house meant new work, new people, and all the same old questions.

With a determined grunt, I pushed myself upright and reached for the basin. After washing my face and plaiting my hair into a long braid down my back, I rushed out into the dark house to find the kitchen. Kira spotted me immediately and waved me over to where she prepared fish for breakfast.

She had also told the entire kitchen staff about me, apparently, which I suppose was a blessing. It saved a lot of time and awkwardness, and after a few well-meaning but very personal questions, they accepted me as one of their own. The work itself wasn't so different from any other kitchen I'd worked in, just a matter of learning Mahiro's particular tastes. He had a love for rich things, so all his meals were accompanied by, or covered in, thick sauces that often took hours to make, as evidenced by a deeply stained saucepan already simmering on the fire.

Presentation was also extremely important. Each dish that left the kitchen looked like a work of art. Colors and textures complemented and cascaded off each other, turning even the simplest dish into something alive and important. Kira told me Mahiro ate with his eyes as much as his stomach and showed me the closet full of carefully selected dishware, arranged by season as well as use.

The sun had just started to rise as Mahiro's meal disappeared down the hall on a lacquer tray, and we started on our own breakfast. Even the house staff ate well here, it seemed. A simpler version of his meal—minus the sauces, of course—was prepared. The head cook intoned more than once how convenient it was to have "someone like me" around as I ran up and down the narrow room carrying heavy bags of rice and bushel baskets full of vegetables. Convenient wasn't a term I was used to people associating with me.

The staff dined at a long, low table in an adjoining room, and the men were just filing in, yawning and scratching at their matted hair, as we laid out the heavily loaded platters. A few of them narrowed their eyes at me, but most just plopped down on their pillows, grabbing at the food in front of them. Kira patted the cushion next to her, and breathing a little sigh of relief, I lowered myself into it.

Another hurdle cleared, and another layer of tension peeled away.

The table was soon abuzz with pleasant conversation. Warmed by good food and good company, I found myself laughing right along with them, and I almost forgot about the snake pit looming underneath me. When they spoke of Mahiro, they spoke with a respect born of love and not fear, their eyes alight with adoration, and that alone spoke volumes on his character. Perhaps he really was as kind as he seemed to be.

Once the meal was done and dishes cleared away, the staff broke into little groups and headed out to their respective jobs. The women generally tended the house while the men tended the grounds and the stables. I felt a stab of loneliness as I thought of Tsukito running out behind them, bubbling with excitement.

"Asagi-san!" A raspy voice caught my attention from down the hall. It was the old man who had greeted me at the gate, Ryuichi, huffing and waving his hands. "The tailor is here."

"Tailor?" I looked at Kira, who shrugged. "What tailor?"

He looked me up and down, disbelief written all over his face. "My stars! I thought you were a woman!" he exclaimed.

I rolled my eyes. "What about the tailor?"

"Oh, Mahiro-sama called him for you. Likely to do something about those ankles," he said with a laugh.

I blushed deeply, tugging my kimono down around my hips.

"Go on." Kira suppressed a giggle and gave me a little nudge with her hip. "I'll catch up with you later."

I found the tailor, a rough-looking older gentleman with a shiny bald head, in the main room juggling kimono boxes and bolts of fabric. He directed me to a raised platform with a grunt. I stepped onto it, and he grabbed me roughly by the hips, jostling me around until he had me in the position in which he wanted me. He took a few measurements, grunted some more, and then dived into his stack of boxes. Next thing I knew, a heavy swath of bright-red silk was thrown over my shoulders.

"I'm sorry, Goshujin-sama, this must be a mistake," I said, lifting my arm to marvel at the soft material.

"No mistake," he grumbled around a mouthful of pins.

"But, Goshujin-sama, I'm just a house servant," I said. "I can't possibly work in this."

"No mistake," he repeated, fixing me with a glare and yanking the fabric tight around my waist.

"It is my belief," came a familiar voice from behind me, "that everyone, no matter their station, should have at least one fine kimono. Though I suppose in your case, you will need two."

I whipped around, eliciting a yelp of frustration from the tailor, and bowed at my master's entrance. Up on the riser as I was, I towered over Mahiro even more than usual, so I stepped down as he approached.

"This color suits you nicely," he said, taking the edge of what would be the collar between his fingers. His knuckles brushed my skin as he ran his fingertips over the silk. I shivered, not with the usual revulsion, but with a feeling so unfamiliar, I wasn't even sure what to call it.

It reminded me, somehow, of Yutaka.

His gaze flicked up to mine, and he pulled sharply away, clearing his throat and turning his attention to the tailor. "This will do well for the furisode."

The old man grumbled something under his breath and pulled me by the elbow back onto the riser. Kira appeared from around the corner carrying an armload of linens and stopped dead in her tracks.

"Oh, you're so pretty," she said. It almost sounded like an accusation.

"I think this for the other one," Mahiro said, holding up a bolt of silk in hunter green.

"Two kimono!" Kira gasped. "Mahiro-sama, you're doting."

"It is my right," he said with a good-natured smile.

Their casual banter left me speechless. Even with all the proper honorifics, the familiarity with which Kira spoke to Mahiro would bring wrath from any other master. But Mahiro didn't get angry. In fact, he joyed in it, encouraged it, matching her teasing with jabs of his own. Wrapped in fine silk and surrounded by laughter, I felt as though I were in a dream and any minute I'd wake tangled in my own bedsheets.

"Are you all right, Asagi?"

I snapped out of my musing to find Mahiro regarding me with concern. "Yes, Goshujin-sama. I'm just…" I swallowed hard around the lump rising in my throat. "I'm just a little overwhelmed, I think."

Mahiro's eyes softened, and he gave a sympathetic smile before turning back to the tailor. "Well, I will leave you to it, then. Kira." Kira brightened at his call, hopping up to his elbow. "I need you. When you are done with your task, come to my room."

"Yes, Mahiro-sama," she answered with a bow, scurrying back into the bowels of the house.

After about two hours of measuring and tugging and pinning, the tailor left me with a stack of four basic kimono—three women's and one men's—two yukata, and all the required undergarments. The formal kimono, of course, needed much more tailoring and would arrive in about a week. I walked back to my room on a cloud, my new clothes clutched to my chest. To me, they were so much more than kimono. They were a symbol of understanding and acceptance. Not just of some fetishized version of me, but the real me, all of me. I could have wept.

I slid the bedroom door open and was shocked to find a futon unrolled with a lump in the middle of it. A fan of long black hair poured out from the top edge of the blanket, and two small feet poked out from the bottom.

"Kira?" The lump shifted slightly, followed by a moan. "Are you okay?"

She didn't answer. I tiptoed inside and slid the door shut carefully behind me. Kira had the blanket pulled up under her nose, and her forehead glowed unnaturally pale from beneath the fan of her hair, shimmering with a sheen of sweat. I set down my load, lowered myself to my knees beside her, and laid my hand on her forehead.

"You're cold," I said, expecting to find the opposite.

"I'm fine," she whined without opening her eyes, her fingers emerging just enough to shoo me away.

"Has Goshujin-sama called you a doctor?"

"I don't need a doctor," she said with a touch of irritation, rolling away from me. "I just need some rest. Go find Haruko. I'm sure she'll have something for you to do."

Something wasn't right. My stomach twisted, and I remembered how ill I felt after my previous master had his way with me, how I would lie in bed for hours refusing to move, even breaking into cold sweats.

Kira, I need you.

I was such an idiot. I'd been walking around on a cloud, celebrating this new utopia. Never once had the possibility crossed my mind that if it wasn't me being violated, it might be someone else.

FOURTEEN

Even Monkeys Fall Out of Trees

I SAT NEXT TO KIRA, STROKING HER HAIR UNTIL SHE FELL ASLEEP. I changed out of my ill-fitting kimono and, maybe out of some small act of defiance, changed into the one cut for a man. I pulled my long hair into a neat top-knot fastened with a plain leather strap. When I looked in the polished brass mirror, it was like looking at someone else. All sharp angles and hard corners.

By the time I made it back to the kitchen, the girls were already preparing for supper. A rich broth cooked down on the stove, filling the room with the thick smell of pork and scallions. Kaoru sweated over a lump of dough that would eventually become noodles, stretching it and pounding it with her big fists, wide streaks of flour painting her hips where she'd wiped her hands.

"Asagi!" she said with a gasp as I approached, her hand leaping to her chest and leaving a big white handprint. She blinked up at me, looking me up and down. "You look so…"

"So?" I crossed my arms over my chest and held my head up high.

"…so different."

"So handsome is what she means," said Haruko in a nasally voice, appearing with a basket of sweet potatoes. Kaoru went red all the way down to her collar and threw a lump of dough at Haruko.

"I want to take Goshujin-sama his supper," I said.

"Miike usually takes it," Kaoru answered, focused once again on her dough.

"Well, I want to take it today."

"Why?"

"Because I want to."

Kaoru stopped her kneading and narrowed her eyes at me. She exchanged a look with Haruko, who shrugged and turned her back, setting herself to peeling potatoes.

"Where's Kira?"

"In bed," I answered, my shoulders dropping. "She doesn't feel well."

Kaoru's mouth pinched, and Haruko's peeling ceased, though she didn't turn around. A familiar, heavy feeling permeated the air, solidifying my bitterness and disappointment.

"Talk to Miike," she said finally with a long sigh. I gave her a short bow, and she caught me by the elbow as I turned to leave. "Whatever you think is going on here," she said, lowering her voice to just above a whisper, "it's not what you think. This isn't like your other house." Her eyes shimmered, and I squeezed her hand in acknowledgement of her silent plea.

Don't mess this up for us.

On my knees outside Mahiro's door, I took a deep breath and tried to reconcile the conflicting urges inside me. A covered bowl of udon sat on a tray beside me. The image of Kira burrowed into her bed haunted me, but so did Kaoru's pleading eyes. Was it worth it? How many of my fellows had wondered the same thing when I was the focus of abuse? How many remained silent, unwilling to sacrifice their own relative comfort and safety for mine?

My guts twisted again, and a scowl formed on my face. I couldn't do it. Every small luxury I'd been given here became tainted, stained black by Kira's suffering. But what could I do? If I went outside the house, Mahiro might be punished, but everyone who depended on him would be too, separated and thrown to the winds of chance. If I confronted Mahiro, I risked harsh punishments for Kira. Who knew what he'd do if he thought she'd told someone of the violation. What if he decided to get rid of me, instead? I'd be gone, and nothing would change. In the end, there was only one thing I could do.

It had to be me.

"Are you going to sit out there all night, Asagi?"

I jumped at the sound of Mahiro's voice from the other side of the door. Swallowing hard, I slid it open and touched my forehead to the tatami.

"I'm sorry, Goshujin-sama," I said in a shaky voice. I lifted my head and quickly averted my eyes when I saw him lounging in a zaisu in only his nagajuban. "I've brought your supper."

"Well, you better bring it in, then, before it gets cold."

I bowed again and hurried inside.

Mahiro settled himself in front of a low table and studied me as I arranged his meal upon it. "My word, it is like there are two of you."

My breath caught and my hands shook so hard, I nearly spilled the bowl of udon. Mahiro chuckled, his hands brushing over mine as he reached out to steady the bowl. That feeling came over me again, that rush of calmness. What was he doing to me?

"Was something on your mind?" he asked, stirring the noodles around with his chopsticks.

"Goshujin-sama?"

"You sat out there so long, I thought you had frozen to death," he said with a cheerful laugh. "Working up courage, perhaps?"

"Yes, Goshujin-sama."

"So?"

"I forget, Goshujin-sama."

He laughed again deeply, leaning back in his chair and slapping his knee. Embarrassment burned its way through me as I stood to excuse myself.

"Wait. I am sorry," he said breathlessly, waving me back over to him. "You have come this far. Sit with me awhile. Perhaps you will remember."

I wavered a moment, fingers tugging at the edge of my obi, before sitting back down across from him. Back rod straight, head down, hands clutched in my lap, I sat in silence as he slurped his noodles and hummed in appreciation. I searched desperately for the words I'd rehearsed outside his door, but they had evaporated along with everything else. Was it possible I was wrong? Mahiro radiated kindness and decency, and I felt traitorous for my thoughts. Yet…

Kira, I need you.

"It's Kira, sir." His chopsticks stopped in midair, their load of noodles dripping broth onto the table. "She's ill."

"Oh." The word came out a sigh, and his expression darkened as he lowered his chopsticks back into the bowl. He was silent a moment, and when his smile returned, it was brittle and emotionless. "It is my fault, probably. She is my most trusted servant. I ask too much of her."

"She needs a doctor."

"She just needs some rest," he said. "She will be fine."

"I don't think so, Goshujin-sama."

His eyes narrowed, and he frowned again, but this time I didn't look away. Disappointment curled in my gut again, and my resolve hardened. He studied me as I studied him, irritation flashing in his eyes, and my mouth went dry. *Tread carefully, Asagi.*

"Fine." He got up and walked past me to the door. He slid it open a crack, calling out down the hall, and soon it filled with whispers. I stood and silently approached him. When he closed the door and turned, I was so close we nearly bumped noses. He gasped, throwing his hands up defensively, and I took them in mine, placing them flat on my chest.

"What you ask of her, you can ask of me," I said quickly, breathlessly, desperate not to lose my nerve.

"Asagi—" He jerked away, but I followed, backing him up against the wall. "Asagi, no."

"Why? Because she is a girl?" I reached up and tugged at the strap binding my hair, letting it fall in rich waves around my face. "I can be a girl. I can be anything you want. I can make it so you won't know the difference." He groaned, curling his fingers in my collar as I slid my hand between his legs and felt him twitch in my palm. "You don't need her, you need me."

"Stop!" He pushed me hard, sending me across the room. I caught my heel on the table, toppled over backward, and he stood over me, face red and breathing heavy. "Is this what you think of me?" His voice was tight and high-pitched. The look in his eyes hurt as if he'd struck me. "This is not *that* house. I am not *that* master. I would never hurt Kira that way, and you insult us both with your accusation."

I crumpled under his look, hiding my face behind the veil of my hair. I felt naked, all my trauma on full display. I opened my mouth to beg his forgiveness, but my tongue froze.

"Get out," he growled, jabbing a finger in the direction of the door.

"Mahiro-sama—"

"OUT!" His eyes flashed with so much venom, I would swear they changed color. I scrambled out on my hands and knees, and he slammed the door behind me so fast, it nearly clipped my heels. I stumbled to my room where Kira was still resting and collapsed in a trembling heap.

I couldn't breathe, my chest in panic's viselike grip. Darkness clouded the edges of my vision until all I could see was the ghost image of Mahiro's eyes, full of hurt and anger. Kira's voice called to me as if from under water.

"Asagi, breathe," she said, her hands on my shoulders and chest pressed against my back. "Match me. Come on." She took a long, slow breath, and I did my best to follow, the exhale coming out a heavy sob.

"I messed up," I choked. "I messed up, and now he's going to send me away."

"He's not going to send you away," she cooed, stroking my hair.

"I can't do it again. I can't." The ground swayed under me at the thought of yet another new house, another new master with new tortures and abuses. "I'll die."

"You won't," she said, moving around in front of me and taking my face in her hands. "Even monkeys fall out of trees, Asagi. I'm sure he'll forgive you. Besides, what could you have possibly done in one day?"

I cringed and squeezed my eyes shut, dripping with shame. "I...I thought..." I hiccupped, "I thought he was hurting you."

"Oh, Asagi-chan," she breathed. Her eyes went soft, and something about it unnerved me. She looked like a devotee, her gaze on something only she could see. I'd seen that softness in her eyes before, when she looked at Mahiro.

She planted a kiss on my forehead and pulled me into her chest. She wrapped her arms around me, and they were so warm, I almost forgot the dread cooling in my stomach. "He can't hurt me. He needs me."

FIFTEEN

Trust

———

THAT NIGHT, KIRA AND I SLEPT WITH OUR HEADS TOGETHER, HANDS clasped between us. That small bit of contact comforted my frazzled nerves. She was okay. We were okay. The doctor had come and gone, pronouncing her in perfect health but exhausted and left her with a powder to "strengthen her blood." I felt relieved, albeit foolish. What Mahiro had said was true, and she was simply overworked. Maybe I was overreacting. The strange look I'd seen in her eyes was only weariness, and my bright utopia began to shine again.

But there was still the matter of my insult, and it hung heavy over my head the next morning as I helped prepare Mahiro's breakfast: grilled fish with miso and pickled vegetables. I arranged them all meticulously on bright-blue plates painted with white plum blossoms and rimmed in gold. I cleaned away every stray spot of sauce, every wayward grain of rice as if it could somehow make up for what I'd done.

Miike appeared just as I laid them out on the black lacquer tray, and she swept it away without a word, only to be intercepted in the doorway by Ryuichi. "Sorry, Miike-chan," he said with a toothy grin. "He wants Asagi."

"Me?" I gasped in surprise. "Are you sure?"

"I may be old, but I'm not deaf," he scoffed. The old man turned on his heel and disappeared down the hall, leaving Miike and I in an awkward silence.

She blinked twice, frowning before shoving the tray into my hands and returning to the kitchen without a word.

Dread pooled in the pit of my stomach, and a cold sweat covered the back of my neck as I walked toward Mahiro's room. He was going to punish me. It was the only explanation. The memory of old bruises tingled across my back, and my mouth went dry. It wasn't as though I didn't deserve it. As I knelt outside his door, I told myself I should be grateful he'd chosen to do so in private when he could smear my shame over the whole house.

Asagi the pervert.

I tapped on the door and cleared my throat to keep my voice from cracking. "It's Asagi, Goshujin-sama. I have your breakfast." His lamp flickered through the paper walls, but he didn't answer. I tapped one more time, waiting a moment before easing the door open and lowering my forehead to the tatami.

Mahiro sat leaning against the rear wall, a thick blanket over his back. He didn't look up when I entered, his eyes dark and focused somewhere beyond his knees. He looked small, rumpled, and lonely the way snowcapped mountains were lonely, and it made something inside me ache.

He hardly moved as I positioned the tray in front of him. His eyes lifted sluggishly upward, but I didn't meet them. I wanted to say something, needed to, but instead I stalled by adjusting his plates and pouring his tea until there was nothing else to do but stand up and walk away.

"Asagi," he called sharply. I stopped just as I reached the door, took a deep breath and turned. "Sit."

A shiver went through me at the sound of his voice, low and slightly rough. I crossed the room again slowly, swallowing hard, and arranged myself on my knees in front of him. *Here it comes.* I ducked my head and hid behind my hair from his disapproving glare, fingers curled in the fabric of my kimono to keep my hands from shaking.

"I have been doing a lot of thinking." Shadows lurked under his eyes, and his voice cracked. He'd lost sleep. "About your place here."

My heart sank. "Please, Goshujin-sama," I said, desperate tears rising in my voice. "I'll take whatever punishment you see fit to give me. Please, don't—"

"I am not putting you out." Cold relief washed over me, and my shoulders sagged. "Your behavior and what it implied angered me, but not at you. It was not your fault. Given your experience and what you have seen, it was only the natural conclusion."

I peeked through the veil of my hair and saw his face pinch. He clutched the blanket tighter around himself and pulled his knees to his chest. "What angered me," he continued, "is that you could not trust me. And that is my fault."

All the affectations of the stern and angry master broke away, leaving him brittle. His eyes shimmered, and he swallowed around a lump in his throat. Trust. For me, it was a foreign word, but to him, it was more valuable than gold.

"I want to," I said, my voice coming out barely a whisper, "but I don't know how."

"Then I will teach you."

The corners of his mouth lifted in a weak but hopeful smile, and something warm burst open inside me. My heart that had been so heavy now fluttered around in my chest like a moth around a flame. My muscles turned to noodles as the tension drained out of me, turning my bow into something limp and sloppy.

"Thank you, Goshujin-sama." I'd never meant anything more in my life.

"I would like you to bring me my meals from now on," he said, sitting up and plucking his chopsticks from the tray.

"Yes, Goshujin-sama."

"You will inform Miike?" Phrased like a command, but inflected like a question.

"Yes, Goshujin-sama."

"Good." His smile widened, and he lifted a bowl of miso to his lips. "I will look forward to your company."

We spent the remainder of his meal in a comfortable silence, punctuated only by the occasional comment on the food. He inquired about Kira's health, a little twitch of guilt crossing his face. When he finished, I gathered up his dishes and retreated to the kitchen, my heart already skipping with anticipation of his next meal.

Miike took our change in status with the same wordless stoicism as that morning's proclamation, and it all went rather ignored by the rest of the house, all except for Kira, who couldn't mask a huff of surprise. She asked a million probing questions as the day went on, and I told her only that she was right. He had forgiven me.

When I delivered his meal that night, it was as if my transgression had never happened. He beckoned me in with a warm smile, and I sat across from him as he chattered about his day. Like the dutiful conversationalist, I agreed when he asked for it and laughed when it felt appropriate, even though I understood little of what he was going on about. In the end, it didn't really matter. All that was important was he enjoyed my company and I enjoyed his, and when the meal was over, I returned to my room with my feet barely touching the ground.

"You've really made an impression, haven't you?" Kira teased as we readied for bed.

"You think so?"

"Are you kidding?" Kaoru chimed in, tugging her wild hair into a tight braid. "He hardly takes his eyes off you."

I blinked as her declaration released a ball of warmth in my chest. Not the spikey heat born from fear I'd grown so accustomed to, but something softer, and it knocked me off-balance.

"It's just because I'm new." I turned my back on them, pulling a brush through my hair and using it to hide my blush. "His interest will fade." I said the words nonchalantly, but inside my stomach flipped. Mahiro's meals had become the best part of my day, and already I was counting down the hours until breakfast. I remembered Miike's blank look when I told her of my new position and wondered if they had started this way too.

"He wasn't that way with me," Haruko said.

"Well, that's because you're boring," Kaoru countered, sticking out her tongue.

"I think he's just lonely," I said.

"How could he be lonely?" Kira's expression remained light, but her tone was marked with a second meaning. *How could he be lonely when he has all of us? How could he be lonely when he has me?*

I shrugged dismissively. "You're probably right," I said, slipping into my futon. "You know him better than I do."

Kaoru and Haruko exchanged a look before Haruko blew out the lamp, plunging the room into darkness. While the other girls settled into their beds, I could feel Kira's eyes on me, and I knew I'd hurt her somehow.

"You're still his favorite, Kira," I whispered just loud enough for her to hear.

"I know that." Her haughty tone did little to hide the hurt as she crawled into her futon with her feet toward me.

SIXTEEN

Sweat

"HOW DID YOU COME TO BE HERE?"

I froze, a teacup hanging in the air just in front of my face. I'd had almost a week's worth of meals with Mahiro and all sorts of conversations, but they always centered on him or the house and such a personal question caught me off guard.

"You bought me, Goshujin-sama."

"No," he said, chuckling as he chased the last few grains of rice around his bowl, "I mean your position. Were you born into it?"

"No, Goshujin-sama. I was sold into it." My stomach turned, and I lowered my teacup to my lap without drinking.

"Looks like we have something in common." I quirked an eyebrow at him, and he laughed. "Neither of us are where we were born to be. As the first son of a samurai family, I should have been a soldier, but a disease of the lungs prevented it." My eyes went wide, and he laughed again, reaching over to pat my hand. "I am fine now, do not worry."

The image of Mahiro sick in bed with death hanging over him made my hair stand on end. "You were cured?"

"Yes." His expression flickered around the edges. "A miracle of sorts."

"My father died when I was four." I wrapped the ends of my hair around my fingers and gave it a little tug. "My mother…he didn't leave us with anything, and she had no way of caring for me, so she sold me to a local Shinabe family." I gave a short, dry laugh. "Dressed me as a girl. I want to believe it was to protect me. But I think she knew."

"Knew what?"

"That he liked little boys." Rage and resentment burned through me faster than I could stop it. Mahiro's eyes shot open wide, and his jaw dropped in a perfect mask of shock and disgust. I lowered my eyes and unwound my hand from my hair, toying with a few strands that had pulled loose. "Sorry, Goshujin-sama."

He set his bowl on the table with a hollow *thonk*. His hands slid over mine. Instinct told me to pull away, but they were so warm. A confusing mash of hot and cold emotions moved through me: shame over what my first master, and my last, had done to me; anger about how he'd broken me, changed me; despair over how when anyone touched me, I always saw his face.

Except for Mahiro.

I looked at my hands and realized my fingers had intertwined with his. It was improper, exhilarating, terrifying. I pulled back. As our hands parted, the knot inside me that had just started to loosen wrenched tight once again.

"How long were you there?"

"Until I was ten." *Tsukito was ten.* My mouth went dry, and I struggled to swallow. "Can we talk about something else?"

"What happened?" he pressed, leaning forward in interest. "Why did they get rid of you?"

"I don't know," I spat. "Maybe I just got too old. What does it matter?"

"I do not mean to upset you," Mahiro said, leaning back and raising his hands. "I just want to know you."

"Why?"

"Because you…" He paused, licking his lips as if tasting the words. "Because you fascinate me."

There it was again. That burst of warmth and lightness in my chest that made me dizzy. For some reason, I thought of Yutaka, of his secret soft touches. What was he doing to me? It had been so long since someone had treated me this way, treated me like a *person*, that I'd forgotten what it felt like.

I averted my eyes, focusing my attention on clearing his dishes, and they rattled in my hands. "I have to get back," I croaked, picking up the tray and fleeing toward the door.

"Asagi."

I stopped, hand on the door, and turned. Mahiro's brows pulled together, and he drew in a breath. We stood in silence, a frozen stalemate, until finally he released it with a shake of his head.

"Nothing. I will see you at dinner."

The kitchen was thankfully empty, and I collapsed in a breathless heap, my load scattering loudly across the wood floor. Feelings I thought I'd dealt with, memories I thought couldn't touch me, raged to the surface and made me feel sick. *Damn you, Mahiro, and your curiosity.* Panic slithered its way in as I became that confused child again. I took deep, gulping breaths and tried to focus on the happy chatter coming from the dining room. *It's okay. Everything's okay now, and that man will never touch you again.*

"Asagi?"

I straightened at the sound of Kira's voice from behind me, quickly gathering up my spilled plates. "I'm sorry," I said quickly. "I'm a bit clumsy this morning."

"That's okay," she said with a laugh. "Nothing's broken, so no harm done."

She knelt close to help me, her shoulder brushing mine, and I flinched away. She frowned but quickly put distance between us without comment. She studied me closely, a sympathetic shimmer in her eye.

"I'll take care of this," she said. "Go get something to eat."

My stomach rolled. "I'm not hungry."

"So go to work, then. There's a whole heap of washing that needs doing." She leaned in close and lowered her voice. "Besides, nothing chases off troublesome thoughts like hard work."

She gave me a reassuring smile and shooed me away. She was right. I needed some fresh air and a distraction. I didn't bother throwing a haori over my shoulders before shuffling across the garden to a small outbuilding in the back corner. The building was narrow with a low roof. It was used for storage in the summer and washing in the winter when it was too cold to do so outdoors. I threw open the sliding door and ducked inside to find the promised pile of laundry in baskets in the corner.

I took a moment to rub the cold out of my arms before getting to work building a small fire in the brazier set in the center of the room. Once the coals sported a healthy red glow, I grabbed a bamboo bucket and ducked back out into the cold to fetch water from the well. It took about three trips to fill the basin set on a grate over the brazier. The building went quickly from frigid to steaming.

Kira appeared just as I was dumping the first armload of clothes into the warm water, my hair already damp and sticking to my face. Her face flushed immediately in the heat, and she rushed to prop open the narrow windows along the ceiling and let the steam out, huffing and flapping her hands about her face.

"Good grief!" she gasped. "You could steam fish in here."

"I like it like this," I said, giving the tub a stir with a wide bamboo paddle.

"I think you like punishing yourself."

I laughed, but she wasn't wrong. I found the heat cleansing, each bead of sweat carrying away a grain of corruption. Maybe if I sweated enough, my tainted past would be washed away, and I would be whole again, a new person.

"So…" she began, fetching a washboard and positioning it on the edge of the basin, "do you want to talk about this morning?"

"No."

"Okay."

Without even looking at her, I felt her frowning. For a while, the only sound was the sloshing of the clothes in the tub and the crackling coals. A cold gust of air came in through the windows and brushed my damp skin, making me shiver, and I plunged my hands into the hot water.

"Are you…are you and Mahiro…" Her cheeks flushed, and her face scrunched up as if the question tasted bitter on her tongue.

My blood went cold, all the accumulated heat leaving my body in a rush that made my muscles lock and teeth chatter. She didn't have to ask. Her suspicions were written across her face in red ink. "No. We're not...he's not like that."

"I know he's not like that," she said from between her teeth. "I'm asking if *you're* like that."

Everything stopped. I opened my mouth to speak and choked on my tongue. "No, I—I'm..." I couldn't breathe. The past tugged at my consciousness and blurred my vision. I leaned forward and pushed my hands deeper into the water until I was submerged up to my elbows. Heat sizzled across my skin, and I focused on the sting.

"Asagi—"

"I'm not..." I squeezed my eyes shut against an onslaught of images. The twisted, leering faces of the men who broke me. My dishonorable mistake with Mahiro. My skin screamed as I pushed my hands even deeper, closer to the fire. *I'm not like that. I'm not.*

"Asagi, your hands!" Just as I pressed my hands to the searing hot bottom, Kira lurched forward, hooked her arms under my armpits, and yanked me back from the basin. I fell back into her lap, my arms cherry red up to my elbows and blisters rising on my palms. She took one look at them and, snatching up a bamboo pail, ran outside to fetch cold water from the well.

I stared dumbly at my hands, opening and closing them as if discovering them for the first time. The raw skin stretched and cracked, and it hurt. I groaned with a dark relief as the visions receded, the psychic pain of the past banished by the physical pain of the present.

Kira returned and frantically wrapped my hands in a cool, wet cloth. She threw her arms around my shoulders and pulled me into her chest, muttering, "I'm sorry. I didn't mean it. Kuso, I'm so sorry."

I looked longingly over her shoulder at the open windows.

I just wanted to sweat.

SEVENTEEN

Worry

Kira escorted me inside and handed me over to Kikyou, a housekeeper who doubled as a nursemaid. She clucked like a chicken over the minor burns on my hands and wrapped them in strips of linen. I was fine of course, my emotional state notwithstanding, but Kira demanded I take the rest of the day off. I was dismissed to our room with nothing but my misery to keep me company.

I sat in the corner with my knees pulled up to my chest and plucked at the bandages on my hands. I felt so stupid. Kira had asked me a simple question, and instead of giving her a simple answer, I flew into a panic. It was the same with Mahiro. He only wanted to get to know me, to hear something from me besides *yes, Goshujin-sama; no, Goshujin-sama; as you wish, Goshujin-sama.* Something real. But I couldn't even give him that.

Maybe because I didn't want to hear it myself. I'd spent so much time, so much energy, splitting myself in two so I didn't have to feel the pain and shame of what had happened to me. To tell the story was to admit it was mine and not some phantom's. Another child in another place.

But I wanted Mahiro to know me. Completely, desperately. I wanted to cut myself open and show him the most broken parts of me, because somewhere deep down, I knew he was the only one who could make it okay. He could smooth down the splintered edges and make them poke less, make them easier to bear.

I hugged my legs and dropped my forehead onto my knees with a groan. I wanted to be braver. I *needed* to be.

Kira amazed me. She was so strong, so confident, and even though her questions rattled me, I admired her directness. I'd always viewed women as the stronger sex, and I wore my femininity like a shield, but she put me to shame. I wanted the woman in me to be like her.

Why couldn't I be?

I lifted my head and, palms pressed into the tatami, pushed myself up and toward Kira's tonsu on the opposite wall. With a twinge of guilt, I pulled open the top drawer and reached deep into the back in search of a treasure I knew she hid there: a little pot of bright-red pigment. I opened the lid and dipped a finger inside. My heart fluttered as I remembered the look in Mahiro's eyes when he saw me draped in silk of the same color.

Surely, she wouldn't mind.

I carried the pot with me back to my own corner and pulled out my brass mirror. Holding it close to my nose, I smudged the pigment over my lips and across my eyelids. My eyes flashed darkly from beneath them, the contrast making them appear deep and mysterious, like fire at the mouth of a cave. I felt stronger already.

The day wound down to evening, and I poked my head out the door. Careful to avoid Kira, I slid my way into the kitchen ahead of everyone else to start Mahiro's evening meal. The fish was already half smoked by the time the rest of the staff drifted in, and I had it plated and out the door before they could stop me with questions. With every step, I held tighter to that strong personality in my mind until I reached Mahiro's door.

He opened the door before I could knock, throwing me off-balance. We stared at each other in silence, and for a terrifying moment, I thought he wouldn't let me in. "G-Good evening, Goshujin-sama," I stammered. "I have...your..." So much for being strong.

"Yes, of course," he said on the tail end of an exhale, something like relief washing over his features. He stepped back out of the doorway and gestured me in, but didn't take his eyes off me. Gripping the tray tightly to keep the dishes from rattling, I bowed and slipped past him to arrange his table in the usual place. He hovered behind me, casting a shadow over me and making my skin prickle.

"What happened?" he asked, thrusting himself abruptly into my field of vision.

"Goshujin-sama?"

"Your hands." I followed his line of sight to my bandaged hands and quickly pulled them into my sleeves.

"It's nothing, Goshujin-sama."

"You were injured." He went down on his knees next to me, grabbing me by the wrists before I could stop him.

"I'm fine, Goshujin-sama."

He clicked his tongue, brow furrowing as he pushed my sleeves up, revealing the raw skin of my forearms. His scowl deepened as he unwrapped the bandages and examined my blistered palms.

"You are burned," he said from between his teeth. "How did this happen?"

"It was an accident, Goshujin-sama." My voice quivered, and I tried to pull my hands away, but he didn't let go. "It was my fault. I was careless with the washing and let the water get too hot. I'm sorry—"

"You did not break a teacup, Asagi." The sharpness of his tone made me flinch. He took a deep breath and held it, closing his eyes a moment before letting it go. When they opened again, they were softer. "I am not angry." His grip on my wrists loosened. "I just do not like seeing you hurt."

The walls I had spent all morning constructing crumbled, and my heart flipped. I ducked my head as warmth rushed to my cheeks. He scared me, the way he could melt me, make me feel totally exposed with just a look.

He let my hands slip out of his and stood. Drawers opened behind me, and he reappeared with a little pot of something clear and slightly viscous. He held out his hand palm up, gesturing with a flick of his fingers for mine. I laid my hand in his, and he smoothed the gel gently over the blistered areas before replacing the bandages.

"Did it hurt?" he asked in a rough voice, gesturing to my other hand.

"No." I placed my other hand in his, and he repeated the process, the coolness of the ointment and softness of his touch making me shiver. "It felt…better."

"Better than what?" he scoffed.

"Everything else."

His hands froze over mine, and I ducked my head lower, hiding behind my hair. Without thinking, I'd confessed something to him I didn't think I'd even admitted to myself. The world tilted in that moment. Mahiro swept my hair aside and peered into my face. I carefully avoided his eyes, but I felt them on me, soft and sympathetic and deeply troubled.

"I do not have to worry about you, do I?" he asked gently.

"No, Goshujin-sama," I answered. "I won't do it again."

His thumb brushed over my cheek, and I ventured a look at his face. That snowcapped loneliness had made its way in again, and I had the urge to pull him into my arms and warm it away, but it felt an impossible distance to cross. He finished wrapping my hand but didn't let it go, holding it instead in both of his against his chest.

A loud rumble broke the silence, and I yelped in embarrassment when I realized it came from my stomach. I hid my face behind my hands as Mahiro fell backward in riotous laughter. "Hungry?" he asked between gasps.

"I'm so sorry, Goshujin-sama," I said through my hands. With everything that had happened, I'd forgotten to eat.

"Are you ever not apologizing?" Mahiro sat up and reached for the bowl of rice and chopsticks laid out for him. He plucked a bit of white flesh from the fish and, hovering it over the rice, held it out toward me. "Here."

"But your supper—" I started, waving my hands in protest.

"I think you need it more than I do."

"You don't have to feed me," I insisted. I reached for the chopsticks, but he snatched them away.

"It will be awkward with the bandages."

"Oh, just give it to me, Mahiro!" I clapped my hands over my mouth too late.

His eyes snapped open and jaw dropped in surprise. "Mahiro?" he gasped, the rice bowl hanging over his head.

"I'm so sorry, Goshujin-sama," I said, dropping my forehead to the floor.

"On the contrary, I am glad to hear it. Far better than Goshujin-sama." He wrinkled his nose and laughed. "I was beginning to think you had forgotten my name."

"No, Goshujin-sama. Of course not, Goshujin-sama, I mean, Mahiro-sama." I laid the proprieties on thick to make up for my previous familiarity, pressing my nose into the tatami. I wanted to dissolve into it. Could this have gone more wrong? Mahiro sighed and set the rice bowl down next to my head. When I lifted it, he was smiling, but his eyes were sad.

"I think I will miss you."

My stomach sank. "Mahiro-sama?"

"Eat."

I picked up the bowl and chopsticks but didn't eat.

"I have to leave for a few days."

"Where are you going?"

His smile faltered. "Nowhere I want to go."

"Then why go?"

"Because sometimes even free men are not all that free."

All the positive energy left in him drained away, and he wilted like a flower in the cold. Back bent, head hung low, he looked old beyond his years. Worry tugged on his features, all his responsibilities hanging on him like a coat of lead.

"Do you believe in karma, Asagi?"

"Goshujin-sama?"

"Do you think good deeds done here can erase the bad deeds done somewhere else?"

"Are you…okay, Goshujin-sama?"

Mahiro released a heavy sigh and dragged a hand across his face. "I am just…" He paused, the corners of his eyes pinching. "Really tired."

His body collapsed as if he couldn't hold it up anymore. I tensed as his head landed in my lap, a protest lodged in my throat. I sat frozen, the bowl of rice held awkwardly to my chest. He felt so light, so warm. His black hair was just long enough to curl around his ears and fall over his eyes. I touched it, tentatively at first, brushing my fingertips through it, and he relaxed into me.

"This may be selfish, but whatever happened to you before," he muttered drowsily, pushing his nose into my thigh and curling his fingers around my ankle, "I am glad it brought you here."

My throat tightened, and tears pricked at the back of my eyes. Being grateful felt like a betrayal to all I had lost, yet here I was, comforting my master, taking comfort from him.

"Me too."

EIGHTEEN

Magic

I TOSSED AND TURNED ALL NIGHT. WHAT SLEEP I DID GET WAS LIGHT and fitful. I finally gave up when I heard the snap of the front door sliding open and closed. Careful not to disturb my roommates, I tiptoed out of the room and down the hall to the front of the house. The room was dark and empty, but I heard voices outside, and pulling my robe a little tighter around myself, I slid the door open just enough to watch Mahiro mount his horse and ride away.

I still stood by the door when Ryuichi came inside, thrashing his arms to shake off the cold. He jerked and cursed under his breath at the sight of me, grasping his chest. "Are you trying to give me a heart attack?" he snapped keeping his voice low in an effort to avoid disturbing the house. "What are you doing there?"

"He's gone, isn't he?" I asked.

"What?" I pointed with my nose toward the door. "Oh. Yes. I guess you'll have to dine with we lowly servants for a few days."

I thought back to his visit to my previous house and the old man with him who had to have been Ryuichi. "You're not going with him?"

"Not this time."

"Do you know where he goes?"

He shrugged. "Not my business to know. But he'll likely be in a foul mood when he returns."

"Why?"

"Usually is."

I frowned, and he gave me a friendly pat on the shoulder.

"Have you been here a long time?"

"Since I was a kid," he said, absently shaking out his haori and folding it into a neat square.

"A kid?" I asked, wrinkling my nose in confusion. "How is that possible?"

"I wasn't born old, you know," he huffed.

"But Mahiro—"

"It was his father before him that took me in," he said with a brusque wave of his hands, his cheeks going a little red. "My goodness, you are a nosy one." He shooed me off in the direction of my room and disappeared into the dark.

DESPITE THE NEVER ENDING BUZZ OF ACTIVITY, THE HOUSE FELT empty without Mahiro in it. With the old man acting as a sort of foreman, work went on as usual, leaving me feeling a bit out to sea. I found myself drifting toward Mahiro's rooms around mealtime, only to have Kira chastise me for moping and drag me back to the kitchen.

But I just couldn't shake it, the feeling of dread that hung over me. One day passed, then two. I had no reason to believe that he wouldn't return, yet I feared it so much that just the thought of his empty bedroom made my heart pound and my chest tighten. I had to resist the urge to rip the bandages off my hands and tear off the scabs that had formed there. I clenched my fists and focused on the sting, a welcome distraction to my roiling thoughts.

A third day passed, and I lay on my futon staring up at the ceiling, listening to the light snoring of my companions and feeling very alone. I thought often of the sickness he'd alluded to. Was I the only one who worried over our master so? The thought made me angry. Didn't they care about him? No one even knew when to expect him back. What if he was already a day overdue, and instead of looking for him, we were allowing him to die in some awful remote place?

I squeezed my eyes closed tight and clenched my fists, inhaling sharply through my teeth as the new skin stretched and cracked. *Stop it, Asagi. You told him you wouldn't.* I released my breath slowly and willed my muscles to relax. I counted my heartbeats until they slowed, and I eased into a shallow sleep.

I sat straight up at the sound of a door sliding open and heavy, awkward footfalls on the wood entryway. I leaped over my sleeping companions and burst into the main room to find Mahiro leaning against the doorframe, one hand clinging to it, the other yanking at his sandals. His body pitched and swayed as if the whole house rocked. He growled, cursed, and when he succeeded, celebrated by chucking it at Ryuichi, who stood outside, struggling to unload his horse.

He was half bent over and ready to do battle with his other shoe when he spotted me. "Asagi!" he said, throwing up his arms and completely losing his balance. I caught him under his arms before he could fall straight back through the paper shoji.

"Are you all right, Mahiro-sama?" I asked, pulling him upright.

He clung to my collar and gazed up at me, a bright-pink flush across the bridge of his nose. "Fine," he answered with a bit of a slur. "I think my shoes are broken."

I clicked my tongue and, after propping him up against the wall, went down on one knee and slipped off his remaining sandal. His hand never left my shoulder, fingers curled tightly in the fabric of my yukata. Despite his sloppy state, a calmness radiated through me.

My master was home.

"Shall I help you to your room, Mahiro-sama?" I asked, rising to my feet and reaching for his arm.

"You think I cannot do it on my own?" He bristled noticeably, pulling away from me and standing as straight as he could manage. I smirked and stepped back with a slight bow, gesturing for him to lead the way. He huffed and straightened his collar, taking one unsteady step forward and then another…and fell head over feet into the unlit brazier. He cursed loudly, and I hushed him as I lifted him up and dusted him off, choking on my own laughter.

"Well, maybe you could just…lend me your arm."

"Of course, Mahiro-sama."

HE CLUNG TIGHT TO MY SIDE AS I ESCORTED HIM TO HIS ROOM, THE heat of his body through his haori making me feel light. Once we made it through the door, I reluctantly peeled myself away from him, unrolled his futon, and covered it with a thick blanket. When I was done, I found him trying to kick his way out of his hakama and getting his feet horribly tangled in the process.

I touched his arm, and with a sigh of resignation, he steadied himself on my shoulder once again and allowed me to extract his legs from the pool of fabric around his feet. His expression took on a soft, dreamy quality as he watched me fold it neatly and put it aside.

"What would I do without you?" he asked as I tugged loose the bindings of his haori.

"Sleep in your clothes, probably." We both laughed. It felt like I hadn't laughed in years.

Joy turned to panic as I pushed his haori back off his shoulders, exposing a long rip under the arm of his kimono framed in a wide ring of blood. "Mahiro-sama, you're hurt!"

"No, I am not," he said, twisting his face in confusion. "I am fine."

"You're not fine. You're bleeding."

"Well, not anymore."

I dropped the haori and yanked at his obi until his kimono fell open over his chest. His nagajuban held a matching stain, this one wider and running all the way down to his waist. Was he so drunk he couldn't even feel it? With my heart frozen in my chest and tears pressing against my eyes, I opened his collar and pushed my hand inside, expecting to find the gore of an open wound, but instead I found…

…nothing.

"See," he said with a cheeky, drunken grin.

"What…how…" I yanked my hand back and stared dumbly at my clean fingers. It just wasn't possible. There was no way blood could be on both layers of his clothes unless it came from inside. I opened his collar again so I could see. Nothing but smooth, fair skin stretched from his armpit to his waist.

"Magic!" he said with a wide flourish that set him stumbling backward and landing on his rump in the futon. He gave a great, bellowing laugh before shivering and pulling the thick blanket up over his shoulders.

"There's no such thing as magic," I croaked around the stone lodged in my throat.

"Oh, I think you would be surprised where you find it if you look hard enough."

"What happened to you?"

"Nothing," he said with a shrug, his smile wavering. "It does not matter."

"It does matter," I said, stomping my foot. "How am I supposed to trust you if you're hiding things from me?"

His face twitched, and I felt a momentary stab of fear. A lifetime of conditioning told me I'd just made a horrific mistake. *Never question your master. Take what he gives you and be grateful or suffer the consequences.*

I shrank back as he grumbled deep in his throat, pulling the blanket up around his nose. He closed his eyes, took a deep breath, and when he dropped the blanket from his face, all the drunken mirth had left it.

"Someone tried to kill me," he said flatly.

My heart jerked. "Why?"

"Because I am...like you," he said with a sad, wry smile. "Different."

I swallowed hard, my skin going cold. "I don't understand."

Mahiro pursed his lips and dipped his nose into the blanket again before standing without so much as a wobble and moving past me to the large cherrywood dresser against the back wall. Adjusting the blanket over his shoulders, he pulled a thin dagger out of the top drawer. He held it in one hand, the other emerging palm up from his blanket.

"I want you to watch this closely," he said in a strained voice, "and remember I would never hurt you."

A pained cry caught in my throat as I watched him drag the blade over his palm, opening an angry red line in its wake. Blood pooled in the hollow of his hand and oozed down his wrist. With the corner of the blanket, he wiped it away, and what I saw underneath made my heart stop.

The edges of the wound shimmered as the skin pulled closed and stitched itself back together, fading into a thin white line, then a pink bruise, then nothing. Mahiro closed his hand, flexed his fingers, and held it up for me to see. Pale, unmarred skin stretched where only seconds ago a wicked cut had been.

"Impossible," I muttered in a voice pitched high with terror. I pressed the heels of my hands against my eyes until I saw bright spots of color. It couldn't be real. He had been cut, but now he wasn't. His clothes had been cut and bloodied, but he wasn't. Electric shots of panic restarted my heart, and it thundered in my ears. My mouth went dry, and my body shook. He took a step toward me, and I flinched away.

"Asagi—"

"Youkai!" I spat the word, and he jerked as if I had struck him. My vision went dark around the edges. My chest seized, and I struggled to breathe. It was all a lie. This wonderful place, my loving master. I'd been dropped into a pit of vipers, and they smothered me in their grip.

"Please, do not be afraid." His voice cracked, and he reached out to me, but I batted him away. I stumbled along the wall, desperately searching for the exit, but he caught me and took my face in his hands. "Do not be afraid," he repeated in an almost whisper, and something happened.

All volition drained out of me, and I fell to my knees. My fear evaporated into a swirling mist, and I remembered my first day here. That tempest with Mahiro as its eye.

"What are you doing to me?"

"Taking away your fear so you can hear me. I know what I have shown you is unbelievable and terrifying, and I am sorry." He dropped to his knees in front of me and pressed his forehead to mine. "I am so sorry, Asagi. I am sorry for hiding this awful thing from you, but you must believe that everything else was true. Everything I said, everything I felt—"

"I believed in you," I choked, clinging to his arms. The fear faded and made room for something like mourning. Tears flowed freely. "I believed you were different. But you're just a monster of a different kind."

I pulled away from him, and just as before, the feelings he'd swept away returned. I lurched toward the door, and he didn't follow me, didn't try to stop me. One final look back found him slouched against the wall, his hand over his face and his shoulders shaking.

NINETEEN

Need

"Asagi! What on earth…!"

Kira found me the next morning slouched on a stool in the corner of the laundry house, barely conscious and soaked with sweat. A pile of dirty laundry sat beside me, and a basin full of water boiled high on the brazier. She threw herself on her knees in front of me and pushed my wet hair out of my face, her mouth puckered and eyes pinched. I saw her in soft focus, my head bobbing.

"I just wanted to sweat."

Kira released a growl of frustration and threw up her hands. "Well, in that, you've succeeded. What if you had fainted with no one out here to wake you?"

She disappeared, and I dropped my head back against the wall. I flinched against a cold blast of air as the door opened and closed, and she reappeared with a bucket from the well. She pressed a cool rag to the back of my neck before tossing the remainder of the water over the fire, dousing it in a burst of hot steam.

"I can't leave you alone for a second," she huffed as she threw open the windows. "I suppose I should be glad you didn't stick your head in the fire this time."

I slouched even further and turned my nose into the corner. The cool air had found its way in, and I hugged myself, clinging to the warmth. As the steam cleared, so did my head. I squeezed my eyes shut as the wheels of my mind that had been so comfortably soggy hardened and started to turn. I thought I could rid myself of my toxic thoughts, that I could push them out of my skin, but they were there waiting for me all along.

Mahiro is a monster.

"We've got to get you dry," Kira grumbled, poking through the pile of kimono next to me. "Strip."

"What?"

"Take off your clothes," she said forcefully, thrusting a kimono into my lap. "Go outside like that, and you'll catch your death." I hesitated, glancing from her to the kimono and back again. She scoffed and turned her back, crossing her arms.

My modesty somewhat preserved, I stood on wobbly legs and tugged off my wet kimono. I braced against the wall as a gust of cold air hit my damp skin, sending a violent, bone-shaking shiver through me. The kimono Kira handed me was only marginally drier thanks to the steam and comically too small, but I wrapped it tight around myself anyway, signaling Kira with a grunt.

"Come on, you big idiot." She threw a supporting arm around my waist and pulled me toward the door. "Let's get inside."

The laundry house was only a few yards from the main house, but my teeth were still chattering by the time we made it inside. Kira rushed me into the kitchen, dropping me down next to the fire and stoking it high. The drastic change in temperature made me queasy, and I shied away from it despite the chill racking my bones. Kira called into the house, and I found myself surrounded by shrill voices and a heavy blanket thrown over my back. Someone thrust a steaming cup of tea under my nose, and I turned my face away.

"What's going on here?"

My stomach dropped. Mahiro, drawn by the commotion, appeared at the door. Fear and shame burned through me, and I fixed my eyes on the fire.

"Nothing, Mahiro-sama," Kira answered quickly, placing herself in his line of sight. "Asagi just caught a chill doing laundry. He'll be fine once he's warmed."

A long, heavy silence gripped the room, freezing everyone in place as they waited for their master's word. I felt his eyes boring past Kira and into me. Part of me wanted to crawl toward him and fall down at his feet, begging for forgiveness. The bigger part felt angry, betrayed, and unbearably empty.

"Be more careful," he said finally in a raspy voice.

The soft sound of his footfalls disappeared down the hall before Kira could push out a hasty, "Yes, Mahiro-sama."

Motion resumed, and I released a breath. The blanket over my shoulders felt made of lead, and I shriveled beneath it. Kira squatted down beside me, shooing the other doting girls away, and pinned me with a stern, but not unsympathetic, look.

"What happened?" she asked softly.

My eyes burned, and I hid my face inside the blanket.

When I didn't answer, Kira inhaled deeply, releasing the breath in a long, slow stream as she rubbed a circle on my back. "You warm enough to move?"

I nodded.

"Good. Let's get you into some real clothes."

She wrapped her arm around my waist again and hoisted me up. I followed blindly, my face still tucked safely behind the blanket until we reached our room. She pushed me inside, lingering in the hall to give me privacy as I changed into my own dry kimono. My skin warmed almost immediately, but inside I still felt cold.

"I know how you feel, you know," Kira said from outside. "Mahiro-sama has this way of making you feel…important. Like you matter. Until you don't anymore, and then it feels like falling." Her feet shuffled, and the door frame creaked as she leaned against it. "But he's very forgiving," she continued, her tone brightening. "I'm sure whatever fight you had—"

"We didn't fight."

She inhaled sharply, and her profile appeared around the edge of the door. I gave her a little nod, letting her know it was safe to come in, and she tucked herself inside, sliding the door closed behind her. I could feel the questions piling up on her tongue. I settled myself in front of my tonsu with my back to her, pretending to be consumed with picking the knots from my hair with a hardwood comb.

"He told you…didn't he?"

My hands shook so hard I nearly dropped my comb. I slapped it down on the surface of the tonsu. She knew. Of course, she knew. I squeezed my eyes shut as I mentally counted all the times she'd disappeared at the words *I need you,* how many times I'd found her pale and cold in her bed afterward. I pivoted on my hip to face her.

"Where does he go when he leaves like that?"

"I don't know. That's why he goes alone. He doesn't want us to know. Sometimes, we don't even know he's leaving until he's gone."

"What does he do to you?"

She flinched and sucked in a sharp breath. She held it for a long moment, curling her fingers in her kimono sleeves, before releasing it and sliding down the wall to the floor. She licked her lips and knotted her brows, opening and closing her mouth a few times as if she wanted to speak but couldn't form the words. "He…takes." At my confused look, she just sighed and tugged down the collar of her kimono. On her shoulder, just above her collarbone, were two scabbed puncture wounds nestled inside a deep-purple bruise.

"Oh, Kira…"

"It's not as bad as it looks," she said quickly, waving her hands. "It doesn't hurt. Feels *good* even."

"How could it possibly feel good?" I asked, nose wrinkled in disgust.

"I don't know, it just does. It's like I can feel the magic in him."

"There's no such thing…" I trailed off. Clearly, I was no authority on what was possible anymore.

"I'm helping him," she insisted. "He needs me."

"He's feeding off you. Your life will surely be shorter because of him."

"I've already lived longer because of him. If he hadn't taken me in—"

"He's a monster," I said, voice cracking.

"Yes," she said. "But he tries very hard not to be."

Conflicting emotions roiled around in my gut until I thought I would be sick. I remembered his talk of karma, this house and his rescued servants who all seemed to come from somewhere awful, his miraculous recovery from illness. We weren't so different, were we? Two people fighting against our natures, trying so hard to be something we were not. Perhaps that's what drew him to me in the first place. And I to him. Two people bound together by their own monstrosity.

"I'm just so tired," I said, unable or unwilling to stop the tears that had been perched on my eyelashes from falling. "I'm tired of being afraid all the time."

"Oh, Asagi-chan." Kira popped away from the wall to sit beside me, throwing her arms around my neck. "There's nothing to be afraid of, you'll see. He would never take from you without your permission. He doesn't have to. He has me."

Her voice lifted as she spoke, tinged with pride and adoration. Meanwhile, my heart calcified. Tears dried, leaving a sticky film on my cheeks. I looked down at my hands to find the bandages dotted with little red crescents.

TWENTY

Arrangements

A WEEK PASSED, AND I HARDLY SAW MAHIRO. MIIKE RETURNED TO her previous position taking Mahiro his meals, and I lost myself in house work. Kira almost never left my side. I think she worried over me, though she never voiced it. I was grateful for her strong, sweet presence. She was my anchor, her smart, cheerful disposition the only thing keeping me sane in this world turned upside down.

But her warmth couldn't melt the ice forming around my heart. Even as the house buzzed with excitement over the approaching New Year. It was the third year of Bunroku, and the wife of Toyotomi Hideyoshi, the Great Unifier, had borne a son just a few months before. We had every reason to celebrate, yet I found myself numb. The entire front room was taken over by the ladies of the house, the floor littered with kimono boxes spilling over with brightly colored fabrics and the air thick with perfumes as they prepared for the first shrine visit of the year.

Kira, as it turned out, was an accomplished hairdresser. She made the rounds among the ladies, constructing the elaborate hairstyles that were the fashion among the higher classes. My formal kimono had arrived just days before. I knelt on the floor with both boxes open in front of me, gazing at the bright-red and green silk and trying not to think about how happy I was the day Mahiro procured them for me. It seemed so long ago now, so far away I thought I might have dreamed it.

"Which one will you wear?" Kira appeared beside me in her nagajuban, her hair already pulled into a tight shimada-mage and face painted with bright cosmetics.

"I don't know," I answered. I closed my eyes and let my fingers trail over each one. I tried to picture myself in them, reaching deep inside for that sliding scale between masculine and feminine, but neither felt right. I found myself wondering which *he* would like. My frozen heart trembled as I curled my fingers around the edges of one box and pulled it toward me.

"Good choice." Kira patted me on the shoulder and smiled as I cradled a handful of red silk in my lap.

Without so much as asking, she planted herself behind me and began tugging and pulling and waxing my hair into a tight topknot like hers. She then fished an elaborate ebony comb out of a box of shared accessories and pushed it into place along with a silver kanzashi dripping with pink flowers.

She giggled sweetly as she swung around in front of me and powdered my face. I felt like her doll, and I had to admit, her giddiness was infectious. With each layer of girlish affectation, I felt stronger, bolder, more myself. Finally, I stood, and Kira helped me shrug the heavy kimono into place, oohing and aahing over me as she wrapped the obi around my waist and skillfully tied the elaborate knot.

"Ohhhh, you make me so mad!" she teased, clicking her tongue and taking a step back to admire her work.

"Why?" I asked with a laugh.

"You're so pretty." She beamed at me, and I couldn't help but smile back, my dark mood obliterated by her excitement.

"Let me see, let me see." I waved my hand toward a brass mirror lying at her feet. She scooped it up and held it at arm's length in front of her. I gasped at my own image in the polished surface. The red silk kimono had been artfully painted with pink cherry blossoms, and they spilled over my shoulder and gathered at the hem. I ran my hands over the bright-gold obi, twisting at the waist to examine the knot at my back, giving a little wiggle to make the trailing ends swing.

I felt like a princess. I'd never worn something so fine, and the power of it was intoxicating. Blinking back tears, I threw my arms around Kira and showered her with words of gratitude before she batted me off, her own eyes shining.

I helped Kira into her kimono, a deep blue that flattered her fair complexion and dotted with red posies, and soon we were all ready. A room full of servants turned into proper ladies for a day. We formed a tight knot, giggling and preening and complimenting until finally our master appeared.

He entered almost silently, the only sound the swishing of his gold hakama around his feet. A bright-purple haori emblazoned with the imperial seal fell nearly to his knees over his black kimono. Our little knot dispersed, lining up instinctively as he ran his warm gaze over us.

"My, my," he said, his small mouth curling into a smile. "You all look so…" My heart skipped as his gaze stopped on me, and a glimmer of pain flashed across his expression. "…beautiful."

Kira wrapped her hand around mine, and I swallowed the icy lump in my throat and bowed along with the others. When I raised my head, the smile was back on Mahiro's face, but it trembled around the edges.

"Shall we go, then?" he said cheerfully. "We mustn't keep the gods waiting."

Mahiro turned and slipped out the door, the rest of us filing out behind him. We met the men outside, all looking rather dashing in their own formal getup, and Ryuichi came around with a bag of coins for prayer offerings, dropping one into each of our hands.

We formed a procession with Mahiro at the head as we made the short walk to the shrine. Stone steps snaked their way up the hillside to the entrance of a squat building with a sloped roof. Red columns draped with paper shimenawa flanked the entrance which housed the slatted offering box under a large brass bell. The air around the building was heavy with incense smoke, its smell making the wind sharp as it whipped through the valley, carrying its load of prayers to the gods.

We stopped and bowed as we approached the torii gate, all idle chattering dying down to polite whispers as we cleansed our hands in the well at the base of the stairs. Kira was at my shoulder, rattling on about all the lofty things she intended to pray for. I fished the little brass coin out of my obi where I had tucked it and rolled it around in my fingers. She had so many hopes. I'd long ago given up on hoping.

"Asagi." I stiffened at the sound of Mahiro's voice from behind me. I turned, and he gave a smile that didn't quite reach his eyes. "Would you lend me your arm?"

I swallowed hard and bowed. Kira gave my elbow a little squeeze as I stepped away from her and placed myself at Mahiro's side. He looped his arm around mine and pulled me gently away from the group and down the path toward the shrine. The air was dense around us, and my heart pounded in slow, painful beats. We ascended the stairs in silence, Mahiro releasing my arm to toss his coin in the offering box and ring the bell.

I knew I should have followed suit, but I could only watch as he pressed his palms together under his nose and closed his eyes. I wondered what a demon prayed for. The prosperity of his house and the people in his care? Good weather and a good harvest for the surrounding farmers? All would have been proper for a man of his position, but he wasn't a man, was he? As his brow pulled together and his lips moved in a silent plea, I got the feeling it was something more desperate, more personal.

His eyes opened slowly, and he clapped his hands, signaling the end of his prayer, and bowed. I did the same, though I didn't pray, and placed myself beside him again so he could take my arm. Kira still stood at the well watching us closely as we descended the stairs again, hesitating when we reached the bottom.

"I have been thinking…" He spoke slowly, carefully, as if each word was a struggle. "…about our last meeting. I behaved inappropriately, and…I scared you. For that I am truly sorry."

I opened my mouth to respond but could think of nothing to say. The ice around my heart cracked dangerously, and I struggled to hold it together.

"The last thing I wanted to give you when I took you in was a life of fear," he continued thickly without raising his eyes, tightening his hand slightly around my arm, "so I have made arrangements for you."

My heart dropped to my feet, its cold protection shattering into a million pieces. "Goshujin-sama—"

"He is a good man. A friend. I trust him. He will take good care of you."

"But—Goshu—Mahiro-sama—" Panic flowered in my breast, and I couldn't breathe.

"He will be here in two days to collect you, so if you have any good-byes to make—"

"Mahiro, please—"

He raised his hand to silence me, unlocking himself from my arm and taking a step away. He had donned the mask of the stern master, but it was fragile, leaking around the edges.

"It is what is best for you. Perhaps for all of us." A tear slipped down my cheek, cutting a track in my thick makeup, and he brushed it away with his thumb. When he spoke again, his voice cracked. "I *will* miss you."

Then, in a rush of purple and gold, he walked away.

TWENTY-ONE

A New World

KIRA WAS AT MY SIDE JUST IN TIME TO CATCH ME BEFORE I collapsed, and she pulled me into a secluded corner of the grounds. I felt like I'd been kicked in the chest by a horse, broken and unable to breathe. She sat me down on a bench and held me, cooing gentle words into my ears and stroking my back until my breathing evened out.

Two days. In two days, I would be gone. In two days, we'd be separated forever.

"What happened?" she asked as my body shook with sobs. I told her everything. How I'd met Mahiro when he arrived home, how I'd fled his room in fear, and the arrangements he'd made. "I don't believe it," she said over and over. "I don't believe it."

Haruko called for us from somewhere in the courtyard. Our little band was leaving and headed for home. Kira wiped the tears from my face, my white makeup staining her sleeve, and pulled me to my feet. She locked her arm in mine, and I walked beside her in a numb state, stumbling and unaware. As our little procession left the shrine grounds, my eyes refused to focus, the shape of Mahiro's back bleeding into a bright-purple blur.

Back at the house, I became Kira's doll again. She escorted me back to our room and helped me out of my kimono. She washed my face, brushed my hair. Haruko and Kaoru came in, and when Kira told them what was happening, Kaoru collapsed into tears. Haruko gaped and slapped a hand over her mouth, her face flushed red with anger. I hadn't realized they cared for me so much.

I wanted to thank them, to tell them I loved them and would think of them every day we were apart, but I couldn't. Already, they felt far away, unreachable, the repressed pain of my recent estrangement from Mahiro and my impending banishment drowning out everything else.

Mahiro. Everything came back to Mahiro. In my despair, I never once thought of the horrible truth he'd shown me, only his kind smile, his warm laugh, his gentle touch. A touch without perversion or pain. A touch that demanded nothing but gave so much. I'd never known a touch like that, but now that I did, living without it felt like dying.

I snapped out of my catatonia to find night had fallen. I sat slumped against the wall, and the girls slept close around me, Kira with her head in my lap, Kaoru with her hand curled loosely around mine. Even stubborn Haruko lay with the bottoms of her feet tucked up against me. Fresh tears painting my cheeks, I carefully pried myself away from them, tucking a pillow under Kira's head and kissing Kaoru's fingers, and tiptoed out of the room.

I dragged my hand along the wall as I made my slow, unsteady way down the hall toward Mahiro's room, stopping every few paces as the house pitched beneath me and knocked me off-balance. By the time I reached his door, I was winded and trembling. I braced against the frame and took a deep breath before giving the door an uneven, staccato knock.

The door slid open, and I lost all composure. His face was pale, eyes red-rimmed and raw, appearance rumpled as if from fitful sleep. I fell to my knees before him, crying and sputtering, all shame gone.

"Please, don't send me away," I cried between hiccuping sobs. "Please. I'm not afraid of you. I trust you. With my life, with everything. Please, I don't want to go."

Forehead pressed against his feet, hands wrapped around his ankles, I pleaded until the words came out garbled and unintelligible. Mahiro was silent, still as a statue, and I grew cold with dread. Was it too late? Had he already closed his heart to me? Thrown me away as so many had before him? My hair fell over my face, plunging me into total darkness, and I thought, *This is it. The end of everything.*

Mahiro took a deep, shuddering breath, and his feet shifted beneath my head as he lowered himself onto one knee. He laid a hand on my head, and it shook. He slipped it over my cheek and under my chin to lift my head, sweeping my hair away from my face and letting the light in.

"I do not want you to go."

I blinked up at him, and it was as if I could see clearly for the first time in days. Pain etched fine lines around his mouth, and tears glistened in the corners of his eyes, hinting at a vast sea of loneliness within. He opened his arms to me, and I fell into them. I buried my face into his neck and sobbed anew as a warm rush of relief washed away the cold despair.

"It is dangerous around me," he said.

"I don't care."

"I do not want you to get hurt."

"I've been so lost without you," I whimpered. I wasn't even sure he could understand me. "I've never felt at home until I met you."

"All I have done is hide things from you."

"To protect me," I said. "Because it wasn't my business to know. Because you are Mahiro-sama, and I'm...nobody."

Mahiro inhaled sharply, pulling me up by my shoulders and pinning me with his eyes. "You are not nobody."

My heart begged to soar, but I dared not let it. Not here, not now, when I was losing everything. Like a fool, I'd fallen in love with the moon, and once again it was out of my reach.

"Let us make a promise to each other, okay," he said, pressing his forehead to mine. "Out there, out in the world, we may have our roles to play, but here, in this room, let us make our own world. One where there is no caste, no social contract. One where we can be open and honest with each other without offense. Where we can act on our feelings without fear of some horrible consequence."

Our own world. One where the toad could dance with the moon. Hope, that dangerous and elusive emotion, flowered inside me. The horrible, heavy pounding of my heart turned into a flutter, light and warm as fireflies.

"Our own world," I repeated through my sniffles, fingers curling in the collar of his yukata, "where we can act on our emotions."

"Yes."

"Starting now?"

He laughed. "Yes, starting——"

He yelped in surprise as I pressed my lips to his. His body went rigid, tightening his fingers on my shoulders, and for a horrifying moment, I thought he might push me away until with a sigh, he relaxed. He slipped his fingers up my neck and burrowed into my hair as he returned my kiss. Softly at first, as if he thought I might break. With each gentle brush of his lips, the fireflies in my chest multiplied and spread, warming my skin until it glowed.

I'd never been high before, and suddenly I found my head in the clouds. The world around us fell away, and we were floating, drifting in a current of our own making. My heart raced and I felt fear. Not the sharp, panicky fear I was used to, but the kind that left you exhilarated, sizzling down to the ends of your toes, and begging for more.

He wrapped himself around me as our kiss deepened. I slid my hands around his waist, over the curve of his back, pulling him into me as if we could become one. I bumped against the knot at his hip, and I froze. That yawning blankness loomed again, ready to consume me at the slightest threat.

"What is wrong?" he asked against my lips, his fingers following the line of my arm until they met mine. I swallowed hard, my mouth dry, unable to speak. "You do not have to do anything you do not want to."

"I want to," I said quickly, breathlessly. "I want to, I want to. I just…" I fought through the euphoric fog in my brain, struggling to find the words to explain what I was feeling. "I don't know how to…be *here*."

Mahiro's eyes softened as understanding settled over him. I could feel it already, my screaming subconscious begging, urging, insisting that I pull back, hide myself away in my safe place so I couldn't feel the pain. He kissed me again, a light, airy kiss just at the edge of my lips that made my mind go soft.

"Do you trust me?" he breathed against my skin.

"Yes."

"You know I would never hurt you."

My head swam as he trailed kisses down my neck. He curled his fingers around mine, urging them around the knot in his obi. My heart skipping in my throat, I tugged at the rough fabric, and it loosened. Mahiro hummed a note of encouragement into my neck, and I pulled harder until it fell away. I slipped my other hand inside his yukata, over his slim waist, and pressed it into the small of his back.

I groaned, my actions becoming frantic as if that first brush of skin flipped a switch inside me. My body screamed for his, and I yanked at my own clothes until my yukata fell open. He pressed his chest to mine, skin against skin, heartbeat against heartbeat, and the fireflies inside me swarmed. Mahiro threw his head back and released a peal of giddy laughter as I wrapped my arms around his waist and lifted him up, carrying him the short distance to the futon and dropping him onto his back.

For a long time, we just looked at each other. Skin fair as soapstone gleamed from within the pool of his open yukata. Long, lean muscles twitched impatiently and his chest heaved. He wore no fundoshi underneath—*scandalous!*—and he swelled beneath me. He found the knot in mine and deftly pulled it away.

I felt a stab of self-consciousness. My body had always been a source of confusion for me. As he held the undeniable proof of my sex in his hand, I felt truly naked. But he didn't hesitate, didn't shirk away with the disgust of an illusion shattered.

"You're beautiful."

With a sound like weeping, I crashed my lips into his again, and they opened to me. I slipped my tongue between his teeth and pressed it against his, shivering as he massaged me, stroked me, stoking a fire inside that flared hot. That voice inside me again screamed—*run!*—but I shoved it down. I wanted to be here, to taste the salt of his skin, hear his gasping breaths, each one making the fire glow brighter.

I traced my fingers along his collarbone and down his sternum. He groaned as I brushed over his nipple, and it hardened under my thumb. I rubbed it, pinched it, and he arched under me, my name pouring from his lips.

He hooked a leg around my hips and pulled me into him. He had a runner's legs, lean and strong. He took us both in his hand, his hardness rubbing against mine, and my mind went white. I was powerless, a boat adrift on Mahiro's sea, but for the first time, I wasn't afraid. He didn't take it from me as so many others had. I gave it to him, completely and willingly. As our bodies rolled together, I let his current take me away to places uncharted. I looked into his eyes and saw the magic inside him as his irises swirled and went white. My hand met his between us, and we stroked together, fingers intertwined.

I don't know who came first. I only remember a great gasping cry, and the fireflies swarming in my gut exploded and filled my vision. Hot pleasure cascaded through me, starting at my groin and filling every cell down to my fingertips. It destroyed my muscles and dissolved my bones.

I didn't realize I was crying until Mahiro brushed the tears from my face and kissed my eyes. It was a strange, dizzying feeling. For the first time in my life, I'd given myself over to another person, and instead of feeling empty, I felt fuller than when I started. For the first time in my life, I believed, truly believed, that magic was real.

TWENTY-TWO

Stay Forever

My tears subsided, leaving me emotionally and physically drained, and I clung to Mahiro, head buried in his chest, the only thing in that moment that felt real. He pulled a blanket up tight around us, cocooning us from the cold, and stroked my hair until I composed myself.

"Are you all right?" he asked gently.

"Yes," I said with a self-deprecating laugh. "I just…didn't know it could be like that." He kissed the top of my head and held me a little tighter. I felt warm for the first time in days. I ran my hands along the curve of his back and over his sides and suddenly remembered the bright splash of blood on his kimono. "Why would someone want to kill you?"

"Because they are afraid of me," he said with a sigh. "Of people like me."

"Why?"

"Because we take." His voice went hard, his expression dark. "That is the unfortunate truth. I do my best to give back in kind, with this house and the people in it, but not all are as conscientious as I."

"So they hunt you. As a hunter does a bear."

He laughed at my stricken expression. "Do not worry, I am not that easy to kill."

"Are you…immortal?"

"It's a little more complicated than that," he said with a drowsy laugh. I pulled back to look him in his face, and he sighed. "I will never get old. I will never get sick. If I am cut, I will heal, but I am not immune to death. I have just…been given a choice."

"I don't understand."

"I was human once, just like you." I gasped, and he gave me a playful knock on the head. "Do not look so shocked! Did you think I crawled out of a pit somewhere?"

"I'm not sure what I thought," I said. "But if you were human, how…"

"I told you I was sick. One day, a man came with a cure. Blood laced with magic." His eyes went a bit dark. "It made me strong but not impervious. Pierce my heart and I will still die, but unlike before, I have the power to return if I choose."

"Doesn't that make you immortal?" I asked. "I can't imagine anyone *choosing* to die."

"Magic always comes at a price," he said ominously, "and it is not without its hardships."

"You regret it?"

He released a long, slow breath. "Sometimes." My eyes widened, and he gave me a reassuring smile. "Don't worry, I'm not going anywhere. I have far too much to live for."

He kissed me gently, and I melted into it. I tried not to think about that horrible blood stain and what could have happened, what maybe *did* happen. In that moment, I was grateful for the magic in his blood. Whatever the price, I would pay it gladly as long as it brought him home.

"What are you going to tell your friend?"

"Hm?"

"You know, since you're not selling me anymore."

"Am I not?" I pinched him hard in the side, and he yelped. "Ow! All right, not funny." He rubbed at the bruise and growled. "Nothing.

When he arrives, I will just give him a warm meal, a place to sleep, and then apologize and tell him there was a misunderstanding. That is all."

"He'll be angry."

"I do not care." I lifted my head and gave him a questioning look. "He is not *that* good of a friend."

I laughed and tucked my head back under his chin. "What about the others?"

"What about the others?"

"They're sure to notice," I said, running a finger absently along the curve of his shoulder.

"It is none of their business."

"And Kira?" He growled again, but I pressed on. "You know, she's in love with you."

He sighed deeply, and when he spoke again, it was tinged with regret. "I know."

"She's my friend," I said. "I don't want to hurt her."

"Then tell her…whatever you want," he said. "I will leave it up to you."

I frowned and buried my nose deeper into his chest. I didn't want to think about it. I didn't want to think about anything but the warmth of Mahiro's arms around me. Suddenly, prying myself away from him and returning to my room seemed more than I could manage.

"Mahiro?"

"Hm?"

"May I stay here tonight?"

"Yes. Please. Stay forever."

I smiled into the crook of his neck, my heart skipping. "Okay."

TWENTY-THREE

Kira

I WOKE THE NEXT MORNING BEFORE THE SUN, AS WAS MY CUSTOM, feeling refreshed and satiated in a way I never had before. Mahiro slept beside me, lips slightly parted, hand resting on my hip. The lines I'd seen around his mouth were gone, and I wondered if I'd imagined them. I swept an errant lock of hair from his eyes and kissed the bridge of his nose before carefully slipping out of bed and hunting in the dark for my yukata.

"Must you get up so early?" Mahiro groaned groggily from behind me. I turned to find him with his nose buried in the futon, his arm stretched out into the space I'd just vacated.

"I'm sorry." I gave his hand a squeeze. "Go back to sleep."

He shivered dramatically and pulled the blanket tight around his shoulders. "Come back in. It is cold."

"I have to get to the kitchen if you want your breakfast on time."

"I need you more than breakfast." He shot his hand out and grabbed my sleeve. He pulled me down to him, inching his fingers up my arm and across my chest. "Just until I am warm. Just a little while."

"A little while?" I said incredulously as he lifted his lips to mine.

He shot me a mischievous grin.

MORE THAN A LITTLE WHILE LATER, I RUSHED OUT OF THE ROOM, a flush on my cheeks and still fussing with my hastily donned yukata. My worries from the night before dropped back on my head one by one with each step away from Mahiro. What would I tell the girls? Surely they would have noticed my absence. Thanks to Mahiro's persistence, I'd lost all hope of sneaking back in before they woke. They were probably halfway through preparing breakfast by now.

And Kira. What on earth would I say to Kira? I had to tell her, didn't I? She'd be hurt either way, but hiding it would only make the hurt worse. If I just got it out of the way, maybe she would understand. She would see that this wasn't just about pleasure, that Mahiro and I actually cared for each other, and she would be happy for me.

It was, in so many ways, like a fairy tale. The poor, abused servant girl rescued by a handsome nobleman. The image, however inaccurate and self-indulgent, made me blush. Didn't every young girl secretly wish for such a fate? Perhaps she would see it as encouragement. Dreams *could* come true.

"Asagi!"

I jumped and spun around at the sound of my name being called from behind me. Blinded by my romantic delusions, I didn't notice Kira coming in from outside carrying a bushel of daikon, the large white roots overflowing the basket she carried them in. Now with her rushing toward me, her wide, worried eyes welling, I felt like a snake.

"Are you okay? When we woke up, you were gone. Where have you—"

I flushed red as she took in my disheveled appearance, my matted hair, my off-kilter obi. Her eyes darted down the hall in the direction I had come from, and her expression shifted dangerously. "Kira, I—"

"Bakayarou!" she spat, shoving the basket into my chest hard enough to knock the wind out of me.

"Kira, it's not what you think," I gasped, dropping the basket to the floor. Broken daikon cut the air with their sharp odor.

"What did you do?" she snapped. "Throw yourself at him so he'd let you stay? You're disgusting. A pervert, just like they all said."

I flinched, her words stinging like bees. "Kira…"

"How could you?" she said, her lips quivering. "He was so good to you."

My heart broke. She thought I was manipulating him, playing with his emotions so he wouldn't send me away. It wasn't a far stretch. Everyone knew he favored me, doted on me even. Why wouldn't she believe that? Especially when it was so much easier and less painful than the truth.

Tears in her eyes, she snatched the basket up and pushed past me. The happy cloud I'd been floating on evaporated from beneath me, and I fell rudely to earth. A door slid open down the hall, and I knew it was him before he appeared, a furrow of concern between his eyes.

"The secret is out then, is it?" he asked.

I nodded gravely. "You heard?"

"Yes." I took a deep, trembling breath, and he pulled me into his arms. "It will be okay. She is just confused. She will come around."

"You don't think I—"

"Of course not."

With that small measure of relief, I relaxed into him. He kissed my cheek, stroked my hair, and gave me one final squeeze before pushing me back up onto my feet.

"Now, go get me my breakfast," he teased. "You are late." The smile he gave me made me believe him, made me think everything would be all right. But the trail of broken daikon suggested differently.

TWENTY-FOUR

Storm

From that day forward, I became Mahiro's shadow. To the outside world, I was his most trusted and loyal attendant. I poured his tea, carried his papers, and, of course, served him his meals. I tended to his guests and became a quiet fixture in the background of every meeting, ready to spring into action at the sound of an empty cup.

In *our* world, we were not only lovers, but also friends. We laughed over house gossip and had sober political discussions. My presence in his meetings gave me an understanding of the outside world and societal workings I'd never had before, and he encouraged my questions. They would often lead to spirited, even heated, debates that would leave us both fuming, but I knew by his actions in those meetings that my opinion mattered. *I* mattered.

My world that had been so small, desolate, and fraught with storms opened up. For the first time, I dared to look to the future and saw only blue skies full of possibilities. I might never be Mahiro's equal, but when I looked into his eyes, I saw myself there, and it made me feel powerful.

Only one dark cloud hovered on my horizon: Kira. Ever since her discovery of Mahiro's and my relationship, she'd grown cold to me. We hardly spoke. She was my best friend, the only real friend I'd had in a long time, and now we passed each other in the halls like strangers. It was more than just petty jealousy. I'd betrayed her, injured her in some deep, irreparable way. Mahiro insisted I leave it alone, but it plagued me like a thorn in my heel, and I missed her terribly.

"What are you thinking about?" Mahiro asked, pinching my thigh to get my attention.

The days had just started to lengthen, and we'd made a habit of sitting on the porch and watching the sky change, a pot of tea steeping beside us. Orange light reflected off his skin, making him glow.

"What? Oh. Nothing."

"Liar," he teased. "Your eyebrow twitches when you feel guilty about something."

"Does not!" I said, my hand flying up to my forehead. Just at that moment, Kira crossed the garden in front of us carrying a load of vegetables bound for the kitchen, and the little muscle at the corner of my eye jumped under my fingers.

Mahiro sighed, following my gaze. "How many times do I have to tell you? You have nothing to feel guilty about. You have done nothing wrong."

"You don't understand," I said, allowing my hand to drop into my lap and shaking my head. "She's afraid."

"Of what?"

"That I've replaced her."

Mahiro scoffed. "As much as I love you, you cannot replace her," he said, touching my hand.

"I know that," I said, a splash of warmth in my cheeks. "I'm sure she knows that too. But that fear...it's like a reflex. Losing your usefulness to your master is like death for us. She probably thought she would never have to feel that fear again, and now she does...because of me."

My shoulders sank under the weight of my admission, and Mahiro scooted closer to me, pressing his side against mine. I leaned into his warmth and let it soothe away the icy lump in my chest.

"Do you want me to talk to her?" he asked gently.

"No." I shifted my legs under me and pushed to my feet. "I'll talk to her."

"Now?" he whined, grabbing onto my hem and pouting.

"Maybe now," I answered with a chuckle. "I have to get to the kitchen, anyway. It's time to start preparing supper." Mahiro growled in protest but ultimately released me. "Will you take your meal in your room?"

"No, I think I will stay out here."

"You won't be too cold?"

"A little cold is good for the soul," he said, bouncing his fist on his chest.

I laughed, and he gave me an affectionate wink. I shrugged my robe off my shoulders and laid it over his on his back, taking the opportunity to place a small kiss on the shell of his ear before disappearing into the kitchen.

MEAL PREPARATION WAS ALREADY WELL UNDERWAY BY THE TIME I GOT there. Kaoru grinned up at me from where she was chopping onions, her eyes red and tearful from the fumes. I gave her shoulders a friendly squeeze as I lowered myself down beside her.

"Apologies for being late," I said, taking the knife from her hand and taking over.

"It's the third time this week," Haruko growled from inside the pantry. "We can't keep doing your work for you, you know."

"Oh, stop it, Haruko," Kaoru scoffed. "You know it's only because Mahiro-sama demands so much of his time."

She gave me a little bump with her hip and a conspiratorial wink. Rumors of our relationship had spread through the house like wildfire, and while most of the staff gave it hardly a passing thought, Kaoru found the whole thing terribly romantic. I felt a prickle between my shoulder blades and glanced over to find Kira loading up a pair of trays with fish and miso, radiating hostility.

"These are done," she said coldly, stacking the trays one on top of the other and dropping them down next to me so hard the dishes clanged together. "You should take it before it gets cold."

"Already?" Kaoru whined. "We hardly see you anymore, Asagi-chan."

"Yours is on top," Kira said, a shake in her voice. I grabbed her wrist to stop her before she could walk away, and she pinned me with an angry glare.

"Can we talk?" I asked in a low voice.

She yanked her hand away. "There's nothing to talk about."

"Please, Kira." She turned her back on me. Caught up in a burst of courage, I followed her. "You don't have to say anything. Just listen."

She stopped but didn't turn, her back rod straight and stiff. I wiped my sweating palms across my hips and raked a dry tongue over my lips. Now that I had her, I was at a complete loss of what to say.

"I love you," I blurted, and her shoulders rose with a gasp of surprise. I didn't know how else to say it. "When I came here, I was… broken. And you were so kind. I felt dead inside, and you taught me how to live again. You saved me so many times just by being there. I hate that I've made you feel this way. The last thing I ever wanted to do was hurt you." Tears burned in my eyes, but I couldn't stop. "I know you're angry with me. That you may never forgive me, and that's okay. I understand. But I just wanted you to know that if that changes, I will be here waiting."

Her hands curled into fists at her side, her knuckles going white. Her whole body shook, and she took heavy gulping breaths. I waited patiently for something, anything, my heart thumping against my ribs.

"Dammit, Asagi," she said in a broken voice. "Why did he have to love you? Why couldn't you have just…gone away?"

She turned and pushed swiftly past me, but not before I saw the tears wetting her cheeks.

TWENTY-FIVE

Doku Zeri

THOUGH I HAD EXPECTED NO LESS OF A REACTION, NOTHING COULD have prepared me for the sting of her words. I stood frozen, staring at the space she'd left as if I could wind back time and make it different. I was jerked out of my stupor by the sound of a dropped pan behind me, and when I turned, half a dozen eyes shifted uncomfortably to the floor. I closed my eyes and took a deep breath to still my nerves before returning to a distraught-looking Kaoru.

"She didn't mean it, Asagi-chan," she whispered, the tears in her eyes no longer from the onions.

"I have to go." I dropped to one knee and planted a kiss on her temple before scooping up the trays carrying Mahiro's and my dinners. I put on a strong face and forced a smile, but my hands shook so bad the dishes rattled as I exited the kitchen toward the front of the house. I could see Mahiro's back silhouetted by the setting sun, made broader than usual by the double layer of robes. I didn't want him to know what happened. If he knew how it had hurt me, he might feel compelled to step in, and that would only make things worse, so I did my best to pull together the shattered pieces of my heart before I reached his side.

"Your dinner, Mahiro-sama," I said, putting on my sweetest smile. He turned on his hip and beamed up at me. I felt better already.

"That was fast. Look, you have not even missed the sunset."

"It was practically done by the time I got there." I set the trays down beside him and settled opposite. I pulled mine off the top and pushed his toward him. He snatched up the chopsticks and, with a quick "Itadakimasu," dug into the fish. I had just scooped up my bowl of miso, thick with tofu and bits of floating nori, when a realization struck me. "Do you even need to eat?"

Mahiro shrugged one shoulder, his chopsticks between his lips. "No."

"Then why…"

"Because I enjoy it," he said with a wink. "Not everything in life should be about utility."

"How decadent," I teased. "I'll remember that next time I'm scraping shit out of your chamber pot."

"Oh, was that really necessary?" he chided, tossing down his chopsticks with a sour face.

I shrugged one shoulder, lifting my miso to my lips. I smiled, and it strained under the weight of my sadness.

"No."

MY COMMENT PUT MAHIRO OFF HIS MEAL FOR EXACTLY LONG enough to pour his tea. Then he was back to drowning his fish in awful sauces and humming in pleasure as he rolled it on his tongue. The sky went from red to deep blue to velvety black. A gentle breeze rustled the branches of the sleeping cherry trees and carried with it the smell of night-blooming flowers. Mahiro pulled his robe around himself tighter and shivered.

"We should go inside." I gathered up our dishes and stacked the trays on top of each other. "I'll clean this up and—"

I gasped as a wave of dizziness nearly knocked me off my feet. Mahiro jumped up, catching the trays before I could drop them. I sank into a nearby beam.

"What happened? Are you all right?" he asked.

"I don't know. I got dizzy all of a sudden." I groaned as my stomach rolled and cramped. "I think maybe the fish was bad."

He swept a hand over my forehead. "You are sweating. I will get you a doctor."

"No, I'm fine," I said, grabbing his sleeve before he could dart away. I felt a stab of panic at the thought of being alone. "It'll pass. I just need to lie down."

His face pinched with concern, but he eventually relented. Leaving the trays behind on the porch, he looped his arm around my waist and pulled me upright. I leaned heavily on him as he led me back to his room. I got the impression he could have carried me but spared me the embarrassment. He whispered to someone as we passed, a sharp command of "Get Kikyou."

I muttered another halfhearted objection.

By the time we reached Mahiro's room, I could hardly stand, and I fell heavily to the floor. "I think I'm going to be sick." I heaved as the floor tilted beneath me, and Mahiro shoved a basin in front of me just as my dinner crawled its way back up my throat. Part of me was relieved. The sooner I got rid of the bad fish, the sooner I'd feel better.

But I didn't feel better. My insides burned, and a pressure like a hot anvil sat on my chest. Mahiro wiped my mouth and urged me into the futon. Kikyou appeared and placed a cool hand on my head. She looked into my eyes, pinched my wrist between her fingers, and laid her head on my chest.

"Asagi was fine before your supper?" she asked, squinting into my sick bowl.

"Yes."

"Where are your dishes?"

"Still on the porch, I think," he said. "Why?"

Kikyou grunted and disappeared out the door. Mahiro took my hand in one of his and held it against his chest as he dabbed a cool cloth on my forehead with the other. He looked pale and scared, and for a disoriented moment, I wondered why. One doesn't tremble and fret over a sick horse. They put it down and sell its meat to pay for a replacement. What made me so important?

Then I remembered. He loved me.

Kikyou returned moments later, her face ashen, my discarded miso bowl in her hand. She swiped a finger along the inner surface, and it came up spotted with flakes of nori. Her eyes trembled as she held it out for us to see.

"I'm so sorry, Mahiro-sama," she said in a halting, broken voice. "Doku zeri."

Water hemlock. I'd been poisoned.

No sooner had the words left her mouth than a sharp pain lanced through my spine and latched onto the back of my head with sharp fingers. My right side went rigid, and my vision black. I was dimly aware of frantic voices and restraining hands. I couldn't breathe, couldn't think.

It could have been seconds. It could have been hours. I regained awareness in Mahiro's arms. He held me tight, as if someone might snatch me away. The blanket he'd tucked around me was tossed and tangled about my legs. Every muscle burned. I tasted blood.

"Send for the doctor! Now!" Mahiro screamed, his voice tight with panic. "Put Ryuichi on our fastest horse—"

"Mahiro-sama, it'll take more than a day—"

"I do not care."

"Mahiro-sama!" Kikyou's eyes glistened as they moved desperately between me and Mahiro. I knew this look. I'd seen it before. Sending for the doctor was useless. I didn't have a day. I didn't have the night.

I groaned as another cramp ripped its way through my gut. My head pressed to Mahiro's chest, I heard his heart race, and he released a whimper of defeat. His normally bright features quivered and collapsed in despair. He looked old, suddenly. My hand twitched in an effort to smooth the lines from his face, but I had no strength to lift it.

"Who did this?" he asked as if to himself as he brushed sweat-damp hair from my face. "He makes our meals. How could this have happened?"

"'Yours is...on top,'" I said in a barely intelligible mumble. Mahiro lowered his head closer, lifting my head so my lips brushed his ear.

"I do not understand."

My eyes overflowed with burning tears, and the anvil on my chest grew heavier until every breath came out a wheeze. I didn't want to say it. Didn't want to believe it. I didn't want to see the anguish in Mahiro's eyes when he knew the truth.

"…Kira."

Pain sliced through me, and my vision went black again, but even through the convulsions, I could hear Mahiro screaming. A scream of rage and despair. He screamed her name, and despite what she'd done to me, I feared for her, for what he'd do. The cold seeped into my veins, and all I could think was, *Don't. Stop. It's not her fault. It's mine.*

TWENTY-SIX

Death and Rebirth

TIME FELT DISJOINTED. I DRIFTED IN AND OUT OF CONSCIOUSNESS, the only constants the warmth of Mahiro's arms around me and searing pain. My guts felt like they were tearing themselves apart, and I heard myself moan as if from far away. I saw faces from the past: my mother, who I barely remembered, her features blurred by time; Yutaka's cold expression that hid such deep feeling; Tsukito smiling wide, his eyes as bright as the sun.

I twitched back to reality with the sound of a sliding door. I blinked bleary eyes and recognized Kira's shape in the doorway, escorted by two men who usually worked in the stables. She trembled, eyes wide, face red and puffy. Mahiro tensed. I rolled my tired eyes up to his face and noticed for the first time his elongated eyeteeth, his lips curled around them in a snarl.

"Leave her."

The two men shoved Kira into the room before bowing deeply and sliding the door closed behind her. She tripped a little, her bad leg momentarily giving out as her gaze bounced around the room.

"Sit," Mahiro barked.

She jumped and clutched her chest before dropping to her knees, back against the wall. "Mahiro-sama, I—"

"Are you one of them?" he growled.

"What?"

"Did *he* send you?"

"I don't under—"

"How could you?" He swung between anger and hurt with every word. "Asagi is your friend. Asagi loves you. *I* love you. How could you do this to us?" Her eyes welled and dropped to the floor. "Do not *dare* look away," Mahiro snarled and her gaze snapped back up. "You have betrayed me. You have betrayed everyone in this house. Now, you will sit there, and you will *watch* until you understand the consequences of your actions."

Fat tears collected in the corners of Mahiro's eyes and dropped down his cheek. I groaned as my consciousness slipped again. I fought it, clinging to Mahiro's clothes as if it could stop the dark. Kikyou appeared from somewhere and tipped my head back, pouring something bitter on my tongue.

"What is it?" Mahiro asked.

"Opium," she replied gravely. "Asagi-chan doesn't need to be in pain."

Then I was gone, dropped into a dark pool of nothingness. The pain was still there, but it felt far away and meaningless. A warm, bright light shimmered in the distance, and I knew it was Mahiro. I reached for it, or I thought I did, but it was too far away, and I sank even deeper. The cold hand of death wrapped itself around me and pulled me down.

I don't want to go.

I do not want you to go, replied a voice from above.

Like a fish pulled from the water on a fisherman's hook, I was yanked back into consciousness. Mahiro's finger was in my mouth, and I tasted something sharp and metallic that sent jolts of electricity through me. His face was close to mine, stoic but bearing the evidence of tears, his eyes white.

"I have the power to refuse death, and I will give it to you."

Kira released a cry of protest as Mahiro plunged his face into my neck. My sluggish brain struggled to comprehend as he opened his mouth wide and latched on. Heat started at his lips and radiated through me. Like the warmth of a fire on a winter's day, it traveled through my veins and banished the cold inside. Down my neck, over my shoulders, into my chest.

It doesn't hurt. Feels good, even.

Mahiro shifted his hold on me, pulling me tighter against him, and I moaned as a pulling ripped at the very moorings of my soul. A small voice in my head rang out like a warning, but it was drowned out by the pleasure of his lips pressed to my skin and the heat in my veins that flowed both out of him and toward him, filling me and draining me at the same time.

I made a choked sound, and he lowered me onto my back on the tatami as my body went limp. I had no power to give in or resist. Just as death tried once again to scratch its way in, something flowed hot and thick into my mouth. Blood. I knew its taste well, but this blood was different. This blood carried something dark with it, infused with something terrible and powerful.

Blood laced with magic.

It filled my heart, my head, my lungs. It coaxed my tired muscles to motion, and Mahiro pinned my body down with his as I spasmed beneath him. A moan built in my chest and burst forth unrestrained when his lips finally released mine. I grasped at his clothes, blinking and disoriented. I saw him in front of me but felt him inside me, vibrating through me, an unmistakable yet impossible connection and then...

Blackness, silent and complete. And no pain. It was as if my body had evaporated into a mist and left me formless. Was I dead? As if in answer, my heart pounded a single, heavy beat. *Not dead. Different. Reborn.*

My body reformed cell by cell, and the first sensation was pain. Not the terrible, gut-tearing pain of the poison, but something sharp and immediate. A pain born from need that encompassed all of me, and instead of dragging me down, it urged me up. My back arched. My veins pumped venom. An ominous, dark voice inside growled *Move. Move or die.*

The sound of scuffling and raised voices came, and I sensed something hot and bright and alive thrown down close to me. I didn't know what it was, but I knew I wanted it, needed it. I opened sightless eyes and clawed at it, balking as a high-pitched cry emanated from it.

"Take her, Asagi." Mahiro's voice cut through the fog. "It will stop the pain."

Blinking, the thing in front of me a smear of white light across my vision, I grasped onto it. Something animal and instinctual rose up in me, and I sank my teeth into the brightest part of it. It burst open, filling my mouth with a sweet elixir that filled every part of me until the pain melted into a dark, deep pleasure.

I drank until the vessel was empty. I moaned again as I let it slip from my hands, blinking and blinking and blinking until my vision cleared. Mahiro. Beautiful Mahiro. He knelt in front of me, his hand outstretched, eyes trembling with fear, relief, and a deep, deep sadness.

I reached a hand out to meet his and stopped short. Blood. Blood everywhere. On my hands, on my face, in my mouth. The stink of it filled me until I thought I would retch. I screamed and pulled away from the thing beneath me—the golden vessel broken and drained.

Kira, her throat torn open.

TWENTY-SEVEN

Red-Eyed Monster

I screamed. The sound ricocheted around the room like something solid, sending me to the floor with my hands clasped over my ears, but I couldn't stop. Even with my eyes squeezed shut, I saw her, felt her, heard her voice whispering through my veins. *Asagi, what have you done?*

Mahiro moved toward me, the scrape of his stockinged feet on the tatami loud as stampeding horses. I jerked away blindly, crashing into the wall behind me. Everything was loud. So loud. Even my skin screamed as my kimono scraped against it, the competing textures of cotton and wool sending electric vibrations that put my hair on end. I didn't want to open my eyes. I couldn't.

"Asagi..." Mahiro kept his voice low, but it still shook the air like thunder.

"She's dead!" I cried, pulling myself tighter against the wall as his hand grazed my arm.

"Yes."

"She's dead. She's dead, and I killed her. I *killed* her!"

Mahiro rushed forward and wrapped his arms around me. A jolt went through me, and I thrashed against him in panic.

"It is all right, Asagi," he said gently despite my fists pounding against his back and shoulders. "I know it is overwhelming. Just breathe."

"I can't," I choked between gasping breaths, but already my body was calming. His heart beat against mine, and something inside me responded. My muscles softened, and I went almost limp in his arms. "It's so loud. Why is everything so loud?"

"Focus on one thing at a time," he said, pressing his palm flat against my back. "Listen to your body."

With a whimper, I buried my face in the crook of his neck and tried to do as he said. I took a ragged, shaky breath and heard it rattle through my chest. I took another and another, each one a little smoother than the last. In the relative quiet, I heard the soft *thump, thump, thump* of my heart and the hiss of blood through my veins. I sounded like a machine made of sinews and steam.

Mahiro's chest swelled against mine with a deep breath, and I struggled to match it. Grief flooded over me with the memory of Kira pressing her chest to my back to ease me out of a panic attack. My deep breath turned into a sob that welled up from my toes.

"What did I do?" I muttered into his neck.

"You did nothing wrong," he answered, stroking my back.

"But I…"

"You took back the life she stole from you," he said coldly.

"But she was…my…"

"She was *not* your friend," he snarled before catching himself. "It was…necessary. It is how we are."

"'How we are?'" I repeated, anger cutting through my grief. "How *you* are!" I shoved him hard in the chest, sending him flying backward. I tried to open my eyes, but sensory overload slammed them shut again. I grasped my head as shimmering pain slid over my skull. "What have you done to me?"

"I have made you," he said, voice cracked and fragile with hurt. "I made you so you could live."

"You made me a monster." Tears wet the blood on my face, and the smell made my stomach heave. I scrubbed at it, scraped at it, finally giving up and collapsing into a rocking, crying mess. I reached out for Mahiro, but he was nowhere. As angry as I was, I needed him, needed him to hold me and rock me and tell me it was going to be okay, and I suddenly regretted pushing him away. He was so silent and so still that for a terrifying moment I thought he had abandoned me until I heard a gentle *pat-pat, pat-pat* just an arm's length away.

I cracked my eyes open. The room was dim, lit only by a single oil lamp, but its light made my head spin and my eyes water. *Focus on one thing at a time.* I blinked hard until the blurriness cleared, focusing on my hands pressed to the tatami in front of me. A man's hands, broad and heavy, the shiny pink of fresh burn scars peeking from between my fingers.

I took a deep breath and eased my eyes up toward the sound. Two round wet spots marred the front of Mahiro's purple-clad knees. I looked up to his clenched fists, his shaking shoulders, his lowered head. Fat tears flowed from his eyes and dripped from the end of his nose.

Pat-pat.

"Forgive me," he said, his voice barely above a whisper. "I was not ready. I was not ready to lose you when I had only just found you."

Something crumbled inside me. The anger burned away, and in the loaded silence that followed, I felt a new sensation rising within. Another heart beat beside mine, within mine, and I knew it was his. The blood he gave me, the blood that made me, warmed me to my core, and within it, I felt his love for me. My blue skies might now be marred by storm clouds, but he would always weather them beside me.

Exhaustion crashed over me, and I crawled on my hands and knees toward him. He gasped in surprise as I crumpled into him, my head in his lap and my arms looped around his waist. I might have been angry about what had happened to me, might always be angry, but it didn't change my feelings for him. Another version of me, a stronger, more stubborn version, might have fought against it, but I was too tired.

I relaxed, and my tears dried as he pulled his fingers slowly through my hair. I felt safe here. The cold hand of death had been turned away and could never touch me again.

I awoke tucked into Mahiro's futon, a thick blanket wrapped

tight around me. The pain of the poison had gone except for a lingering ache in my belly, and I found myself fascinated by the feel of the sheets. I stretched my legs, humming as they slid through the soft fabric, wiggling my toes in the cold air when they poked out the end. I felt like a newborn experiencing waking for the first time. I stretched my arms over my head and listened to my joints pop with a newfound interest. The machine coming to life.

I blinked my eyes open, and the room glowed with the sun pouring in from outside. It reflected off the white bedding and made the painted screens come alive. Details I'd never noticed before stood out in stark relief: the tarnished brass of the oil lamps; the sharp, orderly arrangement of bottles and boxes on the weathered surface of the tonsu; the slightly frayed edges of the tatami around the doorway; the deep-brown stain peeking out from under the edge of the futon.

The room tilted, and I squeezed my eyes shut against the image of Kira lying bleeding on the floor. My hands and face had been cleaned, but I still felt sticky with her blood. The smell of it lingered in the air, and I pressed my face into the pillow to escape it. The door slid open, and Mahiro's hand appeared on my shoulder.

"Are you all right?" he asked, keeping his voice low.

"Yes. No. I don't know," I answered, shying away from his touch. "I think there's something wrong with my eyes."

"What do you mean?" His voice rose a little with concern. "You cannot see?"

"I see everything. Too much."

He chuckled and gave my shoulder a squeeze. "That's normal. Adjusting to the change can be a little overwhelming. Let me see you."

I rolled onto my back, eyes firmly closed until his fingers grazed my cheek. Slowly, tentatively, I opened first one, then the other, blinking until Mahiro's face swam into focus. He gasped, his fingers jumping back before he caught himself.

"What? What's wrong?" I asked, sitting straight up and lifting my hands to my face.

"Nothing," he said, his initial shock settling into something akin to wonder.

I stared at him, bewildered, and he gave me a stiff smile before reaching behind him and dipping his hand into the top drawer of his tonsu. He pulled out a brass mirror and handed it to me. A rock in my throat and butterflies hammering around in my rib cage, I lifted it to my face and looked.

Red. They were red.

Rage bubbled up in me again, and with a choked cry, I threw the mirror across the room. I pressed the heels of my hands to my eyes, and Mahiro had to grab me by the wrists to keep me from gouging them out. Looking in that mirror was like looking at a stranger. My usually deep-brown eyes burned ruby red as if Kira's blood in me had stained them—proof of my sin painted on my face.

Mahiro pulled me into his chest as I shook, crying and cursing his name even as I clung to him. I couldn't shake the feeling that I *had* died, died and been replaced by something dark and repulsive. A red-eyed monster that fed on blood.

TWENTY-EIGHT

First Blood

I SPENT ALL OF THAT DAY CURLED UP IN MAHIRO'S FUTON. WORD OF my poisoning had gotten around, and he insisted I stay sequestered under the guise of recovery until I got a better handle on my new senses. I didn't argue. As much as I missed the girls and however much the thought of them worrying pained me, I couldn't bear them seeing me like this—twitching at every sound, flinching at every touch. The world as I knew it had been erased and replaced with something bright and oppressive. Frankly, I was terrified.

There was something else too. A sinister need rose up in me. It started as a subtle ache in my joints, like fighting a cold and a generalized anxiety. I became irritable, kicking at the blankets and tearing at my clothes as if they'd done me some personal slight. It moved into my muscles and made me feverish. I sensed every warm-blooded thing that moved in the house down to the rats in the walls, and all of them glowed with ethereal light.

What if I lost control? What if I did to Haruko or Kaoru the same thing I had done to Kira?

By the time Mahiro returned from his daily business, I'd worked myself into a paranoid fit. The futon lay wadded up in one corner of the room, the blankets in another, and I had paced a groove in the tatami in between. Mahiro watched from the doorway as I made another circuit, a pair of food trays in his hand and an amused look on his face.

"Restless?" he asked with a sarcastic grin.

"I feel like my skin is on fire." I stomped toward the futon and gave it an angry kick.

"New blood is temperamental. It will calm down eventually." He found an empty patch of floor and settled down, gesturing for me to join him. "Food will help."

"I thought I didn't need to eat."

"You do not. Does not mean it is not comforting." I scowled, and he patted the floor beside him. "I have been worrying about you all day. You could sit with me, at least."

I growled, crossed my arms over my chest, shuffled my feet, uncrossed my arms again. Mahiro watched the whole display with growing amusement until I finally relented and plopped down beside him. He pushed a tray in front of me loaded with fish and vegetables, and I eyed it suspiciously.

"Do not worry. I made it myself," he said, patting my knee as he dug into his own meal.

"That's what I'm worried about," I said, curling my nose, and he clucked in mock offense.

"I happen to be quite useful in the kitchen."

"I've never known Kanjin to be useful at anything."

"Mattaku! You are rude when you are hungry." Mahiro laughed, but the implication gave me a jolt, and my teeth clamped shut.

I sat in silence, the smell of roasted fish itching my nose. Finally, I took up the chopsticks and lifted the bowl of rice. I didn't feel hungry, at least not in the sense I was used to. A need clawed at me that had nothing to do with my stomach, but I poked at my rice anyway and shoved a sticky lump in my mouth.

Mahiro smiled in approval, and I had to admit, the normalcy of the action did make me feel calmer. I plucked at the fish, which was tender and flavorful, and told myself I should apologize to Mahiro. I'd opened my mouth to do just that when my stomach rumbled dangerously, and I clapped a hand over my mouth.

"Oh, come now," Mahiro scoffed. "It is not that bad."

"It's not that. It's——" Pain shot through my abdomen, doubling me over. "My stomach. I think I'm going to be sick."

Mahiro rushed to my side as I lurched for the basin, emptying everything I'd just eaten into it. He lifted my hair and rubbed my back as my body spasmed. "I can't eat?" I said, choking up the last stubborn grains of rice. "Why can't I eat?"

"Your body must still be healing," Mahiro assured me. "The poison did a lot of damage before the change. Once we get some fresh blood in you——"

I cringed and pulled away. "No, I can't. I can't do that."

"Asagi, you have no choice."

"I don't want to hurt anybody," I said, shaking my head furiously.

"I know." His face softened, and he pushed the hair out of my eyes. "But the pain you are feeling will only get worse."

"Maybe I can do it like you," I said. "Like you did with Kira."

"No."

"Why not?"

"Because I said no." The sharpness of his tone made me jump back. In that second, he became my master again. "You have a monster inside you, and if you deny it, it will devour you."

"You've tamed your monster."

"We may have found a truce, but it is a precarious one and something that came with time. Stopping short takes restraint and discipline, neither of which you have right now. And the person you take will be bound to you for the rest of their lives. Kira's love for me was not love—it was obsession, and you see what it drove her to."

"You're saying this is your fault?"

He blinked slowly, pausing for a long time. "Yes."

I gritted my teeth and pushed away from him, swallowing a bitter lump of disappointment. He wanted me to kill, and master or not, I refused. There had to be a better way. *Had* to be.

I stood up with a *humph* and stomped out of the room. Mahiro called my name once sharply, but I ignored him. I could have restraint. I could have discipline. I didn't need to kill anyone. I'd show him.

The rest of the house had settled down for the night, and I made it out without being seen. The outside air hit me like a wall, a damp, biting cold that pierced me to the bone. Horse carts rumbled down the dirt streets. The smell of braziers lit against the chill, crackling and burning fragrant woods, drifted to my nose. I swayed on my feet as I tried to process it all, blinking in surprise at the brightness of the moon.

Come on, Asagi. Concentrate.

I clenched my fists and pushed forward through the veil clouding my senses and out the gate. Mahiro's manor was surrounded by farmland in every direction. Empty rice paddies and wheat fields shimmered with a light layer of frost. A small house perched on the horizon, an oil lamp lighting its window. Even at this distance, I could see the moths circling its flickering flame and a single shadow moving beyond it.

I set my path toward the house. Mahiro followed close behind, but I didn't look back. I covered the distance quickly and easily without even losing my breath. The farmhouse was small and in disrepair, the whole thing slouched to one side. A collection of rusted farm equipment leaned against the outside wall next to bushel baskets half full of vegetables. The resident was a subsistence farmer who likely grew little more than what could feed himself.

Sticking to the shadows, I crept along the house's back side and listened to the shuffling movements within. I closed my eyes as the need rose up inside me. I could feel the farmer glowing through the walls, could hear his heartbeat, could smell the sweat on his skin. My humanity slipped away, and I became a predator, waiting for the perfect opportunity to pounce.

In my daze, I bumped against a scythe and knocked it off-balance, sending it skittering across the wall. The rustling inside picked up a new urgency, and seconds later, the door jerked open. The farmer stood framed in the doorway, his long sinewy frame coiled tight and ready to defend his meager resources. He snatched up a hoe and peered into the dark, his face twisted with malice and a touch of fear.

"Who's there?" he shouted as he spotted my shape in the dark. I stepped forward, and he raised his weapon.

"I'm sorry, sir," I said in as diminutive a tone as my deep voice could manage. "I seem to be lost."

He squinted at me, taking in my feminine appearance, and his guard lowered a little. I took another step forward, and he tensed but didn't retreat. Another and our eyes met.

With a feeling like the snap of a string being pulled taut, a rush of unfamiliar images flooded my mind. Darkly tanned hands working black earth. The sun warming my back. The satisfying burn of muscles pushed to exhaustion. Memories, but not mine. I blinked, and the images receded, curling around my subconscious. The farmer stood in front of me, expression blank, eyes vacant and locked onto mine.

What just happened?

I blinked again, staggering as another wave of memories flooded my mind. A woman. Long dark hair and skin the color of rice paper. A swollen belly and a happy glow. A scream of pain and the memory turned dark, splashed with blood and grief.

My heart raced with his emotions. I saw him, his memories, his pain. I swallowed them up as if they were my own. His empty mind gaped before me, and acting on an instinct I didn't understand, I pushed into it. That string snapped taut again, and his body went rigid.

"Don't be afraid," I whispered, my mind wrapping his in a blanket of soothing thoughts. I took another step forward and laid my hand over his on the hoe. I threw up the stolen image of his woman, and his grip loosened, allowing it to slip from his hand.

"Megumi?" His voice trembled, and his eyes welled.

I touched his chest and felt his heartbeat. A small, guilty voice called out from my subconscious, but the need drowned it out. I ran my tongue over my fangs, small compared to Mahiro's, but sharp as razors, and they tingled in anticipation.

He looked at me and saw her. I pressed my chest to his, and he melted into me, wrapping his arms around my shoulders. I tucked my nose under his chin, and when my fangs pierced his flesh, he felt only the lips of his lost love.

When that first splash of blood hit my tongue, I swooned. Its golden light filled me, carrying with it the farmer's love, his longing, his loneliness. My eyes burned with his tears. In that moment, I loved him the way I imagine Megumi loved him, whole and complete, bound by our very souls.

"Asagi!"

My master's voice cut through the visions, and the string between our minds shuddered and snapped. The farmer's body fell limp in my arms, his breathing fast and shallow, his heartbeat erratic. I released my bite as his weight took us both down.

Head light and body buzzing, my mind a disoriented tumble, I stared dumbly at his pale face. A cold knot formed in my chest as his eyes clouded and rolled away from mine. Mahiro appeared behind me, his hands on my shoulders.

"Time to go," he said, low but firm.

"No," I said, shaking him off and peering into the farmer's dull eyes. "He's still alive."

"He is dead."

"His heart's still beating." I cupped the farmer's face in my hands, brushing away the tears that dropped onto it. "I didn't kill him. I didn't."

"You did. Listen."

The farmer's heart sputtered once, and with a final, gasping breath, he went silent. "No," I muttered, giving his shoulders a hard shake. "No, no, no. I didn't—"

"Asagi…"

"Do something!"

"There is nothing to be done."

"He was alive!" I cried, my voice taking on a hysterical pitch. I gathered the farmer's body up in my arms and crushed him to my chest. "I didn't mean to kill him. I didn't want to…"

"I know." Mahiro's hands were on me again, gently prying the farmer's body out of my grip. "We have to go now, before…"

We both froze at the sound of movement from inside. Light clumsy footsteps shuffled toward us, and a small face appeared in the doorway.

"Papa?"

Despair slammed through me, blacking out my vision. Mahiro grabbed me up and spirited me away. By the time my awareness returned, we were back in our room. A great, wailing cry ripped from my chest. I took that man's blood, his life, and it buzzed through me. The beast had stilled, but at what cost? Mahiro was right. I had no choice. The choice had been made for me, and while I didn't want to die, living suddenly felt like a terrible, irreversible mistake.

TWENTY-NINE

Elevated

I COULDN'T SLEEP. I SPENT THE WHOLE NIGHT STARING AT MAHIRO AS he slept beside me. The longer I looked into his face, the more twisted it became, stretching and morphing until all I saw was a snarling, bloodthirsty animal. My heart split in two. I wanted to love him, needed to love him, but with the farmer's death so fresh on my hands, all I could do was blame.

I was fully dressed and sitting formally at the edge of his futon when he started to stir. He gave a start when he spotted me, rubbing his eyes and squinting against the morning sun.

"You know, some may find this creepy," he said with a drowsy laugh.

"I need my own room."

He blinked. "What?"

"I can't go back with the girls. Not like this."

"And what is wrong with this room?" he asked cautiously.

"You're here."

He flinched, and I felt a stab of guilt. He sat up slowly as if his body ached, those lines around his mouth carving a deep frown.

"You do not love me anymore?" He laughed, but his eyes were dark.

"No, it's not that. I just...after last night, I..."

"Cannot stand to look at me."

I released a long, heavy sigh, my shoulders slumping, and he nodded.

"All right. If it is what you need." He rotated on his hip, putting his back to me, and reached for the pitcher and basin. Silence hung thick as he scrubbed his face and hands. "You should at least visit them, you know. The girls. They have been worried about you."

"All right. I will."

He nodded again and stood. Without looking at me, he crossed to the closet and pulled out a kimono box. I hated this broken feeling between us, but I knew the only way to fix it was to come to terms with myself and what I had become. The longer I spent cooped up in this room, the more the resentment built. I had to find a way to stop it before it overpowered me and ruined us for good.

I stood and took the kimono box from Mahiro's hands. Without a word, I shook it out and draped it over his shoulders. It was a deep hunter green that brought out the hazel in his eyes. I plucked up a bright-gold obi, and he leaned back into me as I wrapped it around his waist. The knot tied, I let my hands rest on his hips and my forehead drop onto his shoulder.

"I love you. I do," I said firmly.

"I know."

"I just need time."

"Then you will have it." He lifted a hand to touch my cheek and pressed a kiss to my temple. "And I will wait patiently until you are ready."

My appearance in the kitchen was met with whoops of joy. Kaoru practically fell over herself in an effort to throw her arms around me, happy tears splashing her cheeks. I squeezed her tight and kissed her hair, ignoring the way her blood slid under her skin and made my veins prickle. Haruko gave me a tight smile and bowed, which is about the most I could expect from someone as tough as her. I dropped down to the floor beside them, surrounded by happy conversation. Drawn by the commotion, even a few men poked their heads into the kitchen to give me rough slaps on the back and express their relief that my health had returned.

"I'm so sorry, Asagi-chan," Kaoru said, gripping my sleeve as if I might disappear. "We knew Kira was jealous, but we had no idea—"

"I hope wherever Mahiro-sama sent her is the worst kind of hell," Haruko growled from the corner, sending a stab of guilt through me. He didn't tell them.

"So what are we to call you now, Asagi-chan?" Kaoru asked, brightening.

"What do you mean?"

"While you were recovering, Mahiro-sama came in and told us you were no longer to be treated as a servant but 'as an extension of himself.'" Kaoru giggled at her own exaggerated impersonation.

"Oh…"

"Do you prefer 'sir' or 'madam?'" Haruko asked with a sarcastic grin. "Certainly, chan is no longer appropriate."

I gasped, and an embarrassed blush painted my cheeks. "Don't be ridiculous," I stammered. "I don't think myself above any of you."

"Think it or not, you've been elevated," she said, lips curling.

"You're his mistress now," Kaoru chimed in, her eyes sparkling.

Something twisted inside me. Two days ago, I would have been happy, ecstatic even. But I was smarter now. Nothing came without a price, and romantic fantasies were no exception.

Conversation shifted thankfully away from my relationship with Mahiro, and despite vocal concerns for my health and recovery, I helped them finish preparing breakfast and accompanied them to the communal table. Fearful of the same reaction I had to yesterday's meal, I didn't eat, but basked in their company. Someone asked about my eyes, and I brushed it off as a side effect of the trauma I endured, which they accepted without question. Last night's events faded into distant memory, and I almost felt normal.

"Does no one work around here?" All eyes lifted, and a collective sigh of relief went through the room at Mahiro's smiling face in the doorway, hands on his hips in mock annoyance. "I am glad to see everyone in such good spirits after the last few days, but I am afraid I must steal Asagi away."

"In more ways than one, it seems," Kaoru said under her breath, giving me a nudge and a wink.

I groaned and pinched her ear as I stood, bowing my thanks for everyone's well-wishes. Mahiro led me out of the kitchen and to the other side of the house, stopping at a door just down the hall from the servants' quarters.

"As requested," he said with a bittersweet smile. "Your room."

I took a deep breath and, with a lump in my throat, slid the door open. I gasped, and my eyes welled at the sight. It was a modest eight-mat room, but more than any private space I'd ever occupied, and full of bright natural light. Blooming cherry trees and bright-feathered birds adorned the painted paper walls, and fresh flowers tinged the air with their sweet scent. A deep closet on one end housed a rolled futon, and a lush stack of kimono boxes and a cherrywood tonsu littered with small bottles and jars sat at the other.

"The outside doors open directly into the garden," Mahiro said in a thick voice. "I thought you would like that."

In my excitement, I threw the doors open wide, letting in a blast of cold air that made Mahiro shiver. "It's perfect, Mahiro," I said, pulling them closed. "Thank you."

"If anything is lacking…"

"This is more than I need. You spoil me."

Mahiro laughed and shrugged one shoulder. "It is my right."

In a rush of emotion and gratitude, I crossed the room, took his face in my hands and kissed him. I loved him. It was foolish of me to think it could ever be any different.

"I have something else for you." He pulled away just enough to look into my eyes, his hands still wrapped around my arms. "I was hoping to save it for when things settled, but…"

His eyes lost focus, and my heart twisted. "But?"

He took a deep breath, and his smile returned. "I think now is a good time."

THIRTY

A Better Place

I had no idea what to expect when Mahiro walked me out to the stables and a pair of saddled horses. One was a black gelding I recognized as Mahiro's, and the other a brown filly, who pawed at the ground with a single white-socked hoof. Mahiro's horse snorted a greeting as he approached, nuzzling his velvety nose into Mahiro's outstretched hand. I hung back, eyeing the other suspiciously.

Mahiro looked over his shoulder at me and laughed. "It is a horse, not a scorpion."

"You want me to ride? On her back?"

"Well, how else would you ride a horse?"

I took a nervous step forward, jumping back again when the filly huffed and tossed her head. "I can't. I mean…I've never ridden before."

"You do not have to worry. She is a gentle soul. She will take good care of you." Mahiro swung himself up onto his horse's back with practiced grace and beckoned for me to do the same. "I will take her reins. All you have to do is hold on."

I swallowed hard and approached the filly once again. One of the stable hands placed a short stool beside her and offered his hand. I took it, wrapped the other around the saddle horn, and leveraged myself onto the filly's back. She snorted and stamped, powerful muscles flexing under the skin of her shoulders as I clung to her neck. The stable hands snickered, and I cast them a withering look.

"Ready?" Mahiro asked with an amused smile.

"No."

He laughed, and with a click of his tongue, we lurched into motion. Mahiro and his horse moved together as one, his back straight and hips balanced with the undulating creature beneath him. I did my best to imitate his posture, but the most I could achieve was a terrified hunch, each step sending a shock through my spine all the way to the base of my skull.

"How much farther?" I groaned. We'd barely made it past our own gates.

"Not far."

"Then why couldn't we walk?"

He chuckled. "Too far to walk."

"Are you ever going to tell me where we're going?"

"To see an old friend," he answered after a pause.

Something about his tone made my heart beat faster. I wanted to probe him further, but I held my tongue, focusing instead on maintaining my balance.

It felt like forever before he pulled us to a stop atop the crest of a hill that edged the bowl-shaped plane. Mountains rose over our heads on one side, and the valley fell to the riverbank on the other while the foothills rolled like ocean waves beneath our feet. Mahiro slid off his horse, shaking the cold and stiffness from his body before raising his hand to help me down. I practically fell into his arms, cursing the whole way as I struggled to uncoil the muscles in my back and thighs.

Mahiro took me by the arm and urged me away from the wretched beast and toward the edge of the road. Confusion settled over me as my gaze swung up and down the mountain path. No villages, no settlements, nothing but frost-covered landscape almost as far as the eye could see.

Almost.

Just below us, nestled in a bend in the river and surrounded on three sides by tilled fields, was a small complex of buildings. They looked like toys against the massive backdrop. A house not unlike Mahiro's, though not quite as extravagant, sat with its back against the riverbank. Outbuildings flanked it on either side, one a storehouse of some kind and the other a modest stable, complete with an adjoining fenced-in paddock.

"Your friend's house, I assume?"

The corner of Mahiro's mouth lifted a touch. "Yes."

"All right." My gaze cut between Mahiro and the house below. "Why are we up here if the house is down there?"

"Just wait."

I frowned and followed Mahiro's gaze back down to the house. Our horses whinnied in the silence, stomping their feet against the cold. The house could have been deserted for how still it was, a thin stream of smoke from a fire inside the only sign of its occupants. I was about to give up and insist we go home when Mahiro tightened his hand around my arm.

The door to the paddock swung open, and a man emerged, leading a stallion on the end of a rope. He released some slack and began working the horse in slow circles, chasing him around the paddock with the brush of a cane against his hindquarters. I squinted down at him. Just a man with a horse.

"I don't under—"

The man beckoned over his shoulder, and my heart stopped when a small body burst out of the stables and into the sun, tripping over his long legs. My chest tightened. My hands shook. It couldn't be. It couldn't.

"Tsu-chan!"

Mahiro wrapped a steadying hand around my waist as my knees gave out and lowered me to the ground. Tsukito. My boy, dancing around on his toes and clapping with glee as the horse ran laps around him. It must have been a dream, but there was no mistaking those bright eyes, his wide smile, the joyous laugh I'd swear I could hear rushing up the valley.

"As it turns out," Mahiro started, "your former master owed a friend of mine quite the gambling debt. Rather than smear his reputation, I suggested he offer a trade."

A thick, wet sound pushed its way out of my throat, and I pressed my fingers against my lips. That part of my heart I'd left with him ached like a phantom limb. Even blurred by tears, he was beautiful.

"They say he is a wonderful boy." Mahiro laid his hand on my back, his own voice thick. "Smart. Great with the horses. He has nightmares sometimes, but he seems to be okay, considering…"

Considering.

"Do you want to see him?"

Warmth burst through my chest, followed by a zing of pain through my veins. Like a reminder. *You are not who you were.*

"I always told him that monsters aren't real. What would he think of me now?"

THIRTY-ONE

Promise

EVEN THOUGH HE MUST HAVE BEEN FREEZING, MAHIRO SAT NEXT TO me on the side of the road and allowed me to watch Tsukito work horses until late into the afternoon. It was nearly dark by the time we made it home. Mahiro leaped from his horse the second we crossed the gates and bolted inside to stoke the fire. I held back, stiff in my body and numb in my heart.

I should have been grateful. I was grateful. Tsukito was out of that awful place. But the tang of bitterness remained. The monster inside me growled and complained at a constant, head-pounding pitch, and though my arms ached to hold him, I knew I never could. Not like this. In so many ways, Kira had succeeded in killing me that day, and even though my heart glowed at the sight of him, it was yet another reminder of what had been stolen from me.

I sank down onto the engawa and watched the sky turn from gray to deep blue to black. The door behind me slid open, and the sharp smell of green tea hit my nose. I looked up to find Ryuichi holding a tray with a teapot and two glasses.

"Mind if I join you?"

I shrugged and turned my gaze back to the sky. He set the tray down between us and lowered himself down to the engawa with a groan. He poured himself a glass, eyeing me over the rim as he blew away the steam.

"You expect me to wait on you, girl?" he growled, gesturing with his eyes down to the teapot.

I laughed and took up the pot to pour my own glass, my chest warming a little.

Girl.

"It wasn't a lie what I told you before," he started after a short silence, "about when I came here, but it wasn't exactly the truth either."

I lowered my glass to my lap and arched an eyebrow toward him.

"I was just a boy when I came to live here, and it was Mahiro-sama's father who took me in." He scraped at a chip in his cup with his thumbnail, a faraway look in his eyes. "Mahiro was very sick, near death I was told, and he looked it too. He couldn't get out of bed. Couldn't even breathe without coughing up blood. My job was to keep him as comfortable as possible in his last days. To keep his linens clean and his room warm."

He wiped a hand over his face and weariness crept into his expression. "I'm ashamed to admit I was scared of him. Every time I went into that room, I was afraid of what I would find. I was just a boy. I'd never seen someone die before. But then…"

"A miracle?"

He snorted and sipped his tea. "All I know is that one day, I went into his room and he wasn't dying anymore."

I blew out a long breath and dug my toe into the earth at my feet. We had never talked about who made him. In my selfishness, I'd never even thought to ask. Now, it was all I could think about. Did he love him? Did he give him his blood in an act of mercy? Did Mahiro still feel his presence in his heart like I did Mahiro's every second of every day?

"His miracle came at a price. I've seen him struggle with it every day for fifty years." He took a long drink of his tea before leveling his hard gaze on me. "I wonder if yours did too."

I jerked and nearly spat a mouthful of tea, triggering a thigh-slapping laugh. "Ryuichi-san—"

"Relax, girl. I've been keeping Mahiro-sama's secrets for half a century. I can keep yours too. Close your mouth. You look like a blowfish."

I clapped my mouth shut. He knew. Of course he knew.

"Why are you telling me this?"

He rolled his eyes. "Because you're sitting out here wondering if it's all worth it."

My throat constricted, and I had to swallow twice to get it working again. "Is it?"

"Look." Ryuichi pushed himself to his feet with a huff. "I don't pretend to understand all of"—he gestured wildly between me and the house—"this, but I do know one thing. He loves you. And unless I've gone senile in my old age, you love him. The two of you finding each other in this world is a miracle in itself. Hell, if things had gone differently, he wouldn't be here to find, and you'd still be getting raped by that monster." I flinched, and he held up his hands. "Pardon my frankness."

Tears pushed hard on the backs of my eyes, and I closed them to keep them from falling. Ryuichi stomped his feet, muttered something about the cold, and disappeared back inside. I reached deep into my heart and felt Mahiro's presence there, warm and patient and accepting. Ryuichi was right. It was a miracle. Not a perfect one, but profound nonetheless, and I would be a fool to turn my back on it.

I took a deep breath to gather myself before rising to my feet and slipping inside. Mahiro sat by the brazier, a blanket wrapped around him and his gaze on the fire. I knelt beside him, and when he looked up at me, his eyes shone. He lifted the edge of the blanket just enough to invite me in. I slid under his arm, rested my head on his chest, and melted into his warm embrace.

"Thank you for today." I slipped my arms around his waist, and some of the tension slid out of his back.

He wrapped the blanket tighter around us and held me as if he thought I might escape. We fell into a silence both thick and soft, broken only by the popping of the coals in the fire.

Mahiro's chest swelled with a breath as if he meant to speak, but the words got hung up somewhere behind his breastbone. I looked up to find him gazing down at me, his eyes pinched and those lines etched deep around his mouth. He brushed his knuckles over my cheek, cupped my chin, and lowered his head just a fraction. An invitation and a promise. When I touched my lips to his, they melted into me, opened up to me, never asking for more than I could give while offering me his whole self.

He would never take from me. Maybe that was worth everything.

THIRTY-TWO

Need

"A-SA-GI."

I glared down at a sheet of rice paper, a brush clutched in my hand so tight I thought it would break. It had been two days since the farmer. Two agonizing, tedious days. My head throbbed. My bones ached. My skin itched as if ants had burrowed their way inside me and were struggling to get out. I did everything I could to ignore it, squinting at the lines on the paper until they writhed like snakes.

"A-sa-gi." My tutor, Suzuki Toshiro, pointed to the three characters of my name in turn.

Apparently, part of my new elevated station meant I should be able to read and write, and Mahiro had brought the tutor in from a neighboring village to teach me. He spoke in soft tones with an expression like a Buddhist monk as he wrote my name across the top of the page and instructed me to copy it. His marks were neat and graceful. Mine were illegible blobs that bled through the paper. I wanted to punch him in the teeth.

"Let's just try the first character," he said, leaning close to me and tapping a thin finger on the paper. He was so close I could smell the spices from his last meal.

"I've tried the first character," I ground out. "I've written it a hundred times, and it still looks the same."

"Try relaxing your hand on the brush." He reached for my hand, and I flinched back, dripping fat ink blots on the table. He gave a soft smile before picking up his own brush and holding it up for me to see. "Too much force, and your line loses its flow. All you need is a light touch. You see?"

I did see. I saw his fingers wrapped delicately around the end of the brush. I saw the bright threads of light under his skin, weaving together into thick ropes as they joined in his wrist and disappeared into the sleeve of his kimono. My breath caught and my mouth watered.

"Asagi." Mahiro's voice shocked my attention away from my tutor. He stood in the doorway, thin brows low over his eyes. He gave me a long, searching look before addressing Suzuki. "I think that will be enough for today, thank you."

Suzuki gave a bewildered shake of his head before clearing away his supplies and leaving with a bow. Mahiro stood over me with his arms crossed, and I shrank under his look.

"I don't understand the point of this." I swiped my hand over the table, sending sheets of mangled calligraphy flying in every direction. "I've gone my whole life—"

"You are hungry."

I blinked. "No." Pain zipped through my veins as if to call me a liar. "I'm fine."

"Then why were you looking at Suzuki-san like a plate of tonkatsu?" He crossed the room to kneel beside me, his expression softening. "It has been two days, Asagi."

"I said I'm fine."

"It has been too long."

"You've gone longer."

"I am also older and more practiced." Anger flared in his eyes when he reached for me and I slapped him away. "Must you always be so stubborn?"

"You call my respect for life stubbornness?"

"You think I do not respect life?" His eyes turned white for half a second before he regained control of himself. "I know it is hard, but it is necessary."

"I can't. I won't." I shook my head and pulled farther away. "There has to be another way."

"What do you think will happen if you keep starving yourself this way?" Mahiro grabbed my shoulders and forced my eyes back onto his. "Today, it's the tutor. What if next time it's Kaoru or Haruko?" He pushed the words through his teeth, and my heart jerked at the implication. "The monster inside you will have what it needs, even if it has to destroy you to get it."

"But—"

"I will not have it, understand me?" His voice raised, and he was no longer my lover, but my master. "Not in my house."

My stomach dropped. "You want to put me out?"

"No." His anger shattered, and it cut the word in pieces. "But I will. For the safety of this house."

My skin went cold. Mahiro held a hand out to me, an ultimatum hanging in the air between us. I didn't want to hurt anyone, but the thought of leaving left a hollow feeling behind my breastbone. This was my home, everyone here my family. I'd never been on my own before, and the world suddenly felt oppressively large. Could I survive it without Mahiro? My lover, my protector. My maker.

Mahiro released a sigh as I slipped my hand into his. He pulled us both to our feet. We stood in silence for a long time, chest to chest, the magnet pull of our hearts drawing us ever closer. I dropped my head onto his shoulder.

"It will get easier, I promise," he said against my temple.

I didn't believe him.

THIRTY-THREE

Take

––––––––––

Mahiro traded his usual flamboyant colors for a plain gray kimono and haori before leading me east to a small town about two miles away. I followed in a daze, sick with dread. The monster had calmed somewhat, as if it knew what I meant to do, and the pain of need died down to a dull thrum.

The town was just populated enough to have a busy market center, and I clung to Mahiro's arm as we melted into the crowd. The air teamed with the smells of grilled fish and calls of "Irrasshai!" rang in my ears. Carts selling sweet cakes and dango on skewers lined the streets. My vision filled with smears of light. Beating hearts swam around me, brushed up against me, drew me to them like a moth. My own heart pounded, and my palms sweated.

"H-How do I…"

Mahiro's hand tightened around my arm. "Take a breath, Asagi."

I closed my eyes against the glare and took a deep, shaky breath. "How do I choose?"

"Let them choose you." I shot him a confused look. He smiled gently and brushed his fingers over my cheek. "Use the power in your eyes. Look at them. Find the one who is suffering and bring him peace."

I swallowed thickly, turning my attention back to the crowd. I blinked as I struggled to focus on a single point of light: a young man looking at elaborate combs made from wood and bone. We made eye contact, and just like with the farmer, there was a snap followed by a rush of images: the face of a girl, young and sweet and beautiful, followed by a swell of hope and affection.

No.

I yanked my gaze away, and Mahiro laid a steadying hand on my shoulder. "What do you see?"

"Everything." I pinched the bridge of my nose and tried to shake the images loose. "Their whole lives. Do you see it, too?"

He shook his head. "No. But I feel things. When I get close to them. When I touch them."

I remembered all the times he'd touched me, every accidental graze of fingers around teacups, and that unnatural calmness that followed.

I pushed it from my mind as my gaze snapped onto someone else: a mother, a soldier, a merchant. Vibrant lives filled with love and possibility. Over and over and over until my head ached and I grew dizzy.

And then I saw him, a boy on the edge of becoming a man wearing a faded kimono ragged along the edges. Dark, sunken eyes beseeched people from within a gaunt face. He slipped among the crowd, hands outstretched, begging for coins and scraps of food, only to be ignored, invisible in this world of relative plenty. In an act of desperation, he attempted to steal an apple from a pile of bruised ones to be discarded, receiving a bloodied nose for his trouble. In the end, he only managed to nick a small end of bread from a food cart before slipping into an alleyway.

I followed. Breath raspy and vision tunneling, I staggered away from Mahiro and into the alleyway after the boy. I found him sitting on a discarded crate, cradling the bit of bread in his hands with a vacant look. He startled a bit when I approached but didn't try to run or even hide his ill-gotten gains. I knelt in front of him.

"Look at me."

Our eyes met, and his life opened up to me. A mother dead from disease. A baby sister dead because he couldn't feed her. Himself starving and tired and barely alive. Ink-black despair blinded me and chilled me to my bones. I knew him. I knew his pain and his hopelessness. I felt it as if it were mine, because it was mine. I had taken it.

I leaned forward and placed my hands on his knees. His face went slack as I took his pain, folded it up like an origami bird, and stashed it away inside me. The need surged as the veins in his throat pulsed with ethereal light. I remembered the farmer. The rush of blood as his skin popped.

Get control, Asagi.

I felt Mahiro hovering nearby, but I ignored him as I fought the urge to rip into the boy's throat. Instead, I ran one hand up the inside of his arm. Light ran there, too, less forceful, less urgent. The boy shivered as I touched the tender spot inside his elbow and lifted it to my lips.

"Don't be afraid. I'll take care of you."

It feels good, even.

The skin broke under my fangs. The boy gasped but didn't pull away, his other hand grasping at my shoulder. A slow, thick stream of blood flowed over my tongue and filled me with a euphoric warmth. Every cell lit up brighter than the sun, burning away that dark need. The world fell away, and it was just him and me, our hearts pumping in rhythm together, locked in a deadly embrace.

Get control.

I groaned, the sound muffled in the crook of his arm as I fought back the fog. I focused on the bite of the gravel on my knees, the cold wind cutting through the alley. Pain ripped through me when I released my bite, the monster raging so hard I saw black. I doubled over, my head on the boy's lap and a scream building in my throat.

"Oneesan…"

I raised my head, and the boy was looking down on me with hooded eyes. He swayed in his seat, blinking twice before crumpling entirely. With a curse, I pulled him into my lap and cradled him in my arms. *No, no, not again.* His skin was pale and slightly clammy with two bright splotches of pink high on his cheekbones. His breathing was slow but steady, as was his heart. I gave him a little shake, and his eyes rolled aimlessly before settling on me.

"All right. You're going to be all right." My eyes burned, and I tucked him tighter against my chest. I'd done it. I'd stopped. Even the pain of hunger had settled into something more manageable, laced with a mellow high like being slightly drunk.

My back stiffened at the sound of Mahiro's stomping footsteps. He was pale and wild-eyed with something between rage and panic. "What have you done, Asagi?"

"I've done it. I can stop. Can't you see? I don't have to take lives——"

He cut me off me with a raised hand. "Finish this."

"No."

"You have no idea the danger you bring on yourself. On both of you." His eyes flared white, but his voice was almost pleading.

"I'm sorry, Mahiro, but I can't live the way you want me to."

He rocked back on his heels, his eyes pinched. He half turned back toward the street, his chest and shoulders heaving. My mouth went dry as I felt something irreparable between us break.

"He is your responsibility now," he said before walking away.

AFTER A BIT OF REST AND SOME DANGO PURCHASED FROM THE vendor on the street, the boy recovered enough to walk, and we made our slow, unsteady way back home. Mahiro was conspicuously absent as I escorted him through the front doors and into the back of the house. I found Ryuichi in one of the storerooms, and he stared, jaws agape, when I presented the boy.

"This is Kenta." I gestured to the boy, who gave an unsteady bow.

"Uh-huh." Ryuichi squinted at me, then Kenta, and then the wound on his arm. "And what exactly do you want me to do with Kenta?"

"Find him a bed. Some clothes. And have Kikyou-san take a look at him."

"He's staying, then?"

"Yes."

"Mahiro-sama won't like this."

"I don't care."

Ryuichi gave a wheezing laugh and shook his head. He gave Kenta a long up-and-down look and scratched at the back of his neck. Kenta never stopped looking at me, eyes wide and glassy. A sizzle of apprehension ran through me when I realized I'd seen that look before —on Kira.

"Is he here?" I asked.

"Out back." He jerked a thumb over his shoulder. "He's in quite the mood, though. I'm guessing this is why."

I gave him an apologetic bow and, leaving Kenta in his care, headed toward the back porch. I found Mahiro standing propped against a post, a bottle of saké dangling from his fingers and a cup pressed to his lips as if he had begun to drink but forgot how. The sun had dipped low, his profile cutting a sharp silhouette against the pale sky.

"You brought him home." It wasn't really a question.

"Yes."

He nodded and took a deep breath before tipping the saké back. The bottle rattled against the glass as he tried to refill it, and I plucked it from his hand.

"Is this what you do? When you leave the house for days and no one knows where you are?"

He sniffed and sipped from his glass. "In part."

"How many?"

He laughed a joyless laugh. "I stopped counting a long time ago."

"And you're okay with that?"

"What choice do I have?" he snarled, fangs flashing. "When I was lying in a bed drowning in my own blood, what choice did I have?"

I shivered and took a step back, cold to my core.

His expression crumpled, his anger melting into despair. "Did I make the wrong choice for you? Should I have let you go?"

"Mahiro…"

"You will be in pain all the time."

"I know. I can handle it."

"Can you? Or are you just burning your hands so you do not have to think about what really hurts?"

I sucked in a breath, my hands reflexively clenching around the bottle. He forced a smile, his gaze drifting back to the sky. "I never wanted this for you. I wanted to give you something better."

"You did. You have." I laid my hand on his arm, my voice thick. "I'll always be grateful to you."

"Yes, but will you forgive me?"

I opened my mouth to answer, stopping short when I realized I didn't have one..

He tipped back his saké, dropped the empty glass in my hand, and squeezed my arm before drifting past me into the house.

"Did you ever forgive him? The one who made you?"

He stopped, his shoulders dropping. "No. I did not."

THIRTY-FOUR

Return

Kenta was the first of half a dozen men and women I took into my care. Mahiro referred to them as my "collection," a term I found only slightly off-putting. I took small amounts from each of them in turn, the steady rotation providing them ample time to recover before I needed them again. I tried to learn from Mahiro's mistake. I took as little as possible and went as long as I could without in hopes it would temper their obsession. I didn't really know if it worked, and every now and then, their glassy-eyed adoration would prompt me to withdraw completely, though never for long. They gave me a way to live, and in return I provided them with whatever they needed: a home, food, love. And I did love each of them in a real, profound way.

It wasn't a perfect system, and it wasn't without casualties, but it was a start. As Mahiro had warned, it took enormous restraint and discipline. Take too little, and the monster inside me would rage and tear me down. Take too much, and the person would die with blood still left in their veins. It meant never losing control, never giving in to the dark pleasure of the blood and stopping at just the right moment.

It also meant I was never satisfied, always hungry, and always in some degree of pain. It made me irritable on good days and a downright bitch on bad ones. I often took out my frustrations on Mahiro. It wasn't his fault, I knew it wasn't, but it was always easier to blame him. When things got really bad, he would use his power as my master and my maker to force me to kill. My body might have felt better, but my heart suffered, and with every death by my fang, I felt my love for him start to crack.

Twelve years passed this way. Twelve years in which one set of demons was replaced by another until my humanity seemed like a distant dream. I hardly thought of Kira and the violence she'd wrought on me. I kept it all locked safely behind an iron door where it couldn't mar this new version of me. The slave was dead, their unimportant life faded into the mists of time.

Brokering trade deals and maintaining political relationships often took Mahiro away from home for days at a time, putting me in the uncomfortable position of head of the house. Not that it needed it. Mahiro's house was as efficient as it ever was, leaving me to wander lonely and aimless through the halls, anxiously awaiting his return. I often found myself staring out the windows for hours, hardly moving until some thoughtful soul touched my elbow and offered me a cup of tea.

On just such an occasion, with the house all closed up against the winter chill, I sat in my room with the outside door cracked open and my eyes trained to the road. He'd been gone for four days, and I yearned for his return, every part of me itching for his warm touch and his gentle smile. My heart lurched at the sight of a train of horses in the distance. They were little more than spots on the horizon, but my sharp eyes made out my master's colors, bright purple and gold, adorning his horse.

I leaped to my feet, tossing away my drab winter haori and trading it for something in pale pink and covered with flowers. I loosed my hair from its ties and brushed it out until it shone, hurriedly painting my eyes and gulping my hot tea to add a warm flush to my cheeks. I rushed back to the door, my heart in a flutter, to find the horses had reached the gate. Normally, I would have run outside to greet him, but he wasn't alone.

He was accompanied not only by the servants he took with him, but another nobleman as well. Stocky and muscularly built, the man appeared to be more soldier than a high-ranking official. A tall, lithe man with long, angular features and impossibly big eyes assisted the first man off his horse.

I stood frozen in my doorway as something behind that big iron door started to tap and scratch dangerously. The happy fluttering of my heart turned into a dreadful pounding. I couldn't take my eyes off the familiar curve of his cheek, the awkward tangle of his long limbs. He'd become a man, but there was no denying the boy I once held so tightly in my arms.

Tsukito.

I snapped my door closed and collapsed gasping to the floor. It couldn't be. I'd spent the last decade dreaming of his idyllic life training horses, tucked safely away in the bend of a river. Now, he was here, and my heart thundered with old memories. I heard his cries clearly as the last day I saw him, interrupted as the voices of Mahiro and his companion flooded the house. I pressed myself to the inner door of my room, opening it just a crack and peering down the hall.

"I must thank you again for your hospitality, Mahiro," the nobleman said in a gruff voice, addressing Mahiro as if they were equals.

"No need," he replied merrily. "I have plenty of rooms that I can assure you are much more comfortable than an inn. You will have use of my servants should you need anything."

"The one I have should be more than enough, provided you allow him access to the kitchen and the stables."

"Of course." As if on cue, Tsukito appeared, presumably just done stabling the horses, and took his place a step behind his master. He kept his eyes lowered, his head bowed, and something about the posture made my heart ache. Mahiro signaled to one of the girls waiting in the wings. "Itsuko will show you to your room. The servants' quarters—"

"He'll be staying with me," he interjected sharply, making my guts clench.

"As you wish," Mahiro responded without missing a beat. "The kitchen is down the hall. Make yourself at home."

The party separated with polite bows, and Mahiro released a sigh, the weariness of his travels settling heavily over him. I slipped from my room and padded down the hall to his, slipping inside just behind him. He turned with a start as I slid the door shut behind me, his weariness melting into a gentle warmth that made my heart flutter all over again.

"Welcome home, Mahiro-sama," I said, bowing slightly.

"Ah, Asagi." My name left his lips like a sigh of relief. "I was beginning to think you were not home."

"I'm sorry I didn't greet you," I said, taking a step toward him, "but I saw you were...accompanied."

"That's Matsumoto," he said with a groan, turning so I could help him out of his haori.

"From Kanto?" My heart squeezed, and I struggled to keep my voice even.

"No. Edo."

My mouth went dry. How did Tsukito end up in Edo?

"We met on the road. A dull, boorish brute of a man."

"Then why invite him to stay?"

"Politics, my dear," he said with a laugh, reaching over his shoulder to touch my cheek. "To serve the common good, sometimes you have to find kindness for even the most boring people."

He lowered himself to the floor, and I sat on my knees behind him, rubbing the ache of travel from his shoulders as he shed the trappings of his rank one by one until he was down to just his deep-purple kimono and black hakama. He relaxed back into me with a sigh, his hand resting lightly on my thigh.

"They're staying in the same room?" I asked, my arms wound around him but my mind still on our unexpected guests.

"Mm," he answered drowsily.

"Do you really think that's...appropriate?" No answer. "Mahiro?"

I bent carefully to look into his face and found he'd fallen asleep, his expression tranquil and his lips slightly parted. With a sigh, I gathered him up in my arms and moved him to the futon, pulling the blanket up around his shoulders before slipping in behind him. I ran my hand over the line of his back and settled my nose between his shoulder blades. Everything I needed was here. The man who saved me, gave me everything I could ever hope for, was here. I squeezed my eyes shut and tried not to think about Tsukito and that man, Matsumoto. It was out of my hands. Remnants of a life long past, locked behind an iron door.

I wasn't his mother. The slave was dead.

THIRTY-FIVE

Hospitality

THE NEXT MORNING, I WOKE EARLY, AS I USUALLY DID, AND SLIPPED quietly out of bed to take my morning tea in the kitchen. Adorned with just a thick winter robe thrown over my yukata, scratching at my wildly matted hair and yawning loudly, I padded my way down the hall, nodding to the few servants I passed as they started their morning chores. The room our new guests slept in was on my way, and I paused outside it, staring at the door as if I could see through the rice paper panels.

Did they share a futon? Did he sleep tucked up against his master's chest like a little bird? Did he still smell of stables and sunshine and wild, insatiable youth?

I didn't realize I'd reached out to touch the door until it slid open under my hand, making me yelp in surprise. In the doorway stood Matsumoto, his yukata hanging open over a darkly tanned and muscular chest. Heavy eyebrows bobbed over his eyes as he stopped short, raking them over me in a way that made me pull my robe tighter around myself.

"Pardon me, Matsumoto-sama," I said with a polite bow. "I was just…on my way to the kitchen. I'm sorry if I disturbed you."

"No, quite the contrary," he said with a suggestive grin, making my insides clench and my skin crawl.

"Would you like some tea?" I asked, venturing a glance over his shoulder into his room where Tsukito was busy rolling up their futon. One futon. "I could have some sent to you."

"No need. Just show my man here the way to the kitchen, and he'll take care of it."

Tsukito looked up from his work, and I quickly ducked out of his sight, tucking my face behind my sleeve.

"It's really no trouble…"

"I insist," he said, making a quick gesture inside the room. "Tsukito is well versed in my particular tastes."

My stomach lurched, and I turned my back as Tsukito appeared beside him. "Fine, then. This way."

I kept my head down as I continued down the hall, Tsukito following silently behind. My heart pounded in an excited panic. Would he recognize me? It had been over a decade. He had been only a child. Certainly he wouldn't remember. But what if he did? Would he be happy to see me, or would I only be a reminder of his pain? Not to mention, I should be old by his reckoning. How would I explain that I looked much as I did the last time he saw me?

I had my mind so tied up in knots by the time we reached the kitchen, I could hardly form the words to direct him, simply waving him toward the pantry before turning my back on him to feign looking out the window. He moved swiftly and efficiently through the kitchen, gathering cups and a ceramic teapot as the water boiled on the fire. I couldn't resist a look over my shoulder to watch him. He was almost as tall as me now, his limbs still long and thin but with a new sturdiness to them that made him look like a dancer. Time stood still for me, but it had changed so much in him.

"Would you like me to make you some?"

I jerked like someone waking, quickly lifting my sleeve to my face again and blinking. His voice was strong, confident. He hadn't been beaten down. That was something, at least.

"Don't be foolish, boy, your master is waiting," I said quickly, shooing him out of the room. "I can manage on my own. Now, go."

He gave me a strange look before gathering up his tray and rushing down the hall, leaving me trembling in his wake. I fell heavily against the wall, panting, my hand pressed to my mouth. Itsuko appeared at my side moments later, face pinched with concern.

"Asagi-san, are you all right?" she said, taking my arm to steady me as I started to sway. "You're white as a sheet!"

"I'm fine…I just…I think I need to sit down." I pulled myself off the wall, and she helped me stagger to the next room and lower myself to the table. She produced a fan from her sleeve and handed it to me before rushing to the kitchen to start a pot of tea. I snapped the fan open and waved it frantically, taking deep breaths in an effort to regain my composure. Itsuko returned with the pot and a glass already poured. I took a grateful sip, stopping short at the taste of something…extra.

"Itsuko." I caught her hand as she walked away, noticing a fresh bandage across her palm. I clicked my tongue, giving her a stern look as I removed it, revealing a long cut. "We have guests in the house."

"I know, I just…you looked so pale."

With a sigh and a soft smile, I pierced my thumb on one of my fangs and dragged it across the wound, healing it with my blood. After wiping it clean, I kissed her palm and sent her back to her work.

Her blood-infused tea did wonders to calm my nerves, and it wasn't long before I was on my way back to Mahiro's room with a fresh pot, the whole ordeal more or less behind me. He had just started to stir as I entered, and he gave me a sleepy smile.

"One of the million things I love about you, Asagi, is your timing," he said as I sat the tray down beside his futon and bent to give him a kiss. His lips lingered on mine a moment before pulling back with a questioning grunt. "You have blood on your breath." He sat up straighter in bed, his expression stern. "Asagi—"

"I didn't do anything," I assured him. "Itsuko said I looked pale, so she put some in my tea."

"Nice of her," he said, frowning deeply but relaxing a little. He scooted closer to me, reaching over me for his cup of tea. He took a long swallow. "Nothing in mine. No fair," he said with a teasing grin.

"I made yours."

"Oh, well, I guess this will have to do then," he said, bringing his lips to mine again and kissing me deeply. When I returned his kiss with less vigor than he expected, he pulled away again. "What is wrong? You seem tense."

"I'm sorry. It's your guest, Matsumoto-san." I scowled. "I don't like him."

"Did he say something to you?"

"No. It's the way he looks at me. Like he…"

"Like he what?"

"Like he wants to eat me." My eyes widened with surprise as Mahiro laughed, pulling me close to him again to nip at my neck.

"Well, you are quite beautiful," he breathed into my ear. "I could eat you up myself."

My stomach lurched again, and I slapped him away. I knew it was meant to be a compliment, a clever ploy to lure me into his arms, but all I felt was disgust. I pushed myself up off the floor and stomped angrily away to the kimono closet, leaving him slack-jawed and stammering. I returned with a box in my arms and glared at him over the top of it as I flipped off the lid and shook out the modest gray kimono inside.

"What?" he asked, standing and meeting my stare. "You are not talking to me now?"

I didn't respond, simply held the kimono out at arm's length and waited for him to slip into it. He huffed, turning his back and poking his arms into the sleeves as I draped it over his shoulders, pulling it roughly into place before wrapping his waist with a white obi.

He grasped my wrists as I set the knot, forcing my attention on him. "I understand how you must feel, but—"

"You can't *possibly* understand how I feel." I jerked my hands away, pulling back from him as far as the little room would allow. "You can't possibly understand the fear and the shame triggered by *that* look."

"Asagi—"

"And the boy in his room—"

"He is hardly a boy. And I have no reason to believe—"

"You're a fool if you think that makes a difference." I was seething, squeezing my words through my teeth to keep from screaming, clenching my fists so hard my long nails cut into my palms. "He has no more choice in what happens to him than the horses in your stables. And you just let it happen. You turn your face away and—"

"What would you have me do?" he asked, irritation creeping into his voice and making it hard. "Turn him out?"

"Yes!"

"I WILL NOT!"

I jumped as if I'd been struck, his words carrying a sharpness I'd never heard from him before.

Eyes white, face red with anger, he took a deep breath to steady himself before continuing. "Now, I have to leave on a short trip." I opened my mouth to protest, and he stopped me with a raised hand. "I will be back tomorrow. You *will* be hospitable, or you will *not* leave this room. Understand?"

I trembled under his look, feeling as bruised as if he'd beaten me, and part of me wished he had. Then that terrible sickness I felt would make sense. He was still my master. I might not have been bound in chains, but I had become a slave of another kind, bound by blood and time. Unbreakable and inescapable.

When I finally was able to speak, my words came out monotonous and dull, the voice of a slave. "Yes, Mahiro-sama."

THIRTY-SIX

One Night

M AHIRO SPENT THE REST OF THE MORNING PREPARING, AND BY afternoon, he was gone. As ordered, I remained in his room, stubbornly refusing to even see him off. I just sat at the window, watching his train of horses grow smaller in the distance, and tried to keep the cracked and dented love I had for him from breaking, but it had taken a terrible blow.

Not long after his horses vanished over the horizon, I heard Matsumoto's voice in the hall. By his tone, I could tell he was addressing Tsukito, issuing some rough command or another. Quick feet on the floorboards followed. I pressed my ear to the wall, all my supernatural abilities focused on what lay beyond it, until I heard the footsteps return and the door to their room slide closed. Once inside, all sounds became vague and muffled, the shuffle of feet and indistinct voices. My mind twisted them into lurid scenes of sex and torture, the voices deafening until I had to clap my hands to my ears to block them out. The memory of my last night with Tsukito overwhelmed me, his hands reaching out to me as Yutaka dragged me away.

I pushed away from the wall and paced a mad circuit of the room, stopping every fourth or fifth pass to crack the door open and peek outside. Hospitable. I could be hospitable. How hard could it be? I looked down at myself, still in the yukata I'd slept in, and groaned before diving into the kimono closet. Men's on the left, women's on the right.

Pulling out a box from the right-hand side, I called for one of the servants to help me dress. Before long, I was clothed in bright-red silk, my waist wrapped with a white obi tied in an intricate knot at my back. I painted my eyes and lips, brushing out my hair and parting it low on one side so that it swept over my face, keeping me safely hidden. I topped it off with a delicate kanzashi, from which hung little silver bars that tinkled when I walked. Once fully adorned, I felt powerful, important, armored.

I slipped a white cloth fan into my obi and threw open the door. Hesitating only briefly at the threshold, I marched out into the hall toward our guests' room. Once in front of it, I closed my eyes and took a deep breath, praying for my voice to stay steady as I announced myself.

"Matsumoto-sama?" I called, tapping lightly on the door. For a tense moment, I heard only silence. Had he gone without me noticing? I was about to call his name again when the door abruptly slid open, jarring my already frazzled nerves.

"Well, well. We meet again," he said as he leaned on the doorframe, completely blocking my view of the room behind him and looking me over with a lecherous grin. I instinctively reached for my fan, unfurling it and hiding my face behind a wall of white.

"I'm sorry to disturb you, Matsumoto-sama," I said in a polite, but stern, voice. "I've come to speak to you about your attendant."

"Oh?" His eyebrows bounced up, and he glanced back over his shoulder. He leaned forward, almost touching my fan with his nose. "Did he do something to offend you? He can get a bit feisty."

I wrinkled my nose and turned my face away in disgust, suppressing a violent shiver. "Matsu—" I took a step back, and he took a step forward.

"Maybe you would like to join me for tea." Another step back matched with a step forward until my back was practically to the wall.

"Matsu—" I tried to interject, but my heart pounded so hard I could scarcely speak.

"Mahiro did say to make myself at home." A hand came up, reaching for the ends of my hair. "I'm sure he wouldn't mind—"

"Matsumoto-sama."

In an action so quick it took us both by surprise, I folded my fan and struck him hard across the back of his outstretched hand. Shocked into silence, he took a step back. Just one step, but it was all I needed.

I straightened my back, lifted my head, and looked him squarely in the eye. "You mistake, Matsumoto-sama. I am no slave." I let my voice fall low, almost growling around the otherwise polite words. "I am Mahiro's companion and head of his house while he is away. I must ask that you address me accordingly."

I took a step forward, and this time he was the one to retreat. Another victory, and it struck me like a lightning bolt. I felt at a crossroads. Part of me wanted to squash him, to pin him with my powerful eyes and mix his mind into jam. But the other part thought of Mahiro and his parting words to me: *be hospitable.* I thought of every time I'd ever heard him addressing his high-powered peers, weaving his words in such a way that they had no choice but to obey. I recalled watching them leave with the vague feeling of being cheated, but not able to articulate why.

"About your attendant," I started carefully after a deep breath, "I understand your desire to have him with you in your room, and Mahiro is more than happy to accommodate, but I'm afraid such an arrangement is simply not appropriate." I paused, tasting my words. "We must consider how it would appear if others thought us unable to properly house our guests. To force a man of your station to share a room with his servants…" I let the statement hang in the air, watched it twist his features into a displeased scowl. "Mahiro, of course, thinks only of the pleasure of his friends, so he sometimes forgets such things."

Matsumoto narrowed his eyes and shifted uncomfortably. He crossed his arms tightly over his broad chest, clicked his tongue, and tapped his foot. I caught sight of Tsukito standing wide-eyed behind him and quickly tucked my face back behind my fan as he deliberated within himself. He could agree and lose the company of his servant for the night, or refuse and risk sullying his ally's good name. I felt the corners of my mouth tugging upward with yet another triumph.

"I am happy to show him to a room at the back of the house with the others," I said sweetly. "If he would just follow me…"

Caught like a rat in a trap, I watched with sick glee as he squirmed, his tapping foot turning into a stomp. Finally, with an annoyed grunt, he gestured into the room. Tsukito appeared at his master's side, a confused furrow in his brow as he nudged him out into the hallway. Face tucked carefully behind my fan, I bowed my thanks. Matsumoto huffed and closed the door between us with a loud *snak.*

Matsumoto forgotten for the moment, I couldn't help but smile behind my fan as Tsukito stood frozen and blinking in the hallway, his gaze darting between me and the closed door. I simply turned and started walking, and he, like the obedient servant he was, hesitated only a moment before following. My heart skipped and fluttered as I led him to the far corner of the house where the other servants' rooms lay. I pulled back a door, gesturing vaguely toward it. It was not unlike the room given to me by our previous master. A small twinge of guilt moved through me.

"It's not much, but…it's private," I stammered, my gaze fixed to the back of my fan as the confidence of my victory leaked away.

"Thank you, but this isn't necessary—"

"You deserve better." The words came out sharper than I intended, and I cleared my throat to shake loose the barbs.

When I raised my gaze, Tsukito stood a few steps away, his eyes narrowed and his brow pinched. His mouth opened slightly, and he took a breath as if a question perched on his tongue.

"I've gone against Mahiro's wishes in doing this," I said quickly, ducking my head and pushing past him in the direction from which we came, "so it may only be for one night."

"I'll relish it, then. Thank you, Goshu—Oku-sama."

Are you a boy or a girl?

I didn't stop. On the contrary, I all but bolted, my pace picking up steadily until I stumbled back into Mahiro's room, slamming the door shut and collapsing behind it. Heart pounding, mouth dry and shaking all over, I became overcome by a sort of mad giddiness, erupting from my throat in a stream of elated giggles. With each gasping breath, they grew in intensity until I was practically roaring.

I'd done it. I'd spoken, and somebody listened. Not only listened, but obeyed. I'd been with Mahiro twelve years, and for the first time, I didn't feel invisible. Even if it was only one night, I'd given it to him. One night away from that awful man. One night of peace.

And one night could change everything.

THIRTY-SEVEN

Where have you been?

EVEN AFTER THE INITIAL EUPHORIA OF MY ACCOMPLISHMENT HAD passed, I felt charged. I ran down the road to the local market, using the allowance Mahiro had left me to buy a whole bushel full of candies and sweet treats to share with the house. When I got home, I gathered all the servants in the dining room and dumped my haul onto the table, earning squeals of delight. Eager hands picked out their favorite things, and though I didn't eat, I bathed in their happiness and sticky smiles until I thought I might float away.

I held back a little for Tsukito, of course, and I felt a pinch of nostalgia as I arranged a pile outside his door. All the things he used to love as a child: sakuramochi, youkan, and several rice paper–wrapped habutai mochi. Once done, I drifted back to Mahiro's room in a rose-colored haze, exhausted but extremely happy. I couldn't remember the last time I slept so soundly.

At first, I wasn't sure what woke me. It was dark as tar and silent, the house still drenched in the thick of night. I rolled onto my back and blinked at the ceiling, trying to figure out the sudden tension in the air, the beams slowly taking shape as my eyes adjusted to the dim light.

Light. Someone else was in the room.

I jerked up onto my elbows, squinting toward the door and the faint light of a small oil lamp shielded behind a long-fingered hand. "Who's there?" I said in as deep and strong a voice as I could manage. The hand dropped, filling the end of the room with pale-yellow light.

"Tsu—" I nearly choked as his name lodged itself in my throat. I swallowed hard and tried to pull myself up a little straighter. "Are you— did you need…"

My heart pounded and my palms sweat as he took a step forward, giving me the same curious look he had in the hall. When his toes touched the foot of my futon, he sank to his knees, setting down his lamp and leaning forward until he was hovering over me.

"What are you doing, boy?" I sputtered as he went down on all fours and crawled up the bed over me, his legs straddling mine and an arm on either side of my waist. My feet scrabbled at the futon under me as I tried to back away. He pushed his face close to mine, and I felt a shot of panic. Did he misunderstand? Did he think I'd removed him from his master's bed only to bring him into mine?

I reached up to grab him by the shoulders when his forward motion stopped. Time froze. My mouth went dry. I couldn't breathe. With his nose less than a centimeter from mine, there was nowhere to hide. He lifted a hand slowly to my face, his eyes trembling as he pushed my hair aside.

"Asagi?"

The iron door inside me bulged and flexed under the weight of those trapped emotions. My held breath came out a whimper, and I squeezed my eyes shut against the tears rising up behind them. When I opened them again, his face was pinched, his big eyes flooded and trembling.

"Don't you remember me?"

I couldn't hold it back anymore. That door inside me burst open and all the pain, fear, and desperate love I felt rocketed through my every fiber and made a quivering, weeping mass of me. I threw my arms around Tsukito and pulled him against my chest. "Of course I remember you," I said as I peppered the top of his head with frantic kisses. "Of course I do. For as long as I live, I'll never forget you."

"I thought I'd dreamed you," he said, his voice shaking and broken by hiccuping sobs. "How is this possible?"

"I told you I was magic."

He gave a little tearful laugh before settling deeper into my chest. "Where have you been?"

"I've been here."

"I needed you, you know," he said, a tinge of resentment in his voice.

"I know. I'm sorry."

"But you're a master now. You could've——"

"I'm no longer a slave, but that doesn't make me free."

He raised his head, his eyes briefly touching mine, before dropping his nose into the crook of my neck with a soft sigh. My arms wrapped tight around him, our legs tangled together, it was as if time had wound itself backward. His hands might have been bigger, but they still balled themselves up tight in my collar, his back broader, but still made the same curve under my fingers. Even his heart fluttering against mine felt the same. I didn't realize how much I hurt without him until he was here.

"Aren't you going to tell me to go back to my own bed?" he asked softly.

"No."

He smiled against my neck, and I ran my fingers through his hair as he drifted off to sleep. My own eyes grew heavy, but I forced them to stay open. If we had only one night, I didn't want to miss a second of it, didn't want to miss a single breath against my skin, and I secretly wished I *was* magic so I could push the sun farther away and make this night last forever. But magic didn't exist, only monsters, and part of me feared his reaction when he figured out which one I really was.

THIRTY-EIGHT

Common Good

I MUST HAVE FALLEN ASLEEP. THE SNAP OF A SLIDING DOOR STARTLED me awake, and I jerked upright, pulling Tsukito instinctively behind me as I blinked in the bright morning light. We had long overslept our night together, which could mean only one thing. We'd been caught. With my heart thumping a dreadful rhythm in my chest, I squinted against the sun as I struggled to make out the face of our discoverer.

Mahiro.

It was as if every drop of blood in me drained into my feet. He stood just inside the door, his hand still resting on the frame and his travel bag dangling from his fingers. He stared at us in shocked silence, his only movement the quick flick of his eyes from me to Tsukito and back again. Tsukito clung to my arm, both of us afraid to move or speak out of fear of what would come next.

"Mahiro…"

"You should return to your master," he said in a hoarse voice, his gaze dropping to the floor.

As if the spell had been broken, Tsukito scrambled to his feet and, bowing with every step, made an uncertain exit. My mouth went dry, and I struggled to swallow the hard lump in my throat as Mahiro slid the door gently shut behind him. Gently. It would have been less terrifying had he slammed it.

"I'm disappointed in you, Asagi."

"Mahiro, we did nothing inapprop—"

He silenced me with a hard look, his usually gentle mouth twisted into a jagged line. He let his bag drop heavily from his hand as he silently crossed the room to his tonsu, and something spilled out of it and burst open. A little white box holding a silver kanzashi tumbled to the floor, its delicate glass flowers shattered by the impact.

Still in the futon, I curled my fingers nervously in the sheets as he sat with his back to me. Drawers slammed as he stripped out of the garments of travel and angrily shook the dust from his hair. I reached out to touch his shoulders, and he stiffened, making me draw my hand back.

"This is a dangerous game you are playing," he growled, his back still to me.

"Mahiro—"

"You disobeyed me."

"I didn't. I simply suggested—"

"It is not your *place* to suggest!" he said, turning on me with an angry glare. I shrank back into the futon, feeling suddenly very small. "What do you think would have happened if Matsumoto had found you?"

"It's not what you think," I said desperately. "I just wanted to protect him."

"By bringing him into your own bed?" His eyes burned white, and his brow knotted with dangerous jealousy. "Was this your intention all along? To betray me? After everything I have given you!"

"What you've given me?" I repeated, my own temper flaring. "What you've *done* to me." He flinched noticeably, but I kept on. "You're no different than Matsumoto. I'm just your possession, bought and paid for."

"Asagi, you know you stopped being a slave the day I fell in love with you," he insisted.

"Then why do you still treat me like one?" I was up on my knees now, blankets thrown off, my face flushed with anger and resentment. "I

asked you for one thing. All you had to do was put them in separate
rooms, but you put his comfort over mine."

"I told you, sometimes for the common good——"

"Fuzakeru na!" I jumped to my feet, using my full height to tower
over him. "You know what *common good* means? It means men like *that*
get to keep their power. It means people like you quiet their voices and
look the other way so no one has to feel uncomfortable. Well, I've seen
the effect of your *common good*. I've seen it spill blood and break bones.
I've seen it torture and rape. Your *common good* doesn't apply to people
like me."

My words broke as I choked on the sadness and guilt that welled up
violently in me. It poured down my face and made my whole body
shake. Mahiro rushed forward as my knees buckled, catching me just
before I hit the floor. I fell sobbing into his chest, and he wrapped me in
his arms.

"You…you told me…he would be safe." Hyperventilating and dizzy,
I tossed the words out clumsily between jagged breaths.

"Asagi, what are you——" His eyes widened as understanding
dawned.

"I just…I just wanted to protect him. He was just a boy, Mahiro. Just
a little boy."

Mahiro held me, rocked me, wiped my tears as everything I'd held
back the last twelve years burst out of me. And even though I clung to
him, his arms offered no comfort.

"Send him away," I sobbed. "Send Matsumoto away and keep him
here."

"You know I cannot do that."

"Why not?"

"He does not belong to me."

I shoved him away, rage and desperation setting fire to my veins.
"He belongs to me." I pounded a fist against my chest. "I am his
mother."

He sighed and cocked his head, his body saying what he didn't. *You
are not his mother.* In that moment, I felt for him something I never
thought possible.

Hate.

"What are you afraid of, Mahiro?" My words dripped with venom. "That I'll love him more than you?"

His shoulders dropped, and he took a staggering step backward as if he'd been struck. White flashed in his eyes again, but it didn't hold. He turned slowly, and I almost regretted it as he slipped out of the room without a word. A few minutes later, the house filled with the distinct shuffle of packing. Our guests were moving out.

I emerged as the sun dipped low in the sky, eyes red and puffy, a thick robe tossed carelessly over my shoulders. I stepped out onto the porch just in time to see Matsumoto's horses leaving the gate with Mahiro's silhouette bowing behind them. He paused next to me as he returned to the house. Finding nothing to say, he simply touched my arm and moved on. I stood on that porch until long after the sun went down, peering into the darkness as if I could catch one last glimpse of him on the horizon. But not even magic eyes could see so far.

THIRTY-NINE

Boo

A WEEK PASSED WHERE I DIDN'T SPEND A SINGLE NIGHT IN MAHIRO'S room. Somehow, even sleeping next to him felt like a lie. I still took him his meal in the mornings, helped him dress, all the domestic duties to which I'd become accustomed, but there was a coldness to them. The things I used to do out of love I now did out of obligation. My mind was always, always elsewhere, and I watched the sadness in his eyes grow with a detached sort of guilt.

I'd taken to dressing extravagantly, spending my entire allowance on kimono, fancy hair ornaments, and brightly colored cosmetics, and I never left the house without them. If I were invisible before, now I was a star, drawing the eyes of everyone I passed. I'd also, much to Mahiro's annoyance, taken up smoking due to my love of fragrant tobaccos. A long-stemmed pipe soon joined the fan tucked neatly inside my obi and to find me, one only needed to follow the smell of cloves.

Despite my large stature and deep voice, I made a rather convincing woman. As my confidence grew, I found myself flirting with all manner of men with breathy words and high-pitched giggles. I filled the gulf between me and my maker with their shallow affections. The desire in their looks was wholly different than the lechery in Matsumoto's eyes or the eyes of my past masters, and I bathed in their attention. My wit grew razor-sharp, and like Mahiro, I found I had a gift for negotiation. Only instead of rice, I traded information. I held their hearts on a string, and it made me feel powerful. I whispered flattery into the ears of braggarts, seducing them to spill their most close-kept secrets which I exchanged for what I really wanted.

The location of Matsumoto and his young servant.

Their talk led me to the post town of Fuchu, just a short walk away on Koushū Kaidou. I spent two consecutive days lounging in the teahouse in my usual cloud of smoke, throwing coy smiles at a young man at a neighboring table, before a pair of familiar long legs caught my attention as they passed at a quick pace on the street outside. I jumped out of my seat so fast, I spilled my tea and nearly tripped over my long obi in my scramble for the door. I stopped just inside, my breath caught in my throat, eyes darting up the road. Tsukito. He was here.

"Asagi-chan, are you all right?" The voice of the woman who ran the teahouse chimed from behind me.

"Yes, I'm fine. I'm sorry about the mess," I said quickly, dumping a handful of coins into her palm and bolting out the door. My sharp eyes darted through the crowd ahead of me as I swallowed a lump of panic. He was here. He was here, and I'd lost him. In a frantic dash about the village, I searched every face, every storefront, until finally I found him, bartering with the fishmonger.

My heart stopped at the sight of him. A feminine, long-sleeved kimono hugged his slender frame, deep burgundy with a pale-pink obi tied in a delicate knot on his back. A conservative ponytail held back his long hair, tied with a leather strap adorned with glass beads that caught the sun, his big eyes accentuated with wide splashes of color. We weren't family by blood, yet I saw myself in him, and my chest swelled with pride. He was so beautiful.

Shaking myself out of my daze, I quickly traded my pipe for my fan and tucked my face behind it. If Tsukito was here, then his master must be close by. A run-in with Matsumoto was the last thing I wanted, so I watched from a distance, following as he left the fishmonger for the grocer, filling a small bag with vegetables before heading farther down the road in the direction of the inn.

It wasn't until he disappeared inside that I realized Matsumoto wasn't with him. Not only that, the whole thing seemed routine. He knew exactly where to go. He spoke and laughed easily with the proprietors. Then I remembered how Matsumoto insisted only Tsukito make his tea. Did he do this every day? Buying the groceries for that day's meals to please his master's particular tastes?

So the next day, I waited, tucked safely in an alleyway outside the inn with a clear view of the street. My heart leapt when I saw him pass. I watched him as he made his regular stops, the fishmonger, the grocer, even a pharmacist, and my heart warmed as he looked longingly over a cart full of sweets only to pass it by. For three whole days I did this, all the while imagining a different life for him in which he returned not to an abusive master, but to someone who loved him. Maybe even a family. Maybe even…

I shook the thought from my head. What was I even doing here? The constant, nagging pain in my veins was a reminder I had no place in his life anymore. I'd stained my tongue with lies to find him, and now I couldn't even call his name. On the fourth day, I'd resolved to speak to him, even if for just a moment, even if only to say good-bye. I arrived before the sun was fully risen and tucked myself into an alley outside the inn, smoking away my nerves and waiting. But he didn't show.

I stood in that alley for what felt like hours, staring at the door and envisioning all sorts of reasons why he wasn't coming out. Had they left? Had his master discovered I was following him and forbade him to leave? Had he taken sick? Been injured? Or had he—

"BOO!"

"Chikushou!" I screamed as a pair of hands came down hard on my shoulders. I jumped a full meter into the air and spun around to find Tsukito doubled over laughing, his eyes shining mischievously.

"Gotcha!"

"Kuso gaki! You just took ten years off my life, you know that!" I said, swatting him over the head with my fan.

"Seems you have some to spare," he said, still giggling as he dodged my blows.

"You're a terrible boy!"

"You've been following me."

"You knew?" I asked, fan frozen in mid swing.

"You're kind of hard to miss," he answered with a flick to one of my dangling kanzashi, making me blush. "You could have just...you know...said hi."

"I just...I didn't..."

"It's safe. He doesn't follow me."

"He doesn't?"

"Perks of being the master's favorite," he said almost proudly. "He trusts me with these small things." His expression darkened a little before springing back as he hooked his arm in mine and pulled me from the alley. "Come on. Come with me."

I followed him in a daze, my heart slowly returning to its normal rhythm. My presence caused a bit of a stir among the merchants, so used to seeing him alone, and he gave each a different story. To one, I was his master. To another, his mistress. To another, his mother and my chest tightened in a not unpleasant way.

"Still quite the fibber, I see," I said, giving him a playful jab in the ribs. "Good to see some things haven't changed."

"Hey, I have to get my fun where I can get it," he said with a shrug.

We walked along in silence for a while, our arms interlocked and our shoulders bumping against each other. My heart grew wings in that moment, flapping and fluttering in my chest as if it would escape. All the years melted away, distilled down to just the happiest of memories. I could have died just then and counted myself lucky.

"You never asked, you know," he said suddenly.

"About what?"

"About Matsumoto. Or what happened all those years ago...after..."

After. I swallowed hard against the lump in my throat. "Neither did you."

"I know what happened," he said with a cheeky grin. "You got sold off to Mahiro and started living the good life."

"Right," I said with a bitter laugh.

"He loves you, I can tell," he said, his eyes getting a faraway look. "It can be…nice when they actually love you."

Love makes everything hurt less. "Yeah…"

"Do you love him?"

I wanted to answer, *Yes. He saved my life. Gave me everything. Of course I love him,* but the words stuck in my throat. I suddenly felt every inch of that great chasm that had opened between us as if they were marked with razor blades. Tsukito watched me closely, his eyes shimmering slightly before returning to the road.

"It's not so bad. With Matsumoto, I mean," he said. "He gives me a lot of freedoms I never had before. Takes me places with him. And he hardly ever hits me."

My breath stuck, and my lips twitched around the question I couldn't bear to ask. Tsukito laid his hand on my arm and gave me a gentle squeeze.

"I know what you're worried about," he said in a rough voice. "It's not like that. It hasn't been like that since…" His eyes went far away, and he took a deep breath before continuing. "I went someplace good after you left. I'm okay, really."

Someplace good. Tears leaped to my eyes as I pictured him in that paddock in the valley chasing horses and smiling. I released a long breath, and a little of my anger with Mahiro went with it. He'd done what he promised after all.

"I know you're trying to protect me. And what you did for me at Mahiro's house…giving me my own room…that was…" He trailed off, his voice going thick. "But you don't have to do that. In case you haven't noticed, I'm not a boy anymore."

"I had noticed, actually," I said after a pause, my heart lodged firmly beneath my larynx. We pulled to a stop just outside the inn, and he slipped his arm out of mine. In a moment of panic, I grabbed hold of his kimono sleeve, desperate not to let him slip away. "You could run. Get away and start over."

He just smiled, a soft, sad smile that spoke to a darker understanding, and I ached for the innocence that once was. Taking my hand in his, he stepped up and just touched his lips to mine. A sweet, chaste kiss, but it warmed me to my core and left me weak in the knees. He was halfway to the door before I righted myself. He threw a cheerful wave and a wink over his shoulder.

"See you tomorrow, Asagi."

"Yeah," I said, struggling to catch my breath. "See you tomorrow."

FORTY

Home

I RETURNED HOME TO FIND A HORSE TIED JUST INSIDE THE FRONT gate, the stable boys loading and securing the last of the luggage for what looked like an extended trip. The glow of my little walk with Tsukito quickly turned dark as I realized what was going on. Mahiro was going away. Confusion turned to hurt and anger as the stable boys shriveled under my red-eyed glare, the horse twitching and snorting from the sudden tension.

The snap of a sliding door and Mahiro appeared, bag in hand and tugging a long haori over his bright-purple kimono. He stopped short when he saw me, his gaze lowering for a moment before hardening into a scowl as he continued a stomping path toward his horse.

"You're leaving," I said sharply, more of an observation than a question.

"Yes."

"How long?"

"A week."

"A week?" The words came out an exhale, expelled by the force of a blow. "And you weren't going to tell me?"

"I hardly thought you would notice," he said coldly, focused on his hands as he tied his bag to his horse.

"So you were just going to disappear?" I asked, unable to hide the hurt in my voice. "Just leave me to wonder where you'd gone or when you'd return?" The servants retreated a discreet distance, but I still felt them watching. "Why would you intentionally hurt me this way?"

"You disrespected me," he growled.

"What? How—"

"You think I do not hear about all those men you flirt with in teahouses?" He swiveled white eyes onto me.

"Green is a terrible color on you, Mahiro," I said, curling my lips in disgust. "You are awfully old to be acting like such a child."

"And what of your walks with a servant of house Matsumoto?"

My jaw dropped, and my skin went cold. Mahiro took a single step closer to me, his voice dropping low.

"Let him go."

"I can't. He's my son—"

"He is *not* your son. For your safety and his, you will obey me."

Resentment burned hot through my veins. "*Slaves* obey their masters."

Snarling, Mahiro mounted his horse, and it reared under him, making me stumble back. "Be careful, Asagi," he said, his expression twisted with sadness and frustration. "That is the thing about freedom. Your choices have consequences."

But I had already turned my back and, biting back bitter tears, stomped toward the house. I slammed the door shut and leaned on it, covering my face with my hand as I hyperventilated and shook. I cursed out loud, not at Mahiro, but at myself. His jealousy was understandable, and though he handled it badly, he was entitled to his hurt. It was my own fear that angered me.

I took a deep breath and held it, forcing my heart to slow down. I let my hand slip from my face. For the first time, I noticed one of my collected servant girls, Kiyomi, sitting on her knees a few paces away, a bucket nearby and a rag in her hands. Her gaze jerked away from me and back down to her work. Her cheeks went slightly pink as she struggled to hide the concern on her face.

I pulled myself straight off the wall, running my hands through my hair and smoothing my kimono. In three steps, I crossed the room to stand over Kiyomi. She ducked her head lower, scrubbing at the floor a little more furiously.

"Kiyomi-chan," I said softly.

Her scrubbing stopped, and she hesitantly looked up, her eyes trembling slightly as they met mine.

"I need you."

"Y-Yes, Asagi-sama," she stammered, quickly gathering up her things.

I didn't wait. I walked on past her to my room and closed myself inside. I plucked the hair ornaments from my long tresses and laid them out neatly across the tonsu. I felt my heart go still as the door slid open, and she entered with a polite bow, filling the room with the slightly accelerated beating of her heart.

"Are you and Mahiro-sama fighting?" she asked timidly.

"It's nothing for you to worry about," I answered, drawing close to her.

"Forgive me for speaking out of place—"

"You can always speak your mind with me," I assured her, brushing a loose strand of hair away from her eyes.

"Please don't be too angry with him," she said in a rush, her voice thick with emotion. "He loves you so much. He just misses you, is all."

I paused a moment, my hand resting on her cheek. Her words should have affected me, but already, part of me was drawing back into that deep, untouchable place in my heart. "I know." I pressed my lips to her forehead and let them linger there. She sighed and leaned into my touch. "I'm sorry for this." Confusion flashed across her face just as my gaze locked onto hers, that cord between our minds snapping taught.

"Fight me."

As if I'd morphed into something wicked before her, her eyes shot open wide and her mouth opened, a scream building in her throat. She jerked away from me so hard she fell backward, and I allowed her to scramble as far as the door before I snatched her up by the collar. I threw her back against the opposite wall, pinning her against it with my own body. She was petite and fair, but a life of hard work had made her strong. She punched and clawed and kicked with all her might. Panicked tears quivered on her lashes, falling in thick rivulets down her cheeks as I caught her wrists and pinned them over her head with one hand.

Her long hair fell loose from its binding, and I curled my fingers in it, marveling at its softness before yanking her head back and exposing her throat. Everything else faded away as I watched her vein jump and pulse blue under the skin. She emitted a pained cry as I ran my tongue over it. I threw my hips against hers, and she aimed a desperate kick at my groin.

She was a fighter, and my blood burned with her intense will to live. I breathed it in like a drug, loosening my grip just enough to allow one final thrash before sinking my teeth into her. She tensed and spasmed with my first hard pull, tightening her fingers painfully in my hair. Her entire body curled in on itself in an effort to hold on to the life I drained from her, and it hit the back of my throat like opium, sharp and bitter with a head rush that left me reeling. With something between a whimper and a growl, I eased the pressure, and her body unfurled, going almost limp.

A few quick, ragged breaths and she started fighting again, only a bit weaker. Sobbing, she tore at my hair and twisted in my arms. She couldn't move me. I held her life between my teeth, and it made some dark part of me bellow and rage with power. Another long, dangerous pull and I was swooning with it. I wanted to devour her, conquer her, make her life my own, and it was only through sheer force of will that I didn't.

I released my bite and threw my head back with a deep groan. The demon inside me writhed just beneath the surface, and it clawed at my skin as I fought it back down. I held Kiyomi tight against my chest. Breathing rapid and hardly able to stand, she whimpered and pushed against me with weak fists in an effort to break away. I pulled her into me, sinking to the ground with her as she begged for release.

"Look at me," I said, gently cupping her face in my hand and lifting her eyes to mine. The rush of the fight quickly left me as our minds touched again, her fear cutting its way down to my chest, making my throat burn. "It's okay. We're done. It's over."

She trembled as the fear leached away, replaced by that terrible, irrational love. The inevitable byproduct of my bite. Her cries changed from panic to relief as she clutched at my collar and buried her face in my neck, as if the monster of a few moments ago were some other thing and I had come to her rescue.

Guilt slid through me as I wrapped her up tight in my arms and moved her to my futon, tempering my euphoria. I'd let the monster inside me win, even if just for a moment, and it turned my stomach. I bit my tongue to put a bit of my own blood on my lips and kissed her wounds closed. Showering her with gentle words and touches as if it could make up for the wrong I'd done, I stayed by her side until her eyes closed and she fell into a deep, dreamless sleep.

Moments later, I sat alone on the porch, my eyes trained to the front gate but looking well beyond it. My pipe hung limply between my fingers, the fragrant smoke curling around the bowl as I slouched against a beam. Mahiro had left me here alone many times before, but the house behind me had never felt so empty.

Warm and heavy with fresh blood, I touched my fingers to my lips and let my mind drift. Despite all that had happened, they still tingled with the memory of my boy's small kiss. I loved Mahiro despite everything, but he'd made me a monster. I wanted to be better. Tsukito made me better.

I found myself back in my room packing a bag. I didn't know what I was doing or when I would return. All I knew was I couldn't be a slave to the monster anymore, and a little inn in Fuchu I'd never been to suddenly felt more like home.

FORTY-ONE

Convenient

ITSUKO'S WORRIED EYES FOLLOWED ME ALL THE WAY TO THE GATE AS I left, my little bag in hand. I put the care of the house in her hands, assuring her I would be back before Mahiro returned. I felt sorry for the awkward position I was putting her in, but I knew I couldn't be here.

The farther I got from the house, the more the angry pounding of my heart turned into an excited flutter. All the little muscles pulling my face into a long and severe scowl relaxed, each step becoming lighter than the last as I shuffled down the road, my beaded zori kicking up dust. I couldn't skulk around in alleyways any longer, and I'd decided to hide in plain sight by taking residence in the same inn as Tsukito, which made a confrontation with Matsumoto inevitable. My mind tumbled over what I would do, what I would say to win time with Tsukito. Matsumoto was obviously attracted to me. Perhaps I could use it as I did with the men in the teahouse.

By the time I reached the inn, I was so flustered and out of breath, I could barely speak my name to the attendant. She arched an eyebrow at the name Arakawa and gave me a hard up-and-down look but didn't ask any questions before making a note in her ledger.

"Well, look who's here."

I looked up with a start as Matsumoto appeared from the hallway, Tsukito following close behind.

"You and your *companion* get in a fight?"

"Mahiro is away." Flustered by his sudden appearance, I hid my face behind my sleeve. Tsukito stood a step behind him, wide eyes darting between me and his master. "I've never felt comfortable in that big house all alone. I find staying in the inn…convenient."

I flicked my gaze back to Matsumoto, glancing diminutively from beneath my lashes. His lips curled as a low, rumbling laugh vibrated through his chest. I suppressed the urge to pull away as he stepped up closer to me, his fingers just touching my elbow.

"The room next to mine is vacant," he purred, his words directed at the attendant, but his eyes never leaving mine. "I am sure my friend would be comfortable there."

I lowered my head in a shallow bow as he pulled away and continued his path out the front door. Tsukito stared at me over his shoulder as he followed his master out. Once they were out of sight, I released my held breath in a burst of laughter. All the flirty little tricks I'd learned in the teahouse paid off, and instead of hiding and sneaking around, Matsumoto had given me the perfect excuse to hover around his door.

A pile of linens in her arms, the attendant quietly led me down a long hall lined with rooms. The inn itself was relatively small, made up of a block of six spacious and elegant rooms facing a wide, beautiful garden, green despite the chill of winter. Matsumoto's room was on the corner, she informed me, sliding open the doors to the room next door and stepping aside with a bow.

Once alone, I stood staring at the dividing wall between our rooms much as I had in Mahiro's house, only this time I didn't feel powerless. I pictured Matsumoto's shadow moving on the other side and glared at it in challenge. I felt the scales move. They maybe weren't tipped entirely in my favor, but my footing felt more stable as the ground beneath me evened out.

Once I'd settled in, I found my way to the kitchen to take my evening tea. As I'd hoped, Tsukito wasn't far behind, his eyes so trained on his own work that he didn't notice me sitting quietly at the servants' table, watching him over the edge of my glass. He looked tense and tired, but nevertheless nimble as he pinched the tea leaves delicately between his fingers and packed them gently into the filter. In a moment that was both heartbreaking and beautiful, he simply closed his eyes and sighed, taking advantage of this rare moment of peace.

"Boo."

He yelped and jumped, spinning in the air like a cat, tea leaves flying. "Asagi!" he cried once his startled eyes finally found me doubled over the table in laughter.

"Gotcha."

"What are you doing here?" he asked, breathless.

"Having tea."

"You know what I mean." He stomped toward me and dropped into a cross little knot on the other side of the table.

"It's as I said," I answered. "Mahiro is away, and I don't want to be in that house alone. If staying here means I take my morning walk at the same time you do your shopping, or take my tea at the same time you're making his, well, that's…"

"Convenient," he finished. I shot him a sly grin over the edge of my cup. "You're unbelievable." He studied me carefully as I took a long, triumphant sip of my tea. "Aren't you worried?"

"About what?"

"That he'll tell Mahiro."

"No," I scoffed. "Men like him only share information when they have something to gain from it. Thanks to our little chat in the lobby, he thinks I'm here because of him, and his ego will allow him to believe nothing else. Therefore, he has more to gain from his silence."

"Sugoooiii," he drawled with a laugh. "You might be a genius."

I shrugged. His eyes went soft and started to sparkle as tension dissolved, the corners of his mouth lifting into a soft smile.

"We can really do this?" he said, his voice thick and trembling slightly. "See each other every day?"

"If we're careful…" I took a deep breath, the reality of it warming inside me. "Yeah, I think we can."

His smile broadened, and a small tear leaked from his eye. I caught it on my thumb, brushing it along his cheek, and he leaned into it with a sigh. Just like that, his earlier tension was gone.

We both jumped as the kettle whistled. Tsukito leaped to his feet, scrubbing at his face as he ran to repack the tea filter and pour the hot water over it. He carefully arranged the little ceramic pot and matching glasses on a lacquer tray and lifted them, pausing a moment to smile at me before rushing back off to his master. The weariness from before returned, but now it held less weight, made buoyant by the promise of tomorrow. With the shadows of Matsumoto and Mahiro looming over us, it wasn't as we liked, but it was all we had.

The best a pair of slaves could hope for.

FORTY-TWO

Hunting a Bear

I COULD HEAR THEM THROUGH THE WALLS AT NIGHT. MUFFLED voices in conversation filtered through the quiet, and despite all his assurances to the contrary, my mind twisted them into something lurid. Matsumoto's low, animalistic grunts. Tsukito's small voice beneath them. I buried my head under pillows and thick blankets, but they pierced them like gauze. I clapped my hands over my ears and gritted my teeth until they ached. Finally, I could take it no more and fled the room.

I retreated to the relative safety of the engawa, focusing all my attention on packing my pipe. The garden filled with shadows, his young face reflected on every shimmering surface, his tortured voice on the wind. I took a long drag off my pipe and let the smoke burn my lungs. I held it until my eyes watered and my chest screamed, and when I released it, I imagined I was a dragon breathing fire, laying waste to the monsters that plagued him.

"Fancy meeting you here." Jerked out of my vision by a voice from behind me, I coughed out a lungful of smoke before turning to meet it.

"Good evening, Matsumoto-san," I said with a polite bow.

"Good evening…I don't think I caught your name."

"Asagi."

"Ah! How appropriate for you." Every muscle tensed as he settled himself on the porch next to me. "A name without gender."

"Apparently, my mother had a sense of humor." He chuckled, and I responded with a sweet smile. I sneaked a glance toward his room, but it was dark.

"You've picked quite a late hour to be smoking your pipe."

"Spend enough time sleeping next to me, and you'll find I keep quite odd hours," I said, batting my lashes at him. "Remnants of a past life. Sleep doesn't agree with me."

"Perhaps you haven't been properly worn out," he said, his big eyebrows bouncing.

"Why, sir!" I touched my fingers to my lips in mock disgust. "What a thing to say to a lady!"

"Good thing you are no lady," he said, leaning toward me with a wicked grin.

"Hmph." I struck my pipe sharply on the edge of the porch to dislodge the spent ashes before pulling myself primly to my feet.

"Have dinner with me," he said quickly, "tomorrow night."

I stopped short. "Why?"

"Why not?"

"People here know me," I answered in a sly tone. "Know I'm with Mahiro. If they get the wrong idea, it could become quite the scandal."

His eyes flashed, much as I'd expected them to, and he rose to his feet to meet me. Like a puppet on a string. My skin tingled with the same rush I felt the first time I'd confronted him in Mahiro's house. I could control him, not with my eyes, but with my wit. Giddiness trilled through me. Perhaps I could convince him he didn't need Tsukito at all. I turned my face sheepishly away and tucked it behind my sleeve as he stepped close to me.

"I suppose we'll have to take our meal in my room then." Hs voice dropped low. "To avoid prying eyes."

I bowed, a noncommittal gesture I knew he would take only as assent, and his lips pulled into a slow grin. "Good night, Matsumoto-san," I said, deepening my bow before sliding open my door.

"Good night, Asagi-chan."

"Matsumoto invited me to dinner."

Tsukito's arm tightened around mine, and he drew himself slightly closer. "I know." He lifted his shopping bag, giving it a little shake. "A meal for two. I take it you accepted."

"I didn't refuse," I said. "It's just a distraction. If he's looking at me, he's not looking at you."

His cheerful expression flickered before settling into something more neutral. "I told you it's not like that."

"I want to protect you."

"Why? You're not my mother," he said with a dry laugh. "Or my father. It's not your job to protect me. Besides, what if he falls in love with you?" A mischievous gleam returned to his eyes as he poked me in the ribs with his elbow.

"Please!" I scoffed. "It's all about challenge. I challenged his authority at Mahiro's, and now I challenge his prowess. It's no more about romance than hunting a bear."

"You mean he wants to mount and stuff you?"

I gasped, and he darted a few steps ahead of me, just out of reach of my swinging fan. He turned, prancing backward on his toes, every bit the precocious little boy I remembered.

"Or perhaps it's the other way around. It would be quite something to see Matsumoto on his hands and knees for once."

This time, I chased him in earnest, and he yelped as I caught him from behind, wrapping one arm tight around his waist and beating him playfully about the shoulders with my fan. Peals of laughter rang through the streets as he struggled in my arms, his bag of groceries falling and spilling in the dirt. We both dropped to our knees in a panic, brushing off onions and turnips and stalks of greens, giggling all over again every time our eyes met. His gaze darted over my shoulder and a determined look settled over his face as they landed on an apothecary.

"Do you have any money?"

"Yes, a little—"

"Give it to me," he said quickly, holding out his hand. I blinked, hesitating a moment before pulling a purse out of my sleeve and handing him a few coins. He closed his fist around them and jumped to his feet. "Wait here."

Ignoring my confused protests, he ran across the street to the apothecary, returning a moment later with a little vial of clear liquid and a conspiratorial grin. "What's that?"

"Oh, this?" he said innocently, holding the vial between his fingers and snatching it back before I could take it. "This is just in case."

"In case of what?"

"In case you start to look like a bear." He bounced his eyebrows lewdly, and I gave a disapproving frown.

"It's not poison, is it?"

"No, of course not," he said with a laugh. "It'll just put him to sleep. He always has tea after his meal. A few drops of this…" He trailed off as my expression continued to sour. "Relax. I've done it before."

"You have?"

"Sure," he said with a shrug. "Gotta get a break sometime." I curled my nose in disgust, and he laughed, hooking his arm back through mine and pulling me in the direction of the inn. "Oh, come on. Haven't you ever pulled any tricks on Mahiro to get some time to yourself?"

"No," I answered, my voice going distant and my vision a bit hazy. I tried to think of a time when refusing him had even been an option. "Even if I didn't want it, it seems like as soon as he touches me, I forget why."

"That must be what love is like," he said, his eyes shimmering.

"Must be." I felt a wave of something like grief wash coldly over me. "Have you ever felt like that?"

He gave a short, sad laugh. "The only person I ever loved was you."

I stood rooted to the spot as he disengaged his arm and bounded ahead of me into the inn. My heart felt trapped, bound in an endless loop of guilt and love, the two so intertwined I couldn't even tell the difference anymore.

FORTY-THREE

Look at Me

MAHIRO WAS RIGHT. MATSUMOTO WAS A BORE, IGNORANT AND offensive and classless to the point where, every time he spoke, I had to restrain the urge to flip the little table between us on its end and beat him over the head with it. I spent the entirety of our meal together jabbing at the fish on my plate with my chopsticks, severing its head and gouging out its eyes. My only savior was Tsukito sitting quietly in the corner. Every now and then he would cross his eyes and make faces behind Matsumoto's back to make me smile.

Matsumoto placed his chopsticks across his plate and leaned back with a contented sigh, Tsukito's signal to take away our plates. He jumped into action without word or acknowledgement, exiting almost silently with his heavy load. I pulled out my pipe and concentrated on packing the bowl as Matsumoto studied me, picking his teeth and scratching his belly.

"Do you mind?" I asked before bringing the pipe to my lips.

"Not at all." He considered me a moment, sitting a little straighter. "I can't help but notice you travel with no attendants."

"I prefer to do things on my own," I answered through a stream of smoke. "I come from…much more humble beginnings, and I must admit being waited on hand and foot makes me uncomfortable. If it were up to me, we would have no servants at all, but Mahiro insists on it."

"I'm quite the opposite, I'm afraid," he said with a laugh. "I wouldn't be able to get into my own kimono without the help of my servants. I always travel with at least one. Tsukito, for example"—he gestured grandly as the door slid open, revealing Tsukito carrying a tray for tea—"is absolutely indispensable."

Tsukito bowed lightly before lowering himself to his knees and sliding the tray between us. Without ever lifting his eyes, he poured his master's cup first, then mine, nudging my knee with his in signal. I watched Matsumoto carefully as he wrapped his meaty fingers around the cup and drank deeply.

"Doesn't it ever bother you?" I lifted my cup to my lips but didn't drink. "The idea of owning another human being."

"Of course not." He paused long enough to take another sip of his tea. "I'm doing them a favor."

"A favor!" I was so shocked by the audacity, I failed to control the disgust in my voice.

"Yes. I know it sounds absurd, but take Tsukito, for example." He gestured over his shoulder, and I could have sworn he'd already started to sway. "He has no family, no upbringing to speak of, no hope for an education even if he had the capacity to benefit from one."

That protective fire in me sparked to life as I watched Tsukito's shoulders sink under the weight of his insults.

"He'd likely be starving on the street if I hadn't taken him in. He works for me, and in return, he has a roof over his head and food in his belly."

"Isn't it possible," I said, voice carefully controlled, "that his family was taken from him, his upbringing aided by others like him, and his education withheld from him by his masters?"

"Yes, and that is unfortunate," he answered, his eyelids growing heavy, "but the result is the same."

He leaned back with a heavy sigh, rubbing a hand over his eyes. His movements grew slow and sluggish like a drunk as the drug steadily wore him down. Tsukito and I locked eyes as he edged closer to his master, ready to catch him if he fell.

"I must apologize, Asagi-chan," he said with a slow smile. "It seems all this heavy talk has worn me out."

"No need." I smiled sweetly through clenched teeth. "It's my fault for bringing it up." I stood and bowed low. Tsukito dutifully helped him to his feet so he could see me out. I paused in the doorway before turning and drawing close to him where he stood, wobbling drowsily on his feet.

"Look at me."

With a snap, our eyes connected, and I could see everything he was, all the fear, all the raging uncertainty. I saw his fascination with me, the one who'd transcended his birth in so many ways. He actually envied me. But what surprised me the most was his true and honest affection for Tsukito. Not love, exactly, but something akin to it, and it knocked me off-balance. He represented everything I loathed, everything I struggled against, but suddenly I couldn't hate him.

"You can tell the measure of a man by the way he treats his servants," I said softly. Our eyes and minds still connected, I pushed nothing but positive feelings into him. "I know you want to be a good man." He bobbed his head in affirmation, his expression blank. I leaned forward, bringing our faces close together, and breathed against his lips. "Good night, Matsumoto-san."

I turned abruptly, leaving him swaying in the doorway with Tsukito at his elbow, and returned to my room. Once inside, I quickly shed all the trappings of wealth and rank as if it could help me shake off the touch of his mind against mine and the confused way it made me feel. I could have forced him, could have used my power over his mind to manipulate him into handing Tsukito over to me. The monster inside thrilled at the idea, but I pushed it away. I would win him over myself or not at all.

I had just tied the obi around my yukata when I heard a light tap at the door, and Tsukito poked his head inside.

"Well, he's out," he said with a smile, slipping inside and sliding the door closed behind him.

"For how long?" I asked without ever really looking up.

"All night."

I heard his feet shuffle, and even without looking, I knew he'd be tugging at the frayed end of his obi and digging his toes into the tatami.

"Did you…do something to him?"

I froze, my outstretched hand hanging in the air as I reached for my hairbrush. "What do you mean?"

"I've never seen him like that before," he answered. "He looked…empty."

"I didn't do anything. I just looked."

"What did you see?"

"That he's not the devil I thought he was." I let my hand drop back to my side as I turned to face him. "Ignorant and misguided, yes. But he truly believes those things he said. That he's helping people. There's no malice. He's just…" I trailed off, grasping at the air in front of me as if the words I searched for hung there just out of reach.

"You saw all that just by looking into his eyes?" I nodded. "Have you looked at me like that?"

"No, of course not," I said, grabbing up my brush, raking it through my hair, and averting my eyes. "It's an invasion. I wouldn't do that to you." I gasped as Tsukito grabbed my wrists, pulling my body square with his. "Tsukito, what are you—"

"I want you to see me," he said, his voice tinged with desperation. "I want you to see me the way you see him."

"No," I said, jerking my face away, a knot of panic forming in my throat. "I don't want to."

"Please, Asagi," he begged, his eyes going wet.

"No."

"Why won't you look at me?"

"Because I'm afraid!" I said, so sharply he jumped back. "I don't want to see. I'm afraid to see what you really think of me after I failed you so spectacularly."

I squeezed my eyes closed, held my breath, and in the terrible silence that followed, thought of every possible scenario. The strange and intimate touch of my mind might break open the deep pain of an abused child, the hidden resentment, that unnatural connection revealing me for the monster I was. I didn't even realize how tightly I clutched my brush to my chest until his gentle fingers wrapped around mine, prying it out of my shaking hands and setting it aside. My breath released in a whimper as he pulled my face back toward him. With a long, heavy sigh, I took both his hands in mine and held them against my chest.

I raised my eyes and looked.

FORTY-FOUR

Wax Wings

I SLIPPED INTO HIS MIND LIKE A WARM BATH. HE DIDN'T RESIST ME AT all—in fact, he welcomed me, embraced me, and filled me up until there was no separation anymore. I felt the happiness of our reunion, the joy and hope it triggered in him, flow over me like a spring breeze, soft and sweet and full of promise. Somewhere, a heart fluttered and danced, and I wasn't sure if it was his or mine.

But under it all was something so familiar it hurt. Fear, sharp and vibrating just beneath the surface, fear of separation and loss, fear of punishment, fear of something intangible and unnamable that everyone like us carried like a stone on our backs. As I fell deeper inside him, the fear became more concrete and attached itself to memories. It was like watching his life unfold in reverse. The most recent memory came sharp and fast to the surface before making way for the less distinct visions of boyhood, distorted and out of focus. The firm hand of harsh masters. The loss of friends and loved ones. Some to sickness and injury, others simply vanishing into the unknown. And then, he himself becoming the vanished, whisked away from a home he'd become familiar with to start the whole terrible process again.

Even deeper and I became aware of something else, something that pierced the dark in flashes and waves of sensation. A warm body next to mine. Long black hair tangled around little fingers. A song, familiar but somewhat distorted. All of it coupled with a strong sense of comfort and safety and deep, deep unconditional love.

It was me.

Tears wet my cheeks, and my whole body shook. Love. The bright rose-colored love of a child untainted by anger or resentment. He'd brought me deep into his heart, into his safe place, and I found myself there.

Without even realizing it, I'd pulled him closer to me. Face wet with tears, I dropped my head onto his shoulder. His lashes fluttered against my neck as he drifted back into awareness, and his arms tightened around my waist. It felt like melting.

"You've forgiven me," I said, voice filled with awe.

"Forgiven you?" he echoed. "You've done nothing wrong."

"But I—"

"No," he said sternly, pulling away from me and taking my face in his hands. "Do *not* blame yourself for what happened to me. You weren't the one who hurt me. It was *him*. Blaming yourself is like blaming the cane that whips you instead of the hand that wields it."

"But I should have done something. Stood up to him, taken you away…"

"He would have killed you."

"I shouldn't have left you alone with him."

"What choice did you have?" he asked with a dry laugh. "What choice do any of us have in what happens to us? I'm glad he sent you away. I'm glad you ended up with a kind master who loves you. You suffered enough for me. You should never feel guilty when karma rewards you."

Reward? I looked back at my long life spent apart from him and failed to see the reward. Mahiro might have been kind and generous, but his love came at a price. And even that had slowly eroded away without me noticing, leaving me with a shocking emptiness filled only with a dark, primal hunger.

"Maybe this is my reward," I said. "I thought I'd never see you again, and here you are." I threw my arms around him and pulled him into me again. "I just want to hold you and never let you go."

He laughed, a small, childish laugh, and I felt transported. It struck me once again how grown he was, and I felt the time like a wound. I thought he'd be ten years old forever, but he'd become a man out of my sight, and though I lamented all the things I'd missed, my heart swelled with pride.

"I love you, you know that?" I said, pressing kisses into his hair.

"I know that," he said with a giggle that made my skin dance. "And I, you."

WE FELL ASLEEP CURLED UP TOGETHER, AND WHEN I AWOKE THE next morning, he was already gone, off to tend to his master. I groaned into my pillow as the weight of real life bore down on me once again. I buried my face in the sheets and tried to stave it off, but it was no good. They were already cold with his departure, his smell on them faint and waning. I was forced to get up if I wanted any more of him.

Feeling heavy and light all at the same time, I pulled myself out of bed. I washed in the basin, pulling the water through my hair with my fingers and humming merrily as my mind filled with thoughts of Tsukito. In those solitary moments, I dared to dream of a future together, of laughing and playing together, of him telling me his stories, of falling asleep every night with him beside me. I let my heart soar with it, even though I knew better, even though I knew it would be a hard landing when I came down.

I jumped at the sound of a gentle rapping and Matsumoto's voice calling to me through the door.

"Asagi-chan? Are you there?" he called. "May I come in?"

"Yes, of course," I replied sweetly.

In a fit of devilish impulse, I shifted my position to allow my collar to slip off my shoulder and the damp fabric to cling to my chest. He stopped short as the door slid open, cheeks flushing and gaze politely darting away.

"Oh, I'm s-sorry." He did a nervous little dance in the doorway. "I-I can come back…"

"Why?" I asked with a girlish laugh. "As you so cleverly pointed out, I am no lady. There's no need for modesty here."

He blushed again, this time so deeply it was almost endearing.

"About last night," he started, trying not to stare as I wrung out my hair and pulled my collar back into place, "I feel the need to apologize."

"For what?"

"For not being a proper host." He took a deep breath, gathering his courage, and stepped inside.

"I'm not sure what you mean." I stood and put the basin aside, pulling a brightly painted kimono out of a box and stretching it over a rack hanging from the rafters. "I found our meal perfectly pleasant."

"And yet, I feel it was cut short." He gave a long, low whistle as his gaze fell on my kimono. "My, that is quite a thing. You can really get into it by yourself?"

"I manage," I said coyly. "It's getting out that proves difficult."

"It would be easier if you had help."

"But as you see, I have no servants." I took a step forward, running the end of my finger along his collar. "Unless you would lend me yours."

"If you'll have tea with me," he said. "Let me make up for last night's rudeness."

I hesitated a moment before bowing in affirmation. He smiled warmly, letting his hand brush over mine before exiting the room. I had just enough time to slip out of my yukata and into a nagajuban before Tsukito appeared, looking bewildered.

"He just sent me here to help you dress," he said with a tinge of disbelief. His eyes widened as I doubled over in a fit of laughter. "You're scary, you know that."

"You have no idea."

He laughed, squeezing my arm as he moved around behind me, and a moment later, the heavy weight of the kimono fell over my back. I shoved my arms into the sleeves and felt myself warm all over again as I watched him work, his tongue popping out as he fastened the bindings of my kimono with quick fingers and tugged it into place. My heart fluttered as he pushed me down to my knees and pulled a comb through my hair, ridding it of the last of the water and fastening it with pins.

"I think this might kill me," I said around a sudden tightness in my chest.

"Oh, don't be dramatic," he said, giving me a sharp poke in the back before helping me to my feet. "It's only tea."

"That's not what I meant."

"I know."

"It's cruel," I hissed through my teeth. "We've been separated for so long, and now—"

"You're looking at it backward," he said, stopping my rant with a finger on my lips. "We could have gone our whole lives never seeing each other again. Always wondering what happened. Fate was kind to bring us back together." He took my face in his hands and rested his forehead against mine. "You should be thankful for these moments, small as they are. I know I am."

He was right, of course. I was in no position to be selfish, and by holding onto my bitterness, I only tainted the time we had together. I pulled him toward me, drawing him into a warm embrace.

"You have to go," he said. "He's expecting you for tea any minute."

"It's a very complicated kimono. It could take a while."

"Asagi, come on." He wiggled in my arms.

I groaned, planting a kiss on the top of his head before I allowed him to slip out of my grip. He moved to the door, sliding it open with a low bow.

I SPENT THAT MORNING AND EACH MORNING THEREAFTER MUCH AS I had the night before: listening to Matsumoto drone on and on about nothing and trying not to explode at his sheer ignorance. My gaze drifted often to Tsukito, sitting quietly just behind him, and I struggled not to smile every time our eyes met. It only made Matsumoto sit straighter, his ego making him believe it was all for him.

My days were spent in agony, flirting mercilessly with Matsumoto, all the while searching for ways to spend time with Tsukito. For someone who had just professed their independence, I played quite the damsel in distress, begging Matsumoto—and by extension, Tsukito—for help with everything from imaginary insects to rearranging furniture. Anything to have Tsukito in my sight.

And every evening, he would slip his little drug into his master's tea to ensure our time together. Sometimes, we would just talk for hours, fantasizing about how our lives would be different if we'd had families that loved us rather than sold us into hell. Sometimes, I dressed him in my kimono, and we went out arm in arm like two fine ladies, walking the glittering nighttime streets. I lived for those nights. At that time more than any other, I lived like a youkai of legend, prowling the night and cursing the sun because it took him away from me.

One morning, I woke to find my bed still warm and an arm flung over my face. I groaned and tried to wiggle out from under it, only to get a knee square in my kidney.

"Tsu-chan..." I pushed at the wiry limbs invading my space, keeping my eyes squeezed shut against the morning light. He snorted once, shifting just enough to wedge his nose into the back of my neck. "Tsu-chan. Back to your own bed, boy. It's—"

My eyes shot open, and I jerked straight up as the light crept in, bringing reality with it. We'd overslept the sunrise, and it came streaming through the rice paper walls, threatening to burn us alive. I grabbed Tsukito by the shoulders and gave him a hard shake. "Wake up, Tsukito!"

He groaned in protest, pressing his fists against his eyes before jerking upright in panic. "*Kuso!*" he cursed. "How long has the sun been up?"

"Awhile, by the looks of it," I said, throwing a robe hastily over my shoulders.

"I have to go." He lunged for the door. "He'll be looking for me."

"You can't just run out there!" I cried, grabbing him around the waist and pulling him back. "If he sees you—"

We both froze at the sound of a tap on my door. "Asagi-chan?" Tsukito clapped his hands over his mouth, his face going white. I silently directed Tsukito to the front corner of the room. In a place like this, there was nowhere to hide, so I would have to be clever. I ran a quick hand through my wildly disheveled hair and, with a deep breath, slid the door open and stepped out into the hall, quickly snapping it shut behind me.

"Matsumoto-san." I let my voice fall low and pulled myself up to my full height. My yukata falling open over my chest, my arms tightly crossed, I must have looked much as he did the first day we met.

"Good morning, Asagi…san," he stammered, his usual diminutives falling away when faced with my natural masculinity. I kept my face hard, my posture polite but uninviting, and he took an uncomfortable step back. "I'm sorry to bother you, but have you seen Tsukito? He wasn't in my room and—"

"Have you checked the kitchen?" I interjected, arching an eyebrow.

"Ah, yes…of course…I should…" He did a nervous little circle with his feet, making like he would head down the hall before pulling back toward me and frowning deeply. "I also wanted to…"

"Yes?"

"I've been called back to Edo," he said firmly. "We leave at first light tomorrow."

I gasped, all the blood rushing out of me as if I'd been run through with a sword. My skin went cold, and I leaned back against the door to keep from swaying.

"I know it's sudden, but I just wanted to thank you."

I swallowed hard to clear the lump from my throat. "For what?"

"For your company." He smiled lightly and took a step toward me as my posture softened. "I know I can be difficult to be around."

"On the contrary, you've spoiled me," I said with a light laugh. "I've grown too used to having someone help me. And as you said, Tsukito is quite…" I lump lodged in my throat, and I swallowed hard to dislodge it. "Perhaps you could lend him to me."

"Asagi-chan…"

"Just for a while." My voice wanted to waver, and I let it, forcing a weak smile. "It would give you an excuse to come back."

His eyes trembled, and for an agonizing moment, I dared to hope. He let out a sigh, his shoulders falling, before taking one of my hands in his. "I'm sorry, Asagi-chan. I can't help but think this is fate telling us our time is over."

"I don't understand what you mean."

"I mean Mahiro." His eyebrows bounced in surprise. "Doesn't he return today?"

Mahiro. I released a loud exhale, touching my fingertips to my brow. He was right. I'd lost count of the days. Mahiro would likely be back by midday, finding his house empty if I didn't return. I squeezed my eyes shut as they began to burn with guilt, and Matsumoto touched my elbow.

"It's been a pleasure getting to know you, Asagi-chan," he said softly, placing a small kiss on my temple. "I do hope we meet again."

When I opened my eyes, Matsumoto was making his way down the hall away from me. I slipped back inside my room and found Tsukito slumped in the corner, his cheeks already wet with tears.

"He's on his way to the kitchen," I croaked, my voice barely above a whisper. "If you hurry, you can—"

"Tell me we'll see each other again," he hiccupped, his big eyes swimming and desperate, ten years old all over again. "Tell me our time isn't over."

I wanted to. I wanted to tell him that nothing could keep us apart, that no matter where he went, I would find him. But I couldn't. My soaring heart had crashed back down to earth, broken and bloodied, its wax wings melted by the sun.

FORTY-FIVE

Run

I STOOD IN FRONT OF THE HOUSE, EYES LOWERED, HANDS FOLDED primly before me, when Mahiro's horses appeared at the front gate. In the quick bustle of activity that followed, I stayed still, a knot forming in my stomach as the stable boys took the reins and helped him down from his horse. A few slow, heavy steps and his feet appeared in my field of vision.

"Asagi." My name came out a sigh as he brushed his fingers over my cheek. "I was afraid you wouldn't be here."

"Welcome home, Goshujin-sama," I said robotically, bending into a deep bow.

He withdrew his hand and inhaled sharply, taken aback by my formality. He pulled back the curtain of my hair with one finger, and I kept my face carefully blank, gaze trained to my toes. He was my master now, and I his prisoner, nothing more, nothing less. Perhaps that's how it had always been. Bound by blood and obligation, I had been living on false promises.

I felt as much as saw the sadness settle over him, weighing down his limbs and flattening his features. Without a word, he let my hair fall back into its place and walked past me into the house. I straightened and followed just a few paces behind, all the way to his room where I helped him out of his dusty haori like I must have done a hundred times, folding it into a neat little pile and leaving it by the door for the servants to collect. He lowered himself to the tatami, and I went to my knees behind him as he continued to shed his outer garments.

"Are you angry with me?" he asked without turning, his words sounding sharp in the silence.

"No."

"But you don't exactly love me either." He turned stiffly to look at me over his shoulder, and I averted my eyes, clenching my hands in my lap to keep them from shaking. He studied me for a long moment and, when I didn't answer, jerked his gaze forward. His room, usually so warm with his presence, went icy cold.

"I am sorry, Asagi," he said in a cracked voice, his rigid posture crumbling under the words. "This is all my fault." I started to protest, but he continued anyway. "I have been doing a lot of thinking while I was away, about you, about us. And you were right. I built myself up in my own mind like I was a hero, that I had saved you from the evils of cruel men. But really, I am no different. I told you over and over you were free, but I just put you in chains of a different kind. Made of silk instead of iron, but chains nonetheless.

"And then, Matsumoto came with that boy, Tsukito," he continued, voice tight with emotion, "and all the resentment you carried for me that I had kept myself blind to became undeniable. I thought Matsumoto and I were so different, but in your eyes, we were the same, and I proved it to be true."

My chest burned with guilt, and my vision blurred. I laid a tentative hand on Mahiro's back and, when he didn't pull away, rested my forehead between his shoulder blades. "I'm sorry, too," I started. "I never meant to hurt you. You've been so good to me…"

"You've been spending time with him, haven't you?"

"Yes."

"Good." He released a long breath, his shoulders rolling forward. "He *is* your son, and I was cruel to try to keep him from you."

I squeezed my eyes shut to stop the tears, but I couldn't keep them out of my voice. "They're leaving."

"And you are just going to let him go?"

"What else am I supposed to do?" I asked, a note of surprise in my voice. "He needs him. He won't let him go. How does someone like me stand up to someone like Matsumoto?"

"You do not," he said simply. "You run."

My eyes snapped open, and I sat up straight with a gasp. Mahiro turned on his hip to face me, smiling softly at my slack-jawed expression.

"I...I can't. I mean, we—"

"Why not?"

"It's too dangerous. I can't risk…" I swallowed hard, heart pounding at the thought. "We both know what they do to slaves who run."

He released a long sigh and, with a gentle pat on my thigh, pushed himself up off the floor. Sliding the door open just a crack, he called down the hall for Itsuko, who appeared almost instantly. A few quick, whispered words and she was gone again. He eased the door shut and leaned back on it, looking down on me with a sad, but warm, expression.

"When do they leave?" he asked.

"Tomorrow."

"Do you think Tsukito can sneak away for a bit?"

"Yes," I said, brows furrowing. "Matsumoto trusts him."

"Good. Bring him here."

"I don't...I don't understand." My palms began to sweat, and I bunched my hands up in the fabric of my long sleeves.

"You will be safer if you leave Musashi." He closed his eyes a moment before continuing. "By the time you get back, I will have everything you need."

Something broke inside me, and I clapped my hand over my mouth to stifle the sob forcing its way out. The tarnished love I had for Mahiro suddenly shone bright as polished bronze, and I found myself torn. I'd cursed him a hundred times for the life he'd given me, but without it, none of this would have happened. I would have died a slave, and Tsukito would have been lost to me forever. But to be with him, I'd have to turn my back on the very man who'd made it possible. The one who, even though he told me to go, desperately wanted me to stay.

"Why...?" I asked as I tried to steady my shaking shoulders.

He lowered himself back down to the floor beside me and cupped my face in his hands. "Because all I ever wanted to do was make you happy." His voice wavered as he brushed a tear from my cheek with his thumb. "Maybe this is my chance."

FORTY-SIX

Happiness

I HALF RAN, HALF TRIPPED MY WAY BACK TOWARD TOWN, MY HEART beating so fast I thought it might explode, alternately laughing and crying with every step. By the time I reached the inn, I must have looked a mess, makeup smeared and hair falling down. I didn't even think about how I would get Tsukito away. All I cared about was finding him.

My heart sank when I reached Matsumoto's room and found it empty. One of the maids politely informed me that he was preparing for his journey, so I hit the streets once again, kicking up an unladylike cloud of dust in my wake. I rushed down every street and ducked my head into every shop until I found Tsukito at the farrier waiting beside his master's horse.

Without stopping to think, I grabbed him by the wrist and pulled him through a cloud of soot into the alley behind the stables. "Asagi?" he yelped as I pushed him out of view of the street.

"What if I told you I could take you away?" I said as quickly as I could manage between great gasping breaths.

"What?" he asked, taking me by the shoulders as my legs threatened to collapse. "Calm down! What has gotten into you?"

"What if I told you that you didn't have to go?" My vision blurred, and my voice cracked as tears bubbled up inside me once again. "What if I told you I could take you somewhere far away from here? Somewhere you wouldn't have to work for nothing. Where no man would ever touch you unless you wanted him to. Would you go with me?"

"You…you want to run?"

"Yes!" I said, taking his face in my hands and pressing our foreheads together. "Let's run, like we should have years ago. You don't have to be afraid anymore. I'm stronger now. I can protect you. Our time isn't over. Just say you'll go with me."

Time stood still. Soot from the bellows hung in the air around us, light as snowflakes. The steady clang of metal on metal slowly faded away to nothing as I became aware of only him, of his hands looped lightly around my wrists, his eyelashes tickling my cheeks. My heart jumped and pulled at its moorings, straining against gravity, begging to soar.

"All right," he said breathlessly. "All right, I'll go."

I released my held breath, pulled him to me and squeezed him hard. He threw his arms around my neck, trembling and giddy, tears making streaks down his soot-stained cheeks. Finally, I let him go, grabbing him tightly by the wrist and pulling him behind me out of the alleyway.

"Come on," I panted.

"What, *now*?" he asked, tripping over himself in an effort to keep up with my pace.

"We're going to see Mahiro."

"Wait. Slow down. Mahiro? You can't tell him! He'll just turn us over to Matsumoto. Asagi, stop!" He planted his sandaled feet firmly in the dusty street and yanked himself free of my grip. When I turned, he had his arms crossed over his chest, wide eyes flashing. "I'm not going one more step until you tell me what's going on."

"He knows," I said, taking a deep breath to steady myself. "Everything. About our visits, our history." Tsukito's eyes widened even more, his arms dropping back down to his sides. My throat tightened and eyes welled. "He knows I can't abandon you, not again. And he loves me enough…he loves me enough to let me go."

I crumpled, hiding my face behind my hands as a wave of guilt crashed over me.

Tsukito looped his arms around my shoulders, pulling me close, and I melted into him. "Are you sure this is what you really want?" he asked gently. "You don't have to rescue me. If you don't want to—"

"I am your mother," I said quickly. He released a wet laugh and squeezed a little tighter. "I do want it. After twelve years away from you, I don't think I can take another day."

"Even if it means never seeing him again?"

Never. For me, there was no such thing. Time was endless and full of possibilities. If Tsukito and I could manage to meet again in his short lifetime, then surely Mahiro and I would meet again in ours. My tears stopped, and my resolve solidified as I took Tsukito firmly by the hand and led him toward the house of my master.

THE HOUSE WAS QUIET WHEN WE ARRIVED, AND WE TOOK ONE LAST, nervous moment outside the gate to scrub the soot from our cheeks and straighten our clothes. My heart and stomach felt like they were trading places inside me, and I had to take several deep breaths to calm down. I didn't even know what I was afraid of. Would Mahiro take one look at us together and change his mind, rip us apart and send Tsukito back to his master branded a fugitive? I knew no matter how angry he was, he would never betray me that way. Yet some small, nagging part of me wondered if I wasn't making a terrible mistake.

Once all my organs had settled back into their normal places, I led Tsukito through the gate. We crossed the garden, pausing just outside the door for one more deep breath before sliding it open. Mahiro sat at a little table in the center of the main room with a stack of papers in front of him and a brush in his hand. A teapot steamed merrily on a tray beside him, flanked by three glasses. His gaze flicked up, and he smiled warmly.

"Oh, back so soon!" he said, his eyebrows bouncing in surprise. He gestured to a pair of mats arranged along the table opposite him. "Have a seat. I am almost done."

Trading a nervous glance, Tsukito and I stepped out of our sandals and crossed the tatami floor to sit. We waited in uncomfortable silence as Mahiro's brush sped over the papers with expert strokes. Despite his efforts with the tutor, I could hardly write, let alone read, and the act always seemed somewhat magical to me—words and thoughts spilling from the end of a brush. Finally, he reached for his hanko, the red stamp that acted as his signature.

"Well, that is that," he said with a sigh, pressing the hanko to the bottom of the page and slipping his glasses off his nose. Out of instinct, Tsukito reached for the teapot only to have Mahiro shoo him away. "Please, allow me," he said, taking up the pot and filling each of our glasses, leaving his for last. "Tsukito, was it?"

"Y-Yes, Mahiro-sama," he answered with a low bow.

"Asagi tells me you met when you were only a boy," he said, taking a sip of his tea and eyeing Tsukito shrewdly over his glass. "Do you not think it strange?"

"I'm sorry, Mahiro-sama?"

"Asagi is awfully young for an old man."

My heart stopped, and I nearly dropped my tea glass. I opened my mouth to interject, but was cut off by a sharp flick of my master's eyes. I knew exactly what he was doing. I could almost see that supernatural fog growing denser around him, reaching out for Tsukito as he quietly considered the question.

"Asagi's magic," he answered simply. "I've always known it to be true."

"Yes, I suppose," he said with a gentle smile. "But every magic has a price." His smile fell, and his face grew hard, every angle sharpening into a point. "You are a smart boy, Tsukito. You must know that the more powerful the spell, the higher the cost. Sometimes, that cost can spill over into the people around us. Asagi's magic is very strong. Are you prepared to help shoulder the price?"

Tsukito's already fair complexion went absolutely pale, and my own skin grew cold. His focus went hazy as he pondered the meaning of Mahiro's words. I had to clutch my hands in my lap to keep them from shaking. There was another meaning to them, one meant only for me, and I heard it as though he whispered it in my ear: *Do not forget you are different. Throw away your romantic ideals and face the truth. He will grow old*

alone, and whether it is next week or fifty years from now, you will watch him die
while you remain. That is the price of your magic.

I didn't even realize I'd squeezed my eyes shut until I felt Tsukito's
long fingers brush over mine. I opened them slowly as he pried my fists
open and knotted our hands together, his doll eyes soft and glistening.
My chest warmed, and I realized I wasn't scared. Neither was he. We
were stronger together. I looked at Mahiro and found his expression had
softened. We didn't need to speak. He had his answer.

"This," he started, blinking furiously and forcing his voice steady,
"will help you on your journey." He curled the papers he'd been writing
into a tube and slipped them inside a leather cylinder. "They are notes
of title."

"Title!" I spewed in astonishment.

"You are now Arakawa Asagi, a son of my house. That should open
a few doors and silence suspicious tongues should you run into trouble."
He tipped the tube toward me but pulled it back just as my fingers
grazed the leather. "That is *my* name on these. Take care not to dirty it."

"Y-Yes, Mahiro-sama."

He released a long breath, tipping the scroll back toward me and
into my waiting hands. He then reached into his kimono and pulled out
a silk bag heavy with coins.

"This should be enough to buy you a horse and a few provisions. If
you are careful, you can use what is left along with the good name I
have given you to procure a small farmhouse on credit far away from
here. You will have to work the land, raise livestock, something to make
your way. It will not be glamorous, but…"

He trailed off as Tsukito struggled to hide a giddy burst of laughter
behind his hand. My heart did a little hopeful skip. He was right—it
wouldn't be glamorous. There would be no more gaudy jewelry or fancy
kimono. The work would be hard and pickings slim, half our yield or
more likely going toward our note. We would break our backs for little
to no gain, but it didn't matter. It was a life, a life that was ours.

"I have arranged a distraction that will keep Matsumoto busy the
entire day and into the evening. It will give you at least a day's head
start. Keep your head down and ride as far as you can. For now, you

should get back to your master before you are missed," Mahiro said, clearing his throat and rising to his feet.

"Yes, Mahiro-sama. Thank you, Mahiro-sama," Tsukito gushed, bowing so low his head touched the floor. "I promise I will find a way to repay your kindness."

"Make Asagi happy," he said softly, touching his shoulder, "and your debt is paid. Now, go."

We scurried to our feet as Mahiro corralled us toward the door. I stopped on the porch, my heart full to bursting, and threw my arms around Mahiro's neck. Happy and sad in equal measure, I clung to him, my maker, my master, my father, the one who saved me and destroyed me.

"I *do* love you. I do," I sobbed into his neck, "and I swear I will return to you one day."

"Then I will wait patiently until that time," he said, pressing kisses into my hair before pushing me away and into Tsukito's waiting hands.

FORTY-SEVEN

Hello, Youkai

I WRAPPED MY ARM TIGHT AROUND TSUKITO'S WAIST AND, DESPITE my conviction, relied heavily on his strength to walk away from the only happy home I'd ever known. The purse Mahiro had given me hung heavy in my sleeve, bumping against my elbow with every step as if in reminder. I found myself wondering how much he had paid for me, if it even approached the amount in this bag.

Tsukito gave my hand a squeeze as we found ourselves back at the farrier, Matsumoto's horse freshly shod and tied to a post. "What now?" he asked in a shaky voice. "What comes next?"

"Go home to Matsumoto," I said, the words coming out strained and breathy. "Continue your preparations as normal. If you have any good-byes to say, do it discreetly. Then, tonight when you serve him his tea…"

"What will I say to him?"

With a heavy sigh, I turned him to face me, my hands resting on his trembling shoulders. I knew he wanted to go, but unlike me, his leaving had the stink of betrayal, and it weighed on him. "Say whatever you need," I said gently, "but say it as he sleeps or leave him a note if you can write. If he truly is a good man, and I believe he is, he will forgive you."

His eyes glistened, and I pulled him to me. My chest swelled with all the things I wanted to say, so many they jammed themselves into a tight knot in my throat. But for the first time, I didn't feel a flutter of panic as he pulled away. There would be more of this, more embraces, and we had all the time in the world to say the things that piled up in my throat.

"I'll meet you tonight in the alley in front of the inn," I said, reluctantly releasing my hold on him.

"The one where I scared you?" he asked, a mischievous glint returning to his eye.

"Yes, the one where you scared me." I scowled and gave him a playful knock on the head. He giggled and took a few steps backward before turning on tiptoe back toward the farrier. He looked lighter, buoyed by hope, glowing even in the soot-darkened air from the smithy.

I SPENT THE REST OF THE DAY AS MAHIRO SUGGESTED. I BOUGHT A horse, a handsome dapple-gray gelding, and loaded it down with provisions—for one, of course, no need for me to eat along the way—and even splurged on a little gift for Tsukito. A leather strap for his hair adorned with glass plum blossoms that tinkled and caught the sun as they moved. I smiled to myself as I imagined giving it to him. At just the right time, to lift his spirits when the road got hard or boost his confidence when he felt out of place, his big eyes sparkling as he touched the little flowers. He'd likely never owned anything of such luxury.

With the trinket tucked into my sleeve and hours to kill before sundown, I decided on one last visit to my favorite places. Dusty roads packed to the brim with life. Carts in the market were overfilled with livestock and produce. Merchants shouted merrily to everyone that passed. Girls smiled coyly behind brightly colored fans. It all held a fresh beauty to me now, and I wondered, if I came back in fifty years, would it all be the same? A hundred?

I watched the sunset from the window of my favorite teahouse, savoring the rich aromas of matcha and steamed buns. I enjoyed my green tea and the golden light spilling in the window. I wanted to sear this moment into my memory. These were my last moments in a place that, under Mahiro's teaching, I'd learned to love. Even though I was already a grown when I came here, I would always think of it as the place I grew up. I would tell stories of it with soft, nostalgic affection, and when I returned, I would embrace her in whatever form she took.

As the darkness thickened, I dropped too many coins on the table and pulled myself to my feet. Tsukito would likely be serving Matsumoto his evening meal right about now, meaning the game would soon be afoot. My skin tingled with electricity born from nerves and excitement. After tonight, our lives would never be the same.

My horse snorted and stamped his hooves as I untied him and led him toward the inn. Tying him to a post nearby, I tucked myself into the alley to wait, the firefly glow of my pipe the only thing betraying my presence. I counted the stars to pass the time. Surely, their evening meal was done and Tsukito would soon serve his spiked tea, if he hadn't already. Any minute Matsumoto would be sleeping soundly, completely unaware of Tsukito's escape. Any minute, he'd come skipping out the front door, his pack in hand, and we'd be on the road to a new life.

Any minute…

The wind shifted, bringing a tension with it that made my hair stand on end. I peered around the corner. All was quiet. A light flickering in the entryway was the only movement I could see. My horse let out a huff and a little whinny, and I reached out to touch his nose.

"You feel that too?"

The wind shifted again, and adrenaline cut through me like a heated blade. Every one of my heightened senses rang in alarm, but nothing was out of place. "Damn it, boy, if you're doing this to scare me, I will hang you by your ears." I squinted into the dark with my sharp eyes, searching every shadow, tuned my ears to every movement, and sniffed at the air like a dog.

Blood.

Faint but unmistakable, it tingled just at the end of my nose. The coppery-sweet smell made the darkness inside me stir and set my teeth on edge. It was the thing I needed and hated and wanted and feared, the thing that made my heart shudder and veins burn and could only mean one thing:

Something was wrong.

I bolted toward the inn, abandoning my horse without a thought. I couldn't think. My mind swirled thick with terrifying images, blocking out rationality. We'd been found out. It was the only explanation. We'd been found out, and Matsumoto was beating him, bad by the smell of it. If I didn't get him out…

I burst through the front door to find the receiving area empty and dark save for a small oil lamp flickering just inside. I tried to take a deep breath to calm myself, but it felt like breathing underwater. The row of rooms spread out ominously before me, all of them dark except one.

"Matsumoto-san?" I called into the darkness. I didn't dare call Tsukito's name for fear of making things worse. Heart racing, I took a single step into the breezeway toward the lighted room, my hand trailing along the paper walls. The air shifted again, and I froze in front of one of the darkened rooms. Instincts I didn't know I had fired off so fast I couldn't make sense of them. I pulled away from the door, sure that something was watching me from the other side, waiting, calculating, ready to pounce.

It came from behind, fast and silent. I raised my hand to the back of my neck before I even felt the sting, pulling out a long pin. Not a pin. A dart. Thick at one end and fitted with a piece of black cloth to make it stable. An electric burn radiated out from where it hit me, spreading quickly throughout my back and shoulders. My mind slowed. My vision blurred. The ground pitched and swayed beneath me like a ship in a storm. I turned unsteadily in the direction from which it came just as a figure materialized from the dark.

"Hello, Youkai," it said in a voice all the more menacing for its calm.

FORTY-EIGHT

Live

THAT SMALL AMOUNT OF POISON WAS ENOUGH TO BRING ME TO MY knees. Poison. I knew it, recognized it on some deep, primal level. The heat in my back spread to my chest, and I struggled to breathe as I floundered on the swaying floor. If I'd been human, I might have even retched. In a moment of pure mortal panic, I wondered if I was dying.

My attacker never moved. He loomed over me, his long body pulled very straight, hands clasped behind his back and chest thrust out. Round tinted glasses perched on his thin nose, and his lips curled slightly in disgust while he watched me writhe under the effects of his poison.

As I'd suspected, the door in front of me slid open, and two pairs of hands gripped me under my armpits. I struggled uselessly against them as they dragged me down the hall on my knees, my long pink obi trailing behind us. The footsteps of the other were slow and deliberate as a stalking cat. He didn't speak, but somehow I knew he was the leader. Something in his lean posture told me, a subtle confidence I'd seen in Matsumoto and others of his ilk. Likely a soldier, and a high-ranking one.

The other two were definitely the muscle of the group, broad and burly, and completely without finesse. They dragged me all the way down to the room on the end, the room with the light on, the room that had been mine, and tossed me in like a sack of rice. I landed flat on my face, groaning as the smell of blood hit me again, sharp and thick and familiar, combining with the drug in my system to make a sludgy mess of my mind. Something tensed inside me, something dangerous, and I bared my teeth and growled against the tatami. My eyes rolled in their sockets, and they struggled to pierce the fog. Something else, something warm and familiar, drifted behind the thing that made my fangs ache. Something that made me think of horses and bright eyes and stolen moments.

"Tsukito."

Everything snapped into focus, and I saw him lying prone just a few feet away, everything at awkward angles and dreadfully still. His long hair fell over his face, hiding all but his split and swollen lips and the narrow bridge of his nose. My fears had been half right. He had been beaten and badly, only not by his master. His kimono had fallen or been yanked loose, and his exposed chest and shoulders were spotted with deep-purple bruises. A delicate flower flattened by a storm. I fought my way through the nausea and vertigo and lifted my head, reached out, hoping and fearing all at the same time.

"Tie him." That voice again, flat, calm, and unquestionable.

The hard, meaty hands of his underlings jerked my arms behind me, and I heard the unmistakable rattle of chains as an iron shackle snapped shut over my wrists. I clenched my fists and struggled against the cuffs with a wailing cry as they wrapped the chains around my forearms and over my shoulders, completely immobilizing my upper body. Pain tore through my ligaments as weakened muscles strained against my bonds. All I could think was *Tsukito*. Tsukito with his blood splattering the tatami. Tsukito with his body broken. I kicked and screamed and clawed at the tatami, crying his name over and over. I just wanted him to move, twitch, something to tell me he lived.

The leader sighed wearily as he watched his henchman struggle to contain me. He crossed the room with that same unhurried stride to stand over Tsukito. He pulled a black katana from his belt, unsheathed it, and pointed it directly at Tsukito's neck.

I froze, throat clamped down. While my human mind told me to stop, think, be reasonable, the sleeping monster inside me rolled over in its cage, cracked its eyes, and licked its lips. Our captor's thin mouth twisted into a smile, eyes glinting behind tinted glass.

"Oh, good," he said. "You do care about him. That will make this much easier."

"Let him go," I croaked.

"I don't think so."

"Who are you?" I asked. "What do you want?"

"You don't remember me?" he said, cocking his head to the side. "I certainly remember you."

A tremor went through me, and I squinted up at him through the haze of pain and fear, searching for something familiar. He was too confident, too smartly dressed to be a servant. He was young, in his early twenties at most, far too young to be one of Mahiro's contemporaries. Did I flirt with him in the teahouse? Was he a jilted would-be lover acting out of some misguided jealousy? No. He knew what I was and how to subdue me. A memory flickered to the surface: Mahiro returning home bloodied. *Someone tried to kill me.* My heart clenched.

"H-Hunter," I gasped. There was no other word for it.

His mouth twisted into something like a grin. "You're so close," he hissed. "The Hunters did find me, train me, gave me a home." He lifted the weapon in his hand, and it flashed strangely. "Even gave me this sword specially made to kill you."

He paused, his focus shifting to Tsukito's prone body. Very slowly, very deliberately, he lifted the toe of his right foot and rested it on Tsukito's obviously broken arm. Very slowly, very deliberately, he applied pressure. A sound emanated from Tsukito, thin at first, like air escaping a balloon and then quickly building into a razor-sharp scream.

"Stop!" I cried as his body twisted and contorted against the pain. The monster was bolt upright now, claws wrapped tight around the bars of its cage. Nausea ripped at my gut as I threw my whole weight against the grip that held me, chains groaning in protest.

He lifted his foot, and Tsukito collapsed back into himself, shivering and panting.

"Remember yet?"

My shoulders dropped, and he sighed, shaking his head in disappointment.

"I suppose I should expect this from a demon like you," he said with a shrug, stepping over Tsukito's suffering body and sheathing the sword with a metallic pop. "You must have killed hundreds, *thousands* in your lifetime. You couldn't possibly remember every one."

"But…I don't…" Something scratched hard at my subconscious, but I couldn't quite grasp it. He had me all wrong. I didn't kill, hadn't for a very long time, and I had the faces of every one nailed to my heart. "You have the wrong person."

"Unlikely," he snarled. He dropped down to one knee in front of me and grabbed me by the hair, yanking my face up level to his. "I will never forget the red-eyed demon that killed my father."

Papa…

My skin went cold as my mind jerked back to that first disastrous kill over a decade ago. The farmer's latent memories swam up from the depths of my subconscious. His pretty, fair-skinned wife who died in childbirth. Her fine features on this young man's face, twisted with anger and bitterness. He already had no mother. I took his father.

I created him.

"I'm sorry," I said in a thin voice. I meant it, meant it down to my bones. My eyes welled and overflowed, my chest squeezed tight in a vine of regret. "I was new. I didn't mean to…"

"What did you see?" he asked, his voice hoarse.

"W-What?" I winced as he gave my hair another hard yank.

"I saw from the door. When you looked in his eyes, something happened." The words spilled from him in a fast, manic pace. "What did you see?"

"I saw you. And your mother." His face jerked, and something sparked inside me. "You've never seen your mother's face, have you? I can show it to you."

He scoffed and pulled away from me, rising to his feet. But his cool, controlled exterior started to crack. He paced a circuit of the room, his knuckles white around the hilt of the sword. My mind focused on the smallest details. The veins throbbing blue under the skin of his wrist. The weight of the blade on the long hilt. The little silver charm caught in the wrapping. A dragon with red eyes flashing in the light. My ruby-eyed kin, winking and grinning with cruel fangs.

The thing inside me stirred again as if in answer.

Let me out. We'll see who has the longer claws.

"Look at me," I pressed. "Your father's memories are still with me. His final thoughts. Look into my eyes—"

With a feral cry, he reared back and struck me so hard across the cheekbone I saw stars. The thugs' grips on me shifted, and I was yanked upright once again. The change in orientation made my head swim, and for a moment, I lost my bearings, searching the room for something to grasp on to. Tsukito's eyes cracked open and watched me, desperate, pleading.

"Let him go." I gritted my teeth against the rage building inside me. Not just against him, but against myself, against what Mahiro had turned me into, what he'd made me do. How many more were out there just like him? How many brothers, fathers, sons, driven to madness by what I'd taken?

For your safety and his…

Mahiro had tried to warn me. I was no longer meant for this world, for his world. That ride into the valley was meant to be a good-bye. *Let him go.* The slave was dead and should have stayed that way, but in my selfishness, I clung to a life that was no longer mine. Now he would pay the price for my magic.

"You want to punish me, fine." The words came out flat and broken. "Beat me, torture me for as long as you want. I won't even resist you. And when you're done…"

A long, thin sound escaped from Tsukito, and despair cut through me with an icy blade. He reached a hand along the floor toward me, tears flowing down swollen cheeks. We shouldn't be here. *I* shouldn't be here. I should have died when Kira poisoned me.

"I've always been told," the hunter started slowly, his focus swinging between me and Tsukito, "always *believed* monsters like you were incapable of real human connection, real friendship, real love. But looking at the two of you…" I tensed as the end of his sword swung toward Tsukito again. "It's not just affection, is it? You would die for him?"

The monster inside me roared, raged, gnashed his teeth, but it didn't matter. The cold had begun to creep its way in. My human heart was already letting go.

A smile crept across the young hunter's face that made my blood curdle.

"Asagi…" Tsukito's hoarse voice struggled out of him, but I hardly heard it.

I tracked the hunter as he took a backward step toward him. *No.* Another step and then another until he loomed over him, his sword clutched tight in an underhand grip.

No, no, please, don't.

Tsukito squirmed beneath him in a last desperate attempt to get away. My heart froze. He *did* want to punish me. And what better way than—

In one quick motion, the hunter dropped to his knee, yanked Tsukito upright, and held his blade to his throat. My mind went white, awash with panic. I lurched against my captors' grips, screaming wordless obscenities and empty threats. Chains cut into my arms, my wrists, my chest, and they threw their full weight against my back, slamming my face into the floor. I tasted blood.

"Get him up. I want him to watch."

"Killing him solves nothing," I cried. "It will make you no better than I am."

The hunter scoffed. "You expect me to forgive you?"

"No. But he is innocent."

I snapped and growled as one of the thugs wrapped me in a headlock and pulled my head up.

"I will kill you," I spat. "I will peel the flesh from your bones, drink the blood from your still-beating heart. You will beg for death before I'm done with you." The monster spoke with my voice.

"Asagi!" Tsukito's voice cut through the animal rage, thin and tight with panic. "Asagi, look at me."

Snarling, poison burning through my veins, I struggled to focus. All I could see was the blade biting into his frail skin, his broken, bloodied face, the hunter's gleeful smile.

"Asagi, please."

Our eyes met, and with that familiar snap I was transported. In the space of a second, my head filled with memories, bright rose-colored moments that chased away the fear and warmed the darkness inside me. Curious fingers parting my hair. The brush of his sleeping breath against my neck. Sneaking up behind me and laughing. Precious moments strung together like shining glass beads. Memories gave way to fantasies, and I found myself on a small, ragged farm. Tsukito smiling, back bent and skin darkened from the sun, wrinkled but still beautiful. Training horses and selling kimono to make money to buy seed. We were poor and struggling, but happy because we belonged to no one but ourselves, to each other, to the earth under our feet. And under it all, Tsukito's pleading voice crying, *"Live, Asagi. Live and fight. Don't let him break you. Fight for our happiness."* The rattle of a lifted blade sounded and *"love you, love you, love——"*

FORTY-NINE

The Ruby-Eyed Dragon

WHAT HAPPENED NEXT, I REMEMBERED LATER ONLY IN FLASHES. A mist of blood that painted the air red, fat drops splashing across my cheek. Tsukito crumpling as the hunter released him, clutching weakly at a wide gash in his neck. Shock gripped me by the throat, and I couldn't scream, couldn't call his name, couldn't even move as his life spilled from him in a great fan of red. One final choking gasp, and his eyes—his big, bright doll eyes—went dark.

I broke the monster's bonds and set it free. With a feral cry, I shed my human skin and became the beast, the youkai. Iron links gave way as if made of rice paper, and I exploded into violent motion. I felt separate, disembodied, watching with a detached coldness as my hands flung out and wrapped around the henchman's swords, drawing them from their sheaths and bringing them down over their heads. One dropped to his knees, blood spraying from a long gash across his chest. The other crumpled as his severed head bounced across the floor.

I swayed on my feet, the dead men's swords slipping from my fingers. I was hungry, ravenous. The smell of their blood, coppery and sweet, sent an electric thrill through my veins. In a daze, I lifted one gory hand up to my nose and breathed it in deep. The monster inside me urged, pleaded, demanded, and I did nothing to resist as he took control. My tongue pushed out and dragged over my bloody fingers. My human parts sank into a deep, dark place, and it felt good, safe, untouchable.

I felt free.

An awkward crash jerked me back to the present. The young hunter, roused from his shock at my escape, clamored to his feet. Black sword raised, he charged me headlong. I sidestepped the end of his blade, and it whizzed through my hair as I caught his wrist and gave it a wicked twist. The blade clattered to the floor, and I watched through the monster's eyes as he wrapped his hand around the hunter's neck and pinned him to the wall.

"Look at me," he snarled in my voice. The hunter squeezed his eyes shut as I plucked the tinted glasses from his nose with my free hand. The monster's grip tightened. "Open your eyes, or I will tear off your eyelids."

Gasping and choking, the hunter forced his eyes open. The monster wrapped his hand around the boy's chin, forcing him to meet his eyes.

"Don't be afraid," he snarled. "I want to show you your mother."

The hunter's body went stiff as our minds touched. Images flowed freely between us, and I knew him. I saw his life on the street, orphaned and starving, and the hunters that took him in, forging his hate into a sharp point and promising him vengeance.

He shrank away as my own memories bubbled to the surface, memories of his father, how he felt, how he *tasted*. The stolen image of his mother, beautiful and pure. The monster pushed it forward, latching onto it with bloody claws until it became distorted. My face loomed over her. My fangs tore into her. My hands, twisted and sharpened into talons, ripped the flesh from her bones.

The boy's voice rose in a shriek of madness. He writhed and kicked in the monster's grip. My human heart begged it to let him go but was drowned out by bloodlust and rage. The hunter clawed at his eyes until they bled, but it was too late. We were already inside him, bending his mind until it broke.

The monster's glee filled me until I was drunk on it. The smell of the hunter's blood poured into my nose, and our hunger surged, setting my veins on fire. A subtle *thump-thump, thump-thump* thrummed in my ears: the hunter's heartbeat. I spread my hand out flat over his chest, and it throbbed under my palm.

My breath quickened. My mouth watered. I wasn't sure who was in control in that moment. I wasn't sure it mattered. With a sharp thrust, my hand crashed through his rib cage in a hot, sticky explosion. The hunter's damaged eyes shot open wide, and blood poured from his mouth as I wrapped my hand around his heart. Something between a growl and a purr vibrated through my chest as I ran my fingers over the twitching muscle, stroking it like a lover, feeling it skip and lurch under my touch.

The hunter convulsed, clawing weakly at my arms as the sinews popped free, his body relinquishing the organ with surprisingly little effort. The monster let the man slip from his grip, cupped his heart in both hands, and brought it to our lips. He groaned, swooning with pleasure as its contents poured down our throat. Still hot, still twitching, we suckled it like a nursing pup. Sparks flashed behind my eyes, and a dark, sensual pleasure slid beneath my skin.

I didn't surface again until the monster, fat and glutted on the blood of our enemies, slunk back into his cage, and I unwillingly emerged, hands, face, clothes sticky with blood, a mutilated corpse at my feet and a still-warm heart in my hands.

Drunk on blood, I dropped the organ, stumbled back away from it, and fell heavily against the wall. I squeezed my eyes closed and pressed my nose against it. I let my legs go out from under me and slid to the floor. I didn't want to look, didn't want to see the ugly reality. That coldness, deep and inviting, opened up inside me once again, and I crept toward it, reaching out with numb fingers to feel at its edges.

Live, Asagi.

With a painful moan, I pulled back. This wasn't right, wasn't fair. Tsukito's bright, beautiful life shouldn't be snuffed out for the sins of a monster. It should be me broken under the hunter's blade, yet here I was, forcing my eyes open and pulling myself off the wall to crawl through the blood toward him.

He lay on his side, his eyes half-open and still pointed at the spot where I had been. I lowered myself into his line of sight. There was a sort of peace in his expression, and I told myself he was still back there, living in that fantasy he had created for us. Numbness seeped into my bones and wrapped around my heart. The trembling, bloodied hand that reached for him belonged to someone else, the rank smell of my destruction like a terrible nightmare. If I could just hold him in my arms, I could make it all go away.

What if there are monsters?

My hand morphed into a gory claw, and I yanked it back. In a blind panic, I searched for the pitcher I knew would be in the room and ran with it out to the garden well. Bucket after bucket of water I pulled up, plunging in my soiled hands and tossing it tinged pink into the grass. Finally satisfied, I filled the pitcher with clean water and carried it back inside. I found a towel in the tonsu and fell on my knees beside Tsukito, gently rolling him onto his back. I dabbed at his face and chest until they were clean and pulled his clothes back into their proper place. I brushed his hair. I closed his eyes and kissed his eyelids. Ignoring the coldness of his skin and the stiffness that had begun in his limbs, I gathered him up in my arms and held him against my chest.

"The monsters are gone," I whispered in a broken voice. "You can wake up now. I've killed them all."

All but one.

My eyes fell once again on that sword, the dragon's red eyes flashing triumphantly. I wrapped my hand around it and pulled it toward me, feeling my own monster stir deep inside. It would be easy, so easy, to let it out.

Don't let him break you.

I didn't know how long I sat there rocking him before the stench of blood and death drove me to action. I had to get him out of there and away from the carnage. Stiff and ambling like a sleepwalker, I tucked the sword into my obi, scooped up Tsukito, and pulled myself to my feet. I didn't even know where I was going until I stumbled through my master's door. I didn't stop until I made it all the way back into his room, collapsing in despair when I found it empty.

Seconds later, he came crashing through the door, bringing reality with him. His face went ashen at the sight of me, torn clothes blood-spattered, a dead boy in my arms. The numbness that had protected me melted. Here among everything warm and familiar and safe, I broke down. For a moment, he just stared in horror before dropping to his knees beside me and throwing his arms around me.

"Help me, Mahiro," I cried. "Help him like you helped me. Bring him back to me."

"Oh, Asagi…" he said, his own voice thick with emotion. "I can't."

"Please. If you love me…if you ever loved me…"

"I am sorry, Asagi."

With a ragged, hiccupping cry, I shoved him away from me and brought my wrist to my teeth. I didn't know why I didn't think of it before. My blood held the same magic as his. If he could pull me back from the brink of death, then I could do the same for Tsukito. Then he would be like me, and we could be together forever, our happiness firmly within our grasp.

Mahiro righted himself quickly and leaped forward, catching my wrist in his grip. "No, Asagi!" I fought him, snapping and baring my teeth like an animal, but he held fast. "It is too late. Listen to him. Just listen!"

I stopped snarling and turned my supernatural hearing toward Tsukito. I held my breath, closed my eyes, and prayed for some spiritual voice to whisper in my ear, but there was nothing but silence.

"He's gone," I croaked. All strength left me, and I collapsed over him, my face buried in his hair.

That cold numbness rose once again, and I let it take me.

FIFTY

Matsumoto

I FELL INTO A SORT OF INTERMITTENT CATATONIA. THE WORLD MOVED around me, but I was unaware of it. One moment I held Tsukito in my arms, and the next he was gone. My clothes had been changed and my hair washed, and I fell into a panicked weeping all over again. He was gone as if he'd never been.

My next memory was of standing in front of a pillar of granite, Mahiro's hand over mine as we traced the characters of his name and he read them aloud to me.

"Tsu-ki-to."

Blackness descended again after that. Then Mahiro, my master who so detested the cold, dozed against my shoulder as I sat in front of it in the snow, a film of ice forming over a long-abandoned cup of tea.

I took blood only when Itsuko pulled my face into her neck and begged, and then barely enough to keep the pain at bay. I wanted the pain, to wallow in it, to drown in it.

I didn't know how long I spent like that. My first real moment of awareness came from jerking awake in my bed, still trembling and sweating from a nightmare I couldn't remember. Mahiro appeared at my side in an instant, one hand gently stroking my hair and the other thrusting a cup of tea under my nose.

I took the cup and drank desperately, focusing on its warmth and sharp taste and away from the ache in my veins. My monster lurked close to the surface, his voice ringing in my ears. Mahiro urged me into a more upright position and rubbed my back as I struggled to catch my breath, cooing softly as if I were a child.

"How do you feel?" he asked.

"How should I feel?" I snapped, thrusting the empty cup back into his hands and flopping back down into the futon with my back to him. Bitter, that was how I felt. It cut through the numbness like a sharp knife. I squeezed my eyes shut and burrowed my nose into the pillow as pain slithered its way through me. Those men came for me because of what I was, what Mahiro made me. His blood in me wasn't magic. It was darkness, and because of it, Tsukito was dead.

The logical part of me knew it wasn't his fault. Mahiro loved me. He would have never steered me down this path had he known what would happen, yet the taste of it was so strong, I could hardly look at him. It was just so much easier to blame him.

I felt Mahiro shrink, and even with my back to him, I could see those lines etching themselves in his face.

"Matsumoto is here," he said flatly, making my heart trip. "He heard about how you stumbled upon the bandits that raided the inn…"

"Bandits…" I repeated with a dry laugh.

"He is worried about you. He has been camped out on my porch for over a week, refusing to leave until he sees you. You must have made quite an impression."

A week. He's been gone for a week.

Mahiro's tone held an edge of jealousy, but I had no room left for guilt, and it slid off me like water off goose feathers. "If you will not talk to me, you should at least talk to him. Perhaps it will do both of you some good."

I curled into a tight ball and pulled the thick blanket up around my nose. I didn't want to see him, didn't want to see anyone. What could we possibly say to each other that would make any difference?

The decision made for me, the door slid open and closed with Mahiro's exit only to open again less than a minute later. Matsumoto inhaled sharply. I could only imagine how I must look to him, a pale, faded version of the person he once knew. He knelt next to me, laid a hand on my shoulder, and sorrow rolled off him in waves.

"I heard what you did for my poor Tsukito," he said after a long silence, his voice broken. "That you carried him all the way back here and tried to save him. For that, I thank you."

I shivered as a small bit of tension released in me. I wasn't the only one who mourned him after all. "I'm so sorry, Matsumoto-san," I said, my face still pressed into the pillow. He gave my shoulder a gentle squeeze.

"There was nothing you could have done."

"He didn't deserve that."

"No, he didn't," he answered with a sigh. "But I find in this world, people rarely get what they deserve."

I rolled over to face him and pressed my forehead to his knee as he wrapped my hand in his. Matsumoto was a horrible, tedious brute of a man, but in that moment of grief, our hearts connected. Tears welled up in me, and for the first time, I allowed myself to feel, really feel, my loss, safe in the knowledge that he felt it too.

"What about us?" I asked between trembling breaths. "What do we deserve?"

"Me?" he asked with a dry laugh. "Probably less than what I have. You, on the other hand…" He swept a hand through my hair and pressed a finger under my chin to raise my face. "You deserve every happiness," he said, his face hard. "If Mahiro isn't giving it to you, demand it. Fight for it." *Fight for our happiness.* "Do not let this break you." *Live, Asagi.*

On an impulse I couldn't explain, I raised up and pressed my lips to his. Such a small, inadequate gesture, but it was all I had. He made a startled sound before returning it with surprising softness. "Thank you," I said, and he responded with a light, breathy laugh.

"Don't mention it."

FIFTY-ONE

A New Life

MATSUMOTO LEFT SOON AFTER, A LITTLE MORE PINK IN HIS CHEEKS than when he arrived. As much as I was loath to admit it, Mahiro was right. His visit had given me a measure of relief. I was thankful to Matsumoto, for the time he had given us. I knew without a doubt that Tsukito's memory would live on in him, and that alone gave me strength.

That didn't mean the pain went away. In fact, I clung to it like a talisman, a constant reminder of my failure, my loss, the consequences of my actions. But instead of letting it consume me, I used it to make myself stronger, tempering it into an impenetrable armor. My heart grew hard, and I approached every human relationship with a new degree of caution.

There was one caveat to my new coldness: Mahiro. Despite his obvious relief at my gradual recovery, he noticed the change in me, and I felt his disappointment. The gentle, naïve servant who hung on his every word was gone, and with every new assertion of my independence, I felt him shrink. I was right beside him, yet he missed me.

And I missed him, so much that I found myself hovering outside his door in the middle of the night begging for the courage to go in. But I never did. I still loved him, part of me always would, just not in the way he needed. I'd buried my heart with Tsukito, and I just didn't have enough left for him. So as winter turned to spring, I made a decision that had been haunting me for months.

I had to leave.

"I suppose I should have seen this coming," Mahiro said from the doorway of my room as he watched me pack up my few precious belongings.

"I suppose you should have," I answered without looking at him. I felt him wince and regretted my harshness almost immediately.

"And what of your *collection*?" The corner of his mouth quirked into a teasing smile before going serious again. "They will need you."

"I'll send for them once I settle somewhere. Until then, look after them for me?"

He nodded, and I watched him out of the corner of my eye as he found that black sword leaning against the wall. He tipped it upright with his index finger on the hilt.

"They say a sword absorbs a piece of every soul it takes," he said. "Is that why you keep it?"

"I don't know. Maybe."

"Is there anything I can do, anything I can say to make you stay?"

"Why would you want me to?" I asked. "I'm not what you wanted. Not anymore."

"You are *exactly* what I want."

A shiver ran through me as I remembered our first conversation so many years ago when I'd thrown myself at his feet, terrified he'd turn me away. Here we were, history repeating, only this time he was the one afraid. I put down my bags and crossed the room to meet him, taking his hands in mine and pressing our foreheads together.

"I love you, Mahiro. I do," I said quickly, struggling to keep my voice steady. "And I will always be grateful to you for what you've done for me, but I have to find my own way."

He inhaled sharply and opened his mouth as if to argue, but closed it again, releasing a pained sound. He threw his arms around my neck, and I held him tight. "You will always have a home here," he said in a shaky voice.

"I know."

"I truly hope you find your happiness," he said, "and I am so very sorry I couldn't give it to you."

THE NEXT MORNING, I LOADED ALL MY THINGS ONTO THE BACK OF my little gray gelding. Half the house staff turned out to see me off, drenching me in tearful good-byes. Mahiro was conspicuously absent, but I didn't blame him. I was grateful, actually. Despite the firmness of my convictions, my heart shook with fear, and seeing his face fade in the distance might be the one thing that could make them break.

I had no idea where I was going or how I would get there. As Mahiro's gates faded behind me, something inside shifted so sharply that even the most familiar streets felt foreign. So I pointed my horse east toward Edo. A place where perhaps I could disappear, become someone else.

My surprise was profound when I stumbled upon a familiar face.

I didn't recognize him at first when he came tumbling out of an izakaya, landing almost squarely against the flanks of my horse. The gelding snorted and dodged with a jerky sidestep. I grabbed the horse's bridle, preparing to fling a curse as the man righted himself on unsteady legs and grumbled into the mouth of a wine bottle. Something thawed inside me at the sight of the familiar hard lines of his face, the set of his broad shoulders, the line of his back.

"Yutaka-san!"

He pivoted, almost losing his balance all over again, and blinked his bleary eyes. His topknot was shot through with gray, his face wrinkled and weather-beaten, but there was no mistaking his scowl.

"Asagi?" His mouth twisted in disbelief, and I stifled a laugh as he glared into his wine bottle.

A giddy smile stretched across my face. "You won't find the answer in there."

"What...How...Why..." He swayed dangerously backward, and I caught him by his elbows.

"That's a long story."

He continued to stare at me slack-jawed as I steered him toward the porch of the izakaya he'd just fallen out of and sat him down. I secured my horse, muscles straining against a current of conflicting emotions, before settling down next to him. Our knees and hips and shoulders lay millimeters apart, and the heat of the near-touch left me breathless. Was he really here?

"You look…older."

"You look exactly the same. Except for your eyes…" His gaze bounced over my kimono and all its fancy ornaments. "What house do you belong to?"

"I don't." I shrugged, my gaze dropping to my clasped hands. "I'm on my own. I am free."

My voice cracked as the truth of it settled over me. It was both terrifying and liberating. For the first time, I had no one telling me what to do, where to go, who to be. I'd paid a heavy price for that freedom. It was now on me to use it wisely.

"I am on my own too." He gave an ironic laugh. "Seems no one needs an old drunk protecting them."

"I do."

He froze, his wine bottle halfway to his mouth. I blinked and swallowed around the words. They'd spilled out without thinking, and now I couldn't take them back. I didn't want to take them back. I should have hated him, but I didn't, and the thought of another parting made my chest ache.

"I'm going to Edo."

"What's in Edo?"

"A new life." I plucked the bottle out of his hand, and it fell limply to his lap. "Come with me."

He released a long breath as he struggled to maintain that shuttered expression I knew so well, and failed miserably. Maybe it was the wine.

"I heard this story once about a toad that fell in love with the moon." His eyes shimmered when he looked at me, every muscle in his face tense. "It didn't end well."

A smile tugged at my lips, and my own eyes burned. "Maybe it isn't over yet."

He sucked in a breath as if to speak, but instead lifted his hand and touched the pad of his thumb to the space between my eyes. My throat constricted as he traced it all the way down the bridge of my nose. All the years, all the little spaces between us closed, and my body warmed with his nearness. The pieces of my heart began to stitch themselves back together. A little ragged perhaps, but it beat all the same.

"A new life." The words came out a sigh, and he dropped his forehead against mine. "A new life sounds good."

つづく

Thank you for reading! Did you enjoy?

Please Add Your Review! You can sign up for the City Owl Press newsletter to receive notice of all book releases!

And don't miss more dark paranormal fantasy like SOUL OF THE UNBORN by City Owl Author, Natalia Brothers. Turn the page for a sneak peek!

Sneak Peek of Soul of the Unborn

BY NATALIA BROTHERS

The pleasure of Chris Waller's first morning in Moscow turned into annoyance when his younger cousin, Debra Alley, emerged from her hotel room carrying an overnight bag despite her promises not to stay in the village.

"Just in case all evening trains are canceled." Debra patted her bag.

"That would be convenient for you, wouldn't it?" Chris asked.

"Go pack your trunks. A couple days on a beach—doesn't it sound *mahvelous, dahling?*"

"We'll take that tour, have lunch, and I don't care what your friends decide to do next. You're returning with me to Moscow." Chris slapped at the elevator call button.

"If Moscow is all you want, then what's the point in you wasting any time on Vishenky?" Debra sounded sweeter than a wooing salesman.

"I'm glad you grasped the part about wasting my time."

"You're thirty-three, not ninety. Be adventurous."

"I was—when I signed up to chaperone you across the Atlantic. You mom said, quote-unquote, 'Promise me you'll watch her every step, breath, bite, and blink.'"

Chris understood Debra and her friends' desire to be on their own. Four college seniors, assisted by the English-speaking escort, Valya

Svetlova, wouldn't get lost on their way to the village thirty miles from Moscow. The guide had rave recommendations from her visitors last year. *Vishenky's Legends and Supernatural Phenomena*, some countryside tour offered by the hotel—good luck with that. The whole thing irked Chris only because the airheads had the *Legends* on their list all along, but Debra didn't bother to tell him until last night. Maybe his overprotective Aunt Rita had a point when she had initially refused to pay for her daughter's trip to Russia.

"Playing babysitter in front of your students...." Debra clicked her tongue. "Must be embarrassing."

"Let me tell you about embarrassing. Your mother also asked me to make sure you don't lose your purse and check your room for a deadbolt lock. No food from street vendors, and, please, don't stay out after nine o'clock."

"And floss my teeth?"

"I was saving that detail until we joined your buddies."

"I'd kill you."

"Then stop being an ungrateful brat." Chris took hold of her skinny elbow, steadying Debra on the sinking floor of the high-speed elevator.

"Too bad your Beth is such a homebody," she cooed. "You two in Gorky Park—oh, so romantic, and off our backs." She turned sideways as a flock of silver-haired ladies invaded the cabin.

Beth Vogel. Another wave of jet lag swept over Chris, an exhausting brew of fatigue and restlessness that had kept him from getting any sleep. There was so much to see, to savor and appreciate, all meticulously selected and crammed into a seven-day trip. For the first time in weeks Beth wasn't on his mind. No, he wouldn't discuss their sudden breakup and endure Debra's tongue-in-cheek "Oh, how disappointing."

"You and Jessie Hunt," he said. "Enjoying your new friendship?" The girls had barely spoken a word to each other since the group had met at the check-in counter at Dulles International.

Debra turned away and studied the control panel, her shoulders positioned an inch higher.

The elevator slowed, stopped, and the doors slid open like symbolical curtains.

The entrance hall of the hotel reflected the same grandeur of the Soviet times as did the metro stations. Tiered chandeliers enticed a woman in a sari into snapping a quick picture as she rushed after her husband rolling his suitcase across the marble floor. Pointing fingers to the high ceiling, teenagers in matching green t-shirts tilted their heads back and giggled furtively, as if in awe of the frescoes that glorified the long-gone era.

Chris spotted Peter Moss and his standoffish girlfriend, Jessie Hunt, by the left wing of the curved staircase. Debra's childhood pal, Luke Higbee, was absent from the rendezvous point; his backpack, stuffed with camping gear, sat at Jessie's feet.

"You both decided to come," Peter said pleasantly, but his thin-lipped mouth twitched.

"I never said I wouldn't." Chris looked around. "Where's Higbee?"

Jessie rolled her eyes as Luke emerged from the gift shop. He shook a plastic bag where the red headdress of a doll peeked out. "A teakettle warmer. I'll tell my sister it's a hat." He tried to get a high five out of Jessie, but she ignored him, her pale eyes fixed on the hotel's entrance. Luke winked at Debra. "So, Deb, is Mr. Waller on board?"

"On board with what?" Chris asked.

Debra shrugged. "Guys, it was your idea. Don't put me in the middle."

"Well, somebody, it's now or never if you're going to bring this up at all," Jessie said. "Valya will be here any moment."

"Okay." Red blotches spread over Peter's cheekbones. "Mr. Waller, we want to ask you for a favor."

Chris turned his hand, palm up. "What?"

"Someone else went on this tour last summer."

"Your brother, yes. Deb told me."

"My half-brother." Peter moved a step toward Chris. "His last name is Ogden, not Moss. The guide has no way of knowing we're related, unless someone warns her."

Jessie raised her arm in front of her boyfriend as if to stop Peter's advancing. "Mr. Waller, please. We just don't want the guide to know how we found her. Maybe you could tell her the tour was your idea and Peter contacted her on your behalf."

"Why?" Chris asked.

"To confuse her." Luke extracted the souvenir doll out of the bag and pointed its pudgy hand at Chris. "You stumbled on Valya's website. Deb doesn't speak any Russian. Jessie will be my girlfriend. We've never heard about last summer's group or seen the footage they filmed."

"And I'm your kindergarten teacher," Chris said. "Why would the guide care who found her website?"

Peter studied Luke and his teakettle warmer as if debating what was more annoying, the doll or his buddy's perpetual grin. "If Valya hears that we saw my brother's film, she might change her program."

"So what?" Chris asked. "Don't you want to learn something new?"

A quick exchange of troubled glances told him that when the real story came out, he wouldn't like it.

"You won't have to lie if you skip the village," Luke said.

"I don't 'have to' anything," Chris assured him.

"Sir, do you believe in psychics?" Jessie asked. "Stuff like mind reading?"

Chris turned to Debra. "What's all this BS about?"

She pouted.

"The guide is like a performance artist, not a psychic," Luke said. "It would be interesting to see if she can read through a load of misinformation."

Chris stared at his cousin. "You told me this was a folklore tour."

"Among other things," Debra said. "Chris, really, you don't have to go. We'll be okay."

A day in a village, in the company of a "psychic" and this bunch of juveniles, seemed like a waste of time compared to the riches of Moscow museums. "See you later" would be a justified reply to Debra's suggestion.

"That's not what I promised your mother," Chris said instead. "And I won't lie about who found—"

"It's her," Jessie said.

A young woman strode across the lobby, a cell phone pressed to her ear, her eyes scanning the tourists congregated around the base of the staircase. For a second her glance met Chris's, but she looked away, searching for someone else.

"Valya Svetlova?" Peter called out.

Silence.

Dressed in beige slacks and a white blouse, with blushing cheeks and a braid streaming over her shoulder and down her chest, Valya could have been a poster girl for any Russian travel agency, except for the fact that not a hint of a smile touched her lips. Watching Valya's widening eyes, Chris thought the guide was startled by the sight of their group rather than glad her guests had arrived.

Don't stop now. Keep reading with your copy of SOUL OF THE UNBORN by City Owl Author, Natalia Brothers.

And find more from Courtney Maguire at www. courtneymaguirewrites.com

Glossary of Japanese Terms

Baka – idiot

Bakayarou – stupid person

Chabudai – small, short-legged table

-chan – familiar honorific often used for women, children, and people with a close relationship

Chikushou – curse similar to "son of a bitch" or "dammit"

Dango – Japanese dumpling made from mochi and served on a skewer

Doku zeri – water hemlock

Engawa – strip of wood flooring that runs around the outside of the house, similar to a porch; can be closed in using wooden shutters during bad weather or when the house is empty for security

Fundoshi – traditional Japanese undergarment made from a strip of cotton cloth

Furisode – long-sleeved kimono, typically worn by young, unmarried women

Futon – traditional bedding that is laid out on the floor for sleeping and then rolled up and stored in a closet during the day

Fuzakeru na – lit. "stop messing around." In this construction, the meaning is harsher, closer to "Fuck off!"

Goshujin-sama – master of the house

Hajimemashite – nice to meet you

Hakama – a type of split skirt worn over the kimono and tied at the
waist

Hanko – carved stamp used as a form of signature

Haori – hip or thigh length jacket worn over the kimono

Irrasshai – a call of welcome said by shop workers to patrons as they
enter their shop

Itadakimasu – lit. "I humbly receive." Traditionally said before a meal

Izakaya – a bar that serves food

Kanjin – Government officials

Kanzashi – hair pin usually decorated with cloth or glass flowers,
engraved metal, amber, etc.

Konpeitou – colorful sugar candy

Koushu Kaidou– one of the five routes to Edo

Kuso - shit

Kuso gaki – lit. shit brat

Macha – green tea powder

Mattaku – as an exclamation, "My goodness!"

Miso – soup thickened with fermented soybeans and barley, often with
added tofu and vegetables

Nagajuban – simple robe worn under a kimono

Ne – article asking for agreement, similar to "isn't it?"

Nori – edible seaweed with a strong flavor

Obi – wide belt worn around the waist over a kimono.

Ofuro - bath

Oku-sama – lady of the house

Oneesan – lit. big sister; often used as a polite way to address a young
woman you don't know

Saké – Japanese liquor made from rice

Sakuramochi – Japanese sweet consisting of a pink rice cake filled with
red bean paste and wrapped in a cherry blossom leaf

-sama – polite honorific used to address someone of higher status

Shimada-mage – elaborate women's hairstyle common in the Edo
period but currently mostly associated with geisha consisting of a
heavily decorated topknot

Shimenawa – "enclosing rope;" lengths of hemp or straw used for purification in Shinto

Shinabe – professionals or tradesmen relevant to court functions

Shoji – Door or window made from a lattice frame covered with paper. Used as both walls and room dividers that can be opened or removed

Sugoi – awesome!

Tasuki – a sash used to hold up the sleeves of a kimono while working

Tatami – mats made from rice straw and rush used as flooring

Third year of Bunroku – Japanese calendar year; roughly 1594

Tonkatsu – breaded and deep fried pork cutlet

Tonsu – storage cabinet

Torii – gateway to a Shinto shrine

Toyotomi Hideyoshi – daimyo that became de facto leader of Japan at the end of the Sengoku period, mid1580s

Udon – thick, wheat flower noodles often serves as a soup

Wagashi – small, sweet cakes made from mochi, anko, and sweet fruits and served with tea

Youkai – "mysterious calamity;" used to refer to supernatural beings in Japanese folklore

Youkan – jellied dessert made from red bean paste, agar, and sugar

Yukata - lit. bathing clothes; lightweight version of a kimono

Zaisu – basically a chair with no legs used on tatami floors

Zori – thonged sandal

Want even more dark paranormal fantasy? Try SOUL OF THE UNBORN by City Owl Author, Natalia Brothers, and find more from Courtney Maguire at www.courtneymaguirewrites.com

One woman battles her own dark secrets—and the pull of her heart—in an award-winning supernatural thriller set in a mystical Russian village.

Posing as a folklore tour guide, Valya Svetlova takes a group of American college students and their professor, Chris Waller, to her summer home in the Russian village of Vishenky for a few nights of supernatural phenomena. She plays the perfect hostess, for Valya doesn't want anyone to discover she harbors selfish motives when it comes to one participant—the only person who can refute a tale declaring her a stillborn resurrected by a paranormal entity.

Her nascent feelings toward the handsome professor inhibit her ability to control the supernatural manifestations and her inquisitive guests. When her unforeseen affection turns Chris into a target, Valya faces an excruciating reality. It's no longer in her human power to ensure her guests' safety. Yet to keep them alive, Valya must brush off her humanity and become the thing she fights so desperately to prove she is not—a soulless monster.

Please sign up for the City Owl Press newsletter for chances to win special subscriber-only contests and giveaways as well as receiving information on upcoming releases and special excerpts.

All reviews are **welcome** and **appreciated**. Please consider leaving one on your favorite social media and book buying sites.

For books in the world of romance and speculative fiction that embody Innovation, Creativity, and Affordability, check out City Owl Press at www.cityowlpress.com.

Acknowledgments

The process of writing and publishing Bloodlaced has been, to put it mildly, a journey. It started even before I decided to pursue writing professionally, the characters and world taking shape in dusty notebooks now shoved in the back of a drawer or in the bottom of a box in the attic hopefully never to be seen again. It is the product of years worth of lessons and mistakes, of arrogance and humility. It is a book almost abandoned, and yet here it is, for better or for worse. A world that was largely mine and mine alone now open to the public. Please wipe your feet.

First, I want to thank my bestie and hetero-soulmate, Kitty. She's been there since the beginning when this world was just a shitty short story with three characters and almost no plot. She held my hand through many a late night brainstorming session and told me I was great even when I'm sure I didn't deserve it. When I say this wouldn't exist without her, that's not an exaggeration. Sometimes, her squealing excitement when I sent her a new chapter was all that kept me going.

Next, I want to thank my horde of beta readers which I won't list individually because I'm sure I will forget someone. It's been a long time and, well, I've slept since then. I do want to give a quick thanks to Hitoshi Noguchi for fielding my very strange questions about Japanese language and cultural context. I also want to thank Jennifer Worrell and Heather Grossart. Both are extremely talented writers in their own right and have beta'd several projects for me with great enthusiasm. Good, consistent beta readers are hard to find and I treasure them both.

Of course, I want to thank the entire crew at City Owl Press for the work they've put in to make this book a reality. I especially want to thank my editor Heather McCorkle. She's a rock star. I was ready to give up on this manuscript when I received a Revise Resubmit from her. If you're not familiar with publishing lingo, that's basically a rejection with editorial notes and a chance at a do-over. I really wasn't sure if I wanted to invest any more time in what I was sure at this point was a futile effort, but when I introduced myself to her at conference and mentioned my book, she lit up. That little bit of positivity gave me the push I needed to keep working and that positivity has continued through every step of the process. If it weren't for her, this book would have joined the notebooks in the attic. And that would suck.

I also want to acknowledge all the help and encouragement I've received in the course of my writing career from members of the Twitter #WritingCommunity and #WriteLGBTQ community. I have learned so much about not just writing, but about examining my own biases regarding race, sexuality, and gender expression. I have interacted with so many people from different backgrounds with unique experiences that have challenged me in ways I didn't know I needed. I hope to continue to learn and grow among you.

Last and certainly not least, I want to thank the readers. Thank you for being readers. Thank you for taking a chance on the unknown. Thank you for leaving footprints on my world.

About the Author

COURTNEY MAGUIRE is a University of Texas graduate from Corpus Christi, Texas. Drawn to Austin by a voracious appetite for music, she spent most of her young adult life in dark, divey venues nursing a love for the sublimely weird. A self-proclaimed fangirl with a press pass, she combined her love of music and writing as the primary contributor for  Japanese music and culture blog, Project: Lixx, interviewing Japanese rock and roll icons and providing live event coverage for appearances across the country.

www.courtneymaguirewrites.com

 twitter.com/PretentiousAho

 instagram.com/courtneymaguirewrites

 facebook.com/CourtneyMaguireWrites

About the Publisher

City Owl Press is a cutting edge indie publishing company, bringing the world of romance and speculative fiction to discerning readers.

www.cityowlpress.com